Bishop's Road

Bishop's Road
by
Catherine Safer

Killick Press
St. John's, Newfoundland and Labrador
2004

We acknowledge the support of The Canada Council for the Arts for our publishing program.

We acknowledge the financial support of the Government of Canada through the Book Publishing Industry Development Program (BPIDP) for our publishing program.

Cover Art: Katherine Munro
Cover Design by Todd Manning

Published by
KILLICK PRESS
an imprint of CREATIVE BOOK PUBLISHING
a Transcontinental Inc. associated company
P.O. Box 8660, St. John's, Newfoundland A1B 3T7

First Printing November 2004

Typeset in 12 point Garamond

Printed in Canada by:
Transcontinental Inc.

National Library of Canada Cataloguing in Publication

Safer, Catherine, 1950-
Bishop's Road / by Catherine Safer.

ISBN 1-894294-78-5

I. Title.

PS8637.A44B48 2004 C813'.6 C2004-906589-0

Dedication

This one is for Andreae and Jennifer, who are so lovely. For Susie, who read and liked it. For Andrew who said, "Go write something. I'll bring home the bacon."

Bishop's Road is long enough. And straight. If you walk back and forth every day you'll lose a few pounds and tighten up but most people around here don't bother with that. Mrs. Miflin's boarding house sits between a Catholic Church, with priest's rectory, and a school - all on their last legs. Now and again the Department of Education threatens to close the school but the parents get upset and have meetings and eventually the talk dies down for a couple of years. The church puts on a brave face but since hardly anyone goes to Mass these days, except for the midnight service on Christmas Eve, maybe, and during Lent when you absolutely have to, its days are numbered as well. A very old priest lives in the rectory with his equally ancient housekeeper who is terrible for getting on his nerves but makes great bread pudding when she's in the mood.

Across the road and down a cobblestone path, the only one left in the city, tucked away behind poplar, maple, birch, aspen and a low stone wall, is what was once an orphanage. It stood empty for years until some enterprising members of the arts community begged it away from the church. The artists are generally happy there except for the ones who work late into the night because no one can get the crying out of the walls and they are thinking of packing up their brushes and going elsewhere.

There used to be a lot of little nuns around in the old days, teaching in the school and the orphanage. Since the ones conceived in sin would surely have a negative influence on those from proper homes, everyone agreed to keep the children separate back then. With the Word of God on their lips and black leather straps on their belts - next to the Rosary beads - the holy women confused several generations of youngsters for a hundred years or more until they all just dried up and blew away. No one remembers exactly when that happened but surely it was a sunny day with just enough sweet wind to whip through the convent and out the back door with those withered Brides of Christ in tow. Once the dust settled and it became apparent that no one in the world was interested in taking over the duties of the recently departed Sisters of Joy, Mrs. Miflin bought the convent for a song. Rumors of devil worship and torture, orgies and the like, didn't entice too many prospective buyers among the locals even if they'd had the money, and the fact that it would take a king's ransom to heat the place kept everyone else away. But not Mrs. Miflin. She had started most of the rumors herself a few years ago anyway, and she doesn't have the furnace on between April and November no matter what the temperature. How she got the old nuns to cooperate is anyone's guess but they weren't gone an hour before she was beating on Father Delaney's door with her offer to buy.

~

Ginny Mustard grew up in the orphanage. And the little nuns tried to hammer things into her soft yellow head. Had her kneel at the front of the room with her nose to the wall for a bit of ridicule now and then. If ever they felt the need for reinforcement they encouraged the other children to find her faults and laugh, though not too loudly, mind, because either one of them might be next - there were no shining stars in Ginny Mustard's world. She moved from the orphanage to the streets and on to Mrs. Miflin's house. If she's not careful she can see the window of the ward where she slept from the front porch in the winter when the trees are bare and so she keeps her eyes the other way until she is down the road and around a corner.

Mrs. Miflin's house is big with many rooms, not accustomed to sudden sound or quick movement though it is quite familiar with haunted dreams. The original furniture is still there. In the walls are nooks and crannies holding statues of Mary the Mother of Jesus and occasionally, Jesus himself, wounded and weary. Mrs. Miflin is what you might call a good Catholic. She makes it to Mass every morning. She takes Communion every day. And every Friday, doesn't matter what that Pope said, there's fish on the dinner table. For Lent she gives up what pleasure she takes in life and when her feet hurt she complains only a little and would have you believe she offers most of her discomfort for the repose of the poor souls in Purgatory. Kneeling at night, she says a Rosary before her head touches the pillow, no matter how tired she may be.

Everything is downhill east of Bishop's Road. It runs parallel to Caine's Street which overlooks Beaton Row which frowns on Water Street which leans closer to the ocean every day. Connecting the lot are many short streets that you don't even want to walk on, let alone drive, when it's icy. Beyond Water Street is the harbour and surrounding it but split at The Narrows are hills. In the morning the sun comes over the one on the left and at this time of year, if there are icebergs about and a little fog, the effect is enough to blind you.

Once there was a big old building messing up the view but it fell apart and no one had money to fix it. After a few hard winters it began throwing itself at passersby every time the wind blew hard. Pigeons nested there in droves and the smell was wicked in summer from tons of droppings and ratty old nests and the bodies of their deceased. So the city decided that it had to go and then put it back on their 'things to ignore' list until the scavengers had their way with doors and windows and the half-decent bricks and then it was simply a matter of bulldozing the remains into the harbour. The government types who had worked there were long gone to a business park on the outskirts of town where there was enough heat that they didn't have to keep their coats on all day come December, and lots of cold recycled air for the five or six really hot days you get sometimes in August.

Caine's Street has houses all smooshed together and holding each other up. Beaton Row has small shops of first and second-hand books and clothing and what-nots, restaurants and galleries. Water Street boasts offices and department stores and more bars than anyone needs. There is no parking space and most businesses do poorly. Every time you turn around there's one closing down and another opening up so there's no point in thinking anything is where you left it yesterday.

The people who live here are an odd mix. Professors from the university rub elbows with low-life who haven't held jobs for two generations. They didn't start out low, mind, but there's nothing like poverty to bring you to that level after a while. Down here children who have not known want since they were born play with urchins whose only hello for the day is the back of a hard hand across a small mouth. One is clean and the other wears last night's dinner on her pretty face. Down here is the Women's Shelter and the Salvation Army Men's Hostel and the brave souls who don't care for the rules in either of those places and would rather take their chances outside - thank you very much - until it's too friggin' cold to breathe. Even then they don't put their things away but keep all worldly possessions in garbage bags to save packing when the spring comes around again. Down here are the artists and the fine plays and the music festivals. People who live up town say they would venture down more often if there were some place to park but no one believes it except the ones who say it. When they do show up they don't really get it and usually bring lawn chairs with arms to the outdoor events so they don't have to sit too close to the riffraff.

On the west side of Bishop's Road things are on a more even keel. The ground is mostly flat and easy to walk. There are a few places where you can get a decent meal of fish if you don't mind going that far, though if you ever want to see a movie or have some brochures printed there's nothing for it but to head on out to a mall. The most interesting places, the ones with any expression in their eyes, are here, below Bishop's Road.

~

Ginny Mustard has never been anywhere else in her life and, like most things, that suits her fine. If it doesn't happen within a fifteen minute walk of Bishop's Road, it might as well not happen at all. She goes to the river beyond the park. Stands on one of the little bridges that cross it and looks at the water rushing. She likes the storms and the snow as much as she likes calm and sunshine. And the river is as lovely when trees are falling over and their roots coming out of the banks and the wind so loud you can't hear another thing, as when it is gentle and whispering low and pretty little finches swarm the willows. She goes to the ocean. Watches the ships come and go. Pulls the cold fog and fishy smells deep into her lungs. Holds them there. Closes her eyes and smiles.

Ginny Mustard has a secret. All afternoon she's been walking up and down Water Street looking for someone to tell but no one ever comes along who might have time to listen. She's not good with words. When she does talk at all they fall over themselves and some are left out so it takes a patient person to know what she is going on about.

The secret is brand new. She ran it around in her head and tried to write it down when she got bits of it clear. Junior Brophy from Harry's Groc. and Conf. gave her a load of paper placemats once to draw her pictures on and at the rate she's going she'll need every last one of them to write her secret because her letters are big and lumpy and backwards and she can't get more than a dozen words on any one sheet.

After cooking and praying, Mrs. Miflin likes cleaning best so Ginny Mustard keeps her papers and coloured pencils between her mattress and box spring, all neat and tidy and hidden. She wears her pen on a chain around her neck along with a medal of the Holy Blessed Virgin and a penny that Joe Snake put on the railway track just before the train came and flattened it thin.

Ginny Mustard has lived here longer than anyone else except Mrs. Miflin. It used to be a beautiful house but now it's just pretty enough to get by. That's what Mrs. Miflin says; me and the house are the same, she says, just pretty enough to get by. She was married once. She has pictures on the walls and a dried bouquet. Her wedding dress hangs in her closet in two green garbage bags stapled together to be long enough to keep the dust off if any dares land. Ginny Mustard has never seen it but Mrs. Miflin tells her all about it sometimes when they wash the dishes. She likes to talk and goes on and on about back in the day when she was pretty and her husband was so good looking and they were young - too young to get married. The pictures show that he had a big nose and glasses and was a lot taller than Mrs. Miflin and his arms looked like they might be really thin under his jacket. And in the pictures Mrs. Miflin was round and smiling as though she'd had a good meal of something tasty and her dress was snug on top, buttoned with pearls that wanted to pop off and scatter. Mr. Miflin must have gone away because no one in the house has ever seen him. Mrs. Miflin sets a place for him every mealtime and even puts food there as if he just went to the store for a newspaper or something and she expects him back any minute now. You might think that wasteful but it's not because when he doesn't show up she eats his share or puts it in tomorrow's soup.

~

Ruth lives at the very end of the house - third story and beyond the linen closet. Not a lot happens back there so she spends much of her time in a chair at the top of the stairs near a window just watching. She can see across the street and through the trees and across another street and into the park. If she squints she can just make out the bodies lying around on the grass tanning or rusting - depends on the weather - and the little kids playing on the swings and in the sandbox after their mothers pick out the glass and dog shit. They have to do it every day. It's that kind of park.

Sometimes Ruth wears the same clothes for a week. She dresses like a bruise. Black leggings and a big black shirt. Purple. Other times she doesn't even bother to take off her nightgown or wash her face, what would be the point, though she's very particular about brushing and flossing and her hair is always clean. She has been on the planet for 50 years and is tired of life and so has given up - except for the sitting. Watching.

Maggie has a room just ahead of the linen closet. It's the nicest one in the house with a huge bay window and lacy curtains that move about easily. At night she lies awake and watches them float across the room - soft and narrow - like thin ghosts with a floral pattern. Maggie is still trying to figure out how she got here and watching the curtains puts her mind at rest. She thinks that if she lies here long enough she will know what came before and after leaving home and being here in this room, in this house. She remembers a suitcase and lots of screaming, her mother's face hard before she turned away from Maggie. A big place with little beds. Before that there's nothing. After that there's nothing either - until this room, this house.

At night she puts her pillow at the foot of the bed under the curtains and they wash across her face on their way to and fro. Sometimes the moon is behind them and when they move it shines all over her. Turns her skin a nice pale blue. When it is full she takes off her clothes and looks at her pale blue body. She holds up an arm or a leg to get as much of the light as she can. She likes to see herself that color and wishes she could show someone how pretty she looks.

The people whose clothes Maggie wears were old and larger than herself. Her underpants are lumpy bloomers and her skirts have to be held with a belt - pulled very tight and even then her blouses are generally hanging out and in her way. All of the spare fabric gives her the look of a sausage. If you could see her face you might be surprised to find that she is attractive.

There is a shoe box under Maggie's bed containing 118 letters. Sealed. Stamped. Never opened. Maggie brought it with her and goes nowhere without it. She takes it to breakfast, lunch, dinner and the bathroom. Only in her room is it out of sight and even then she often pulls up the bedspread and checks to make sure. She thinks sometimes it isn't true - that nothing is - and so she pulls up the bedspread and checks to make sure.

Eve has been alive since God was a youngster. She lives on the second floor - east side - and can see the ocean from her room but mostly she tends the garden out back, a job she hasn't had since her fall from grace with that fool Adam. She has a knack for growing things but sticks to flowers since the zucchini year when everyone got so fed up with zucchini this and zucchini that every meal for a month because Mrs. Miflin can't bear to waste anything. Eve is big and strong with no softness to her bones at all. She is generally content but for missing Adam - mostly in February when the days are so gray and the seed catalogues haven't arrived yet. She's been six years without him this time - he always seems to go ahead of her - but she enjoys the garden. Every spring when the slugs come crawling, Eve buys a hedgehog and sets it loose. And every spring the newest one munches away for a couple of weeks and wanders off. When Eve is not gardening she wears long black dresses, stiff and silk, with here and there a touch of lace, a cameo, a satin rose. But more often than not she's in overalls and rubber boots, a red kerchief holding her hair away while she works.

~

Judy arrived this morning. Mrs. Miflin has convinced the powers that be that her house is the ideal place for wayward girls. Being God fearing and all, who better than herself to shape up degenerate youth? Aside from the weekly visits to her probation officer and a counselor, the bulk of Judy's rehabilitation now rests on the capable, albeit sloped, shoulders of Mrs. Miflin, a position of power that pleases the old doll no end.

Judy is seventeen, a little beyond foster care even if anyone would have her. The last child after three rowdy boys, Judy's only flaw, if you don't count her height of six feet, is that of being too damned smart for her own good. When she dares to dream, her ambition is to become wealthy beyond belief at which time she will go home and burn the place to the ground. If you catch her smiling you can be sure she is imagining the part where they all come running to her for help and she tells them they are shit out of luck, go to hell the lot of you friggers. Judy has been stealing make-up and clothes since she was ten and has a record as long as her wingspan. She has dropped out of school for one reason or another a good seven times already and has the IQ of an Einstein.

Judy owns five pairs of jeans and six tee shirts with things written on them. She has a short black dress and her underwear has seen better days. She has running shoes and hiking boots, socks and a pair of men's pyjamas, never worn, because she sleeps in her day clothes just in case she has to leave in a hurry. On the dresser on a pink plastic doily that Mrs. Miflin bought on sale - five for a dollar - is a black wooden jewelry box that plays a rusty *Fur Elise* when you wind it and a little spring inside goes around and around without the ballerina that used to be there. In the box is a pair of tiny real gold earrings and a few other odds and ends. And there's the cover of another box wrapped in brown paper, with small shells glued on in a daisy pattern and a red velvet lining with two satin strings that once attached it to a bottom that is somewhere else.

If Judy hadn't suggested that Ginny Mustard take a look in the attic this morning when Mrs. Miflin was out and they couldn't find light bulbs, then Ginny Mustard might not be having a hard time of it now. But she did and Ginny Mustard did and there's a tear in the fabric and time tugging the edge. Someone might want to lay a hand on that girl's yellow hair and smooth it back. Tell her everything will be okay.

~

Mrs. Miflin has been away for much of the day, signing papers and assuring the probation officer and Judy's counselor that of course the girl will behave herself and make her appointments on time. Tonight she will formally introduce her latest acquisition to the rest of the household. She has already squeezed another chair into the dining room and if they ever felt tempted to put elbows on the table they can forget about it now. Four might be comfortable here - with six and Mr. Miflin's place it's a stretch. Here they come - right on time. Bladders newly emptied for the duration. Once you're sitting there's room for no other movement but fork to mouth.

The room is the size of a breadbox and packed to the rafters with furniture, old and intimidating, dark and forlorn and smelling always of Murphy's Oil Soap. There's a useless window never opened, its sill crawling with porcelain puppies. From the centre hangs a plastic geranium, bathed weekly in warm soapy water. Sprayed with a bit of air freshener. It is the only plant in the house but Mrs. Miflin is thinking of getting another like it for the front porch. This is where every meal is taken and if you're a minute late and no money in your pocket you'll go hungry until the next one. Breakfast at seven, lunch at noon and dinner at six, that's all there is to it and nothing in between unless you manage to hide a box of crackers in your closet, or an apple.

"Eve," says Mrs. Miflin, "Mr. Abe Hennessy over on Blake Street thinks one of your old hedgehogs could be in his shed. He was cleaning up and it looks like something or other made a nest in a barrel what he had turned over on its side and slept the winter. If you want it back you better go get it because he needs the barrel. It might be a rat he said but it didn't move nearly so fast as one and its more roundish. I don't know why you don't just pour salt on them slugs, you know. Kills them quicker than anything and not nearly so costly as buying hedgehogs every year and they taking off soon as they got their bellies full."

"Well, Mrs. Miflin, I'm not all that fond of killing things. If the Creator wanted me pouring salt on His slugs He would never have come up with hedgehogs in the first place. I think He might have done something about their wandering habits while He was at it but who am I to question His ways?"

Mrs. Miflin does not much care for arguments she can't win. "Okay everybody. Enough of this chit-chat. This here young lady goes by the name of Judy and is living with you now thanks to Social Services who couldn't find anyone else who'd have her being as she's what you'd call a delinquent. She is in the habit of stealing anything that's not hammered down so keep that in mind if you catch her in your rooms. She is supposed to keep her nose clean from now on or she'll be in the jail for the rest of her days. Judy eat them peas. I got no patience for fancy eating diseases in this house. I made a nice trifle for dessert and I'm not bringing it out until them plates is polished."

"Which means," says Ruth, "that our Mrs. Miflin has constructed a sponge cake and flung a can of fruit cocktail at it.

You're welcome to my share, Judy. There's been more than enough trifle in my life already."

"Ruth. Don't be testy. Everybody likes trifle. Don't mind Ruth, Judy my dear. She's always like this, but nice enough if you can manage to ignore her. And Ruth, don't you think for one minute I didn't see you hauling them sheets down to the laundry-mat last night. I go through all the trouble of hanging them in the lovely fresh air and you take them there. I don't know why you can't be like everyone else and sleep on them nice and outdoorsy smelling."

"Because they're like bloody sandpaper, Mrs. Miflin, and it's cheaper to take them for a quick tumble in a dryer than to pay good money for the amount of lotion I'd need to keep my skin from falling off if I don't. Fifty cents and ten minutes makes them at least livable."

"Well don't come complaining to me when they go getting holes in them from all that tumbling. I buy my linens once a year and not a minute sooner."

~

In the attic the rattling of small bones muffled by pink soft knit blanket. Soft knit blanket with hope and dreams set in delicate stitches - seven month's worth of delicate stitches. On a satin pillow. Singing. Low. Ginny Mustard hears it from her place at the table. *Hush little baby don't say a word. Momma's gonna buy you a mocking bird.* And she drops peas from her fork, who loves her food and would never waste a mouthful, drops peas from her fork and they roll under the table. Mrs. Miflin frowns and after that everyone is conscious of her feet and there is no movement from below. The little voice is clear above the plate scraping and Mrs. Miflin going on and on about nothing, but no one takes notice except Ginny Mustard.

Ginny Mustard's mother left her in the hospital where she was born. There was no talk of adoption or anything else. She just up and went when her time was through and she didn't take the baby. She was not a young girl in trouble. She had a toddler and a husband and a fine home and she was thirty-two years old. She kept Ginny Mustard in the room with her but she never nursed her when she woke or changed her wet diaper or bathed her small smooth body. She sang *hush little baby* while she sat and stared but she never stroked her sweet face. Only once did she touch her fingers and frowned when Ginny Mustard curled her tiny brown fist into the centre of her own strong pink hand. Then that woman packed her suitcase and put on her blue dress and make-up and high-heeled shoes and left the hospital and no one ever heard tell of her again. Ginny Mustard cried for a long time before one of the nurses discovered that she was alone and nobody wanted her. And she grew tall and brown and her hair grew long and yellow and most people didn't bother with her after those first few days.

~

When dinner is through, Ginny Mustard tells Mrs. Miflin that she is not feeling so good and can't help with the dishes. Mrs. Miflin says Judy can have her turn tonight and that way she'll stay out of trouble. And while they clean up, Mrs. Miflin fills the girl in on the dos and don'ts of life in her house. What not to touch, where not to go and there's no point in thinking she won't be found out if she crosses the line because Mrs. Miflin has eyes in the back of her head and will be quick enough turfing Judy out on her ear if she messes up. And then she tells everything she knows and more that she doesn't about the other tenants.

Ginny Mustard walks to the harbour. Tries to think things

over but there's a boat in and the gulls are hanging around looking for scraps as the fish are cleaned and life being the way it is for Ginny Mustard, she forgets all about the little song and the tiny bones and sits on the dock to watch the birds awhile. She stays until the sun is down and the moon fat over the water before she trudges back up the hill. Way inside her head, Ginny Mustard knows that she needs to tell someone about all of this - the bones and now the singing - but it is hard to remember sometimes and for all her good intentions she can only keep her mind on one thing at a time and is so easily lead astray by birds and cats or any number of interesting things in the world. Something is wrong and it nags away at her but for such brief intervals in her living that it may be someone else's duty to work it all out.

~

Eve and Maggie are in the sitting room. It is rare that anything happens in this room but for some reason Eve decided to draw Maggie out tonight and has come up with a project that might do the trick. On a white cotton tea towel she has printed large letters. *The kiss of the sun for pardon. The song of a bird for mirth. We're nearer God's heart in a garden than anywhere else on earth* and expects Maggie to embroider the whole thing. Not all at once of course. Eve would never ask that.

Maggie has never embroidered anything that she knows of and is having difficulty with the concept so Eve does a sample. Whips up a blue 't' as slowly as she is able. In a little tin can that once held English toffee, the kind with pretty shiny wrappers, are needles and a dozen skeins of floss and Eve suggests a color scheme. Now she threads a needle and places it in Maggie's right hand. Steers the white cloth to her left, just clear of the shoe box.

"And after you've done the letters you can put little flowers and birds in the leftover space. I didn't draw them. I think you'll have more fun doing them freehand."

Maggie, to whom the concept of fun is as foreign as that of needlework, nods rapidly and takes a stab at an 'h'. The shoe box is in the way and there's a bit of a struggle to get the needle out of it to make the return stitch but it's really only time it takes and neither of them has much else to do tonight. Eve has brought home the errant hedgehog and settled it among the new shoots of the hosta and the moon won't be on Maggie's bed until after ten.

Eve would like to talk about Judy - she's never seen a girl as tall. Or as well decorated, with rings and studs all over her body and that orange hair. But each time she speaks Maggie stops her embroidery and stares straight ahead of herself so Eve gives it up and says nothing until she feels Maggie has had enough drawing out for one night and tells her she can quit until next time.

By moonlight, the moonlight on Ginny Mustard as she walks from the waterfront, the moonlight making its way to Maggie's room to turn her skin soft blue, that irritates Ruth and makes Judy want to do bad things, that Mrs. Miflin never sees, Eve walks to the garden. The hedgehog snuffles by and she can just make out the smile on its pointed little face. Moonlight pushes its way through her hair and into the deep lines around her eyes and mouth. A small wind with summer at its back rustles the lilac and bathes her in perfume. She sits on the damp grass and listens to it grow awhile with her red sweater pulled tight around her and the sleeve ends tucked in the palms of her old hands.

~

Ginny Mustard keeps walking. It's one of those nights when people leave their windows open and she knows of a big house that has music. The kind that starts off slow and sad and grows up and up until it seems she will break from the sound of it. She climbs over the fence to the backyard and waits at the base of a rhododendron, takes off her shoes and rests her bare toes against the back of the marble Buddha that waits with her, has waited with her every spring as far as she can remember for the music to begin. Knees to her chin and arms wrapped around her legs, she is small and hidden.

And at the appointed hour someone walks to the kitchen sink and pours water into a glass. Stares out the window for a minute or two. Ginny Mustard knows that he doesn't see her. Even when the moon is full, he never sees her. And then the music comes. And she closes her eyes and lets it crawl through her for a while until there is no room for anything else. And it becomes an aching so fierce that she trembles all over with the strength of it and the Buddha becomes unbearably hot with her heat and she pulls her toes away and lies folded on the ground.

Sometimes she stays there a long time. Now and then she has fallen asleep and awakened with the sun on her face and the little ants in her clothes. Other times she has had to leave and run as hard as she can to get the pain out and on those nights she promises herself she will never go back but it's been a long winter and here she is again.

~

Ruth sits and stares at herself in the mirror. She brushes her hair that hasn't been colored for two years or more and is streaked gray to her chin and solid black to her waist. It took three bottles of dye the last time she did it and she dripped some in the sink and on the hall rug when she walked back to her room. Mrs. Miflin never did get the stains out and complains to Ruth whenever she's pissed about something and happens to be anywhere near the third floor bathroom at the same time Ruth is. There's nothing to be done about it. She tried bleach and steel wool and gave it up for a bad job.

The moon laughs at Ruth and she becomes more and more irritated. Itching all over. She trudges to the bathroom and scrubs her face. In the shower she turns the water cold and hard on her skin and leaves it that way for a long time. Back in her room she sits again and stares at her hair. The moon is still laughing but not so much at her as near her, inclined to share some cosmic joke if only Ruth will listen.

Ruth's hair has always looked as though it wants off her head and to fly. Her mother had combed and tied and buckled it down in vain. The minute her back was turned it was gone again. Her father called it 'nigger knots' and wouldn't let Ruth out in the summer unless it was raining. If she was tanned she would look like one of those friggin' coloreds and he wasn't having that. When he caught sight of Ruth with her hair all over the place he would go into a rage - yelling and hollering there was no way he could be the father of a youngster with a head on her like that. And he would find a pencil and paper and try to figure out where he was when Ruth's mother got pregnant and who might have been around in his absence. Hours he spent at it, but not being mathematically inclined, never did come up with an answer though he asked the question often enough.

And now here is Ruth with the moon over her shoulder and her hair dries soft and floats about her face. How long since she let it free? How long since she was free? How long since she supported the warm weight of a strong man? How long since she dug her heels into a mattress and howled? And why the hell is she thinking this way? It's that damned moon! She curses as she yanks the curtains to shut it out but they never did close properly and a thin streak of blue winks in the mirror when she turns off the overhead light.

Ruth is wrong, though, and while the moon may be in on it, she is not the cause. This particular disturbance hitched a ride with Judy. It is in her pockets and on her face and finding the inhabitants of Mrs. Miflin's house needing a little more than they had bargained for, has decided to stay awhile. With the moon's blessing it is creeping under doors and through closets leaving a smudge of itself on shirts and underwear, photographs and letters. And it goes to the attic for a quick look around before sliding under Mrs. Miflin's pillow to nap.

~

Tonight Ginny Mustard doesn't leave her nest under the rhododendron until the music stops and the lights go out in the big house. At midnight she walks home with the moon to guide her steps. Lets herself in the front door. Climbs the stairs to her room and crawls under her covers, the creak creaking of a cradle lulling her to sleep.

~

The new day begins with a bang. Judy is furious because Mrs. Miflin has forbidden her to visit friends on Caine's Street. She started off asking nicely for permission and when that didn't work she took to stomping around the house, slamming doors and yelling about what a bitch Mrs. Miflin is and how she's going to report her to the authorities for keeping her locked up. Maggie is hiding in her room with her shoebox tucked under the bed and both hands pressed to her ears and she hums as loud as she can to drown the terrible sounds, lies on the floor and curls in a ball, rocks back and forth, back and forth.

Ruth is pissed. She has been trying to write a quiet letter to someone she hasn't heard tell of in years, who visited her dreams last night. She can't think with that racket going on and twice has pushed pen through paper in exasperation.

Eve is in the garden looking for signs of new life. She went back inside when the fight began and found a pair of blue earmuffs for silence and is quite content to pick away at the earth despite the battle.

Old Father Delaney poked his head out of the rectory at one point and wondered briefly what the fuss was all about but he hasn't been in that house since it was a convent and it will take more than blood-curdling screams to entice him there again.

It would be easy enough for Judy to overpower the round Mrs. Miflin and escape, but she chooses not to. Would rather do some screaming and slamming. Mrs. Miflin is right, of course, though that's the last thing Judy will admit aloud. She just wants to get over to Jimmy's house for a bit of weed, is all. She hasn't been high since last week and Jimmy owes her big time since she's the only one who knows he beat the crap out of Frankie and the cops are still looking. When Frankie gets out of his coma he'll tell for sure but right now only Judy can point the finger. It's killing her to have the upper hand and see it go to waste. Still and all she has to clean up her act. She has had as many chances as she'll ever get. The joke is they don't know the half of it but they might any day now and a bad move will have her in shit so deep she'll never get out again.

So as quickly as she blows up she calms down. Tells Mrs. Miflin she's sorry for calling her names and making such a fuss and heads out to the garden to see what Eve is up to. When she sees Judy coming Eve takes off her earmuffs and smiles hello. Judy had a grammy once who was nice to her and she likes old women though this one is older than anyone she has ever seen before. She asks Eve what she's doing and actually listens to the answer. Judy, who has never noticed a flower in her life, can walk on dandelion and crocus alike and not blink an eye, hears where the primrose will grow and how high the clematis will climb and the best place to plant calendula and morning glory. She touches the curled leaves of monkshood and columbine and when Eve describes the workings of a compost bin and where she'd put one if Mrs. Miflin would only allow it, Judy blows her own sharp mind by volunteering to build one.

"Doesn't sound too complicated," she says. "If we had some wood. Do you think missus might have some in the basement? There's always wood in basements. Probably a saw and hammer too."

Mrs. Miflin follows them to the foot of the basement stairs, yammering all the while about the smells and the flies and the rats more than likely and why can't Eve just get some nice fertilizer instead it's bad enough what with mud being tracked in over the floor all spring she's not putting up with rats on top of it, and that she isn't. Judy says she's bored out of her friggin' skin with nothing to do around here and if Eve wants a compost bin why shouldn't she have one. Judy knows of a boarding house over on Caine's Street where they let the tenants do whatever they friggin' well want and wouldn't it be nice now if Eve decided to pack up and move there. And just think how much you'll save on garbage bags with the potato peels and all going into the bin. And Mrs. Miflin, who prides herself on the rapid growth of her savings account, gives up and grumbles her way to the kitchen to prepare lunch.

The old basement is musty and damp, full of boxes and bags and nuts and bolts, trunks and dead things waiting. Mrs. Miflin never comes here if she can help it, lets the furnace man find his own way around. As Judy reasoned, there is wood. Tools. Nails. The only thing missing is chicken wire and Eve says maybe they can buy it at the hardware store out near the mall but it will be difficult bringing it home on the bus. Judy has a cousin who might have some. He's always collecting junk for one thing or another and after they drag their treasures to the backyard she makes a phone call. Comes out with a grin on her face. Says, "Well now, we got our chicken wire. As much as we need. Harold is going to bring it over this afternoon. I told him make sure he does. I told him if he doesn't get it here by two-thirty sharp I'm going to tell the cops he's been trying to get into my pants since I was ten years old. See, Eve, you just got to know how to talk to people." And Eve smiles the saddest smile. Says, "Thank you."

Mrs. Miflin calls through the kitchen window. "One of you run upstairs and bang on Ginny Mustard's door and tell her to get herself out of that bed and come down for lunch. If she doesn't eat she'll be moping around the whole day with her stomach rumbling and I'll be damned if she's getting anything else before supper. Go on, now, and get her up."

Ginny Mustard has not slept this soundly for a long time. All through the night she was rocked gentle and held so close. When she hears Judy's knock and opens her eyes it is almost noon. She is ravenous. Races to the bathroom to wash her face and practically leaps over the others to get to her seat at table. She even eats the leftovers that Ruth pushes onto her plate. It isn't until Mrs. Miflin goes to make tea that she hears the song from the attic - hears *hush little baby don't say a word* - and when she begins to hum along everyone stares at her and then jumps when Mrs. Miflin drops the kettle on her way from the stove to the counter and screams. They rush to find her flat out on the floor and burning, boiling water splashed all over her chubby legs. While Eve hurries upstairs to find ointment, Judy picks up the whimpering Mrs. Miflin and carries her - with no more effort than if she were a little bird - to the armchair by the kitchen window.

"The best thing now, Mrs. Miflin," says Eve on her rush

back into the room, "is to get yourself into a bath and stay there until the burning stops. And then we'll put this on and you'll be fine in no time. Ruth, you go run a cool bath for Mrs. Miflin, dear, and while the tub is filling tell Maggie everything's okay and she can come out of her room. She gets so upset when there's either bit of noise at all in the house. Ginny Mustard, you go in and start clearing the table and Judy, you help her with the dishes after you carry Mrs. Miflin upstairs so she can have a lovely bath and stop the burning. Now, Mrs. Miflin, don't you worry about a thing. Once you're settled in the tub I'll bring you a nice cup of tea and you can just relax."

And Mrs. Miflin, whose job it has always been to do whatever bossing around needs to be done, is at a loss. No one has every volunteered to look after her that she can remember, and the pain is getting to the point where she feels like crying. She folds and gives in. And here's Judy with the strongest arms picking her up body and bones, carrying her to the bathtub. She sits on the edge while Eve helps her out of her clothes, doesn't even blush with her round body exposed to other eyes and slides with relief into the tepid water.

Downstairs the rattle of pots and pans. Sounds of washing and drying and putting away. Ginny Mustard has a vague feeling that she is to blame for Mrs. Miflin's misfortune but can't quite put her finger on what she did wrong. Maggie stands at the end of the counter, clutching her shoebox and waiting. Ruth sits in the armchair while Ginny Mustard and Judy work. When Eve comes back she tells them that things are probably going to be a little different around here for a few days while Mrs. Miflin recovers. She can do the cooking if they will help out with the cleaning and whatever else it is that keeps Mrs. Miflin on the run day and night.

From the bathroom comes a call. Mrs. Miflin was going to pick up groceries this afternoon and now there won't be anything to eat for a week. She has a list and tells Eve where she keeps her money. Makes her promise not to tell the others, especially Judy, for she might be as strong as an ox but she doesn't trust her any further than she can throw her and Mrs. Miflin won't be put in the poorhouse by the likes of that one.

"Now make sure you go to the corner market for the tinned goods and boxes and Wareham's for the meat and fish and frozen stuff and go to Murphy's for vegetables and apples. God. I can't be making bread in my condition. If I tell you how do you think you can? I'm not paying those prices for bread and rolls. I never did and I won't be starting now. And bring me my radio off the top shelf in the kitchen. I'm not about to sit here and listen to nothing all day." Mrs. Miflin needs some control. For a few minutes there it seemed she was losing it and if that were ever to happen who knows what would become of her so she grabs and clutches what little is left to build on until she is back on top where she should be.

Eve finds the money and the list and the shopping cart and brings Mrs. Miflin a cup of tea. She plans to take Judy with her when she goes but does not bother to mention this to Mrs. Miflin. If she could convince the poor thing to go to the hospital - but no - Mrs. Miflin will have none of it. She doesn't like hospitals. She's heard her share of horror stories from people who went to have gall bladders removed or hearts repaired and came away dead or with holes in their kidneys. No hospitals for Mrs. Miflin and that's that.

Mrs. Miflin has not missed a Sunday Mass since she was born except for that one time. And now she wants to confess she won't be there tomorrow. Ruth is dispatched to the rectory to find Father Delaney. Mrs. Miflin cannot have such a sin on her soul. If she should die before she can get back on her feet and over to the church it's hell for all eternity. Mrs. Miflin knows this for a fact.

~

Father Delaney's housekeeper is not all that fond of living so near such a queer crowd of women. She looks Ruth up, down and sideways before she opens the screen door. Once she does, though, Ruth is past her and down the hall calling out to the old man.

"Father," she says. "Mrs. Miflin has burned herself with the kettle water. She wants to see you right away. She's in a state thinking she might die in the night and needs to confess."

"She confessed this morning. What could she possibly have done since then that she needs me now? I was just having my tea."

'She hasn't done anything. She wants to confess the sin of not going to Mass tomorrow so she can stay out of hell."

"I don't think a person can go around confessing sins they haven't committed yet. Besides, she was at Mass today and if she doesn't get there tomorrow it isn't even a sin. Hasn't been for years. And the Pope went and told everyone there's no such thing as hell anyway so what's her problem? Fool Pope. I don't know how he thinks we're going to get them interested in heaven if we don't have hell to throw at them."

"I think you may have missed the point, Father, but that's none of my concern. Are you coming or not? Hell or no hell, the woman wants to confess and if I go back without you I'll never hear the end of it. I'll wait until doomsday if I have to so you might as well say yes now and get it over with."

Father Delaney trudges down the hall and out into the sunlight, muttering. Looks like he has to go back into that God-forsaken place after all. He follows Ruth. Grumbles all the way to the second floor bathroom. Eve hears him coming and closes the door to hide the naked Mrs. Miflin.

His conversation with the landlady is not unlike the one with Ruth and the little patience he had is gone so he gives in and, through the door, hears Mrs. Miflin confess that she didn't go to church tomorrow to which he replies that she should say the Sorrowful Mysteries and if her legs hurt too much to kneel she can say them in bed or wherever else she wants. He leaves the house and Mrs. Miflin yells to Eve to bring her Rosary beads and since she said the Sorrowful Mysteries last night for no reason at all, decides to say the Joyful Mysteries instead and to hell with Father Delaney. Settles back in the tub to purify her soul.

Eve hasn't shopped for groceries or anything else in six years, not since she moved to Mrs. Miflin's house. She is rather excited by the idea but pleased to have Judy along. She rarely leaves home or garden these days and is not sure what is out there anymore because she hears the news now and then and things don't sound all that pleasant. Eve loves the world but over time she has become cautious.

So there they go to replenish the pantry. Eve tall and strong and gray. Judy taller and stronger and orange-crowned with rings and studs in her ears and nose and tongue. An unlikely pair if ever there was one. They follow the list to the letter until they reach fresh vegetables and then it's a bit of this and a bit of that, green leafy things that neither has tasted but they smell so very good and since Eve will pay for the extras with her own money, and Mrs. Miflin will be abed for a few days, they decide there's no harm in a little change.

At home they are greeted by Ruth in a mood. Mrs. Miflin is still in the tub looking like a prune but her left leg is swelling up fast and she may have broken something.

"Oh dear," says Eve. "She must have hit the floor harder than we thought. I guess there's nothing for it but to get her to the hospital."

"Well, better you than me trying to convince her of that. I've been running back and forth since you left the house and I've had enough of it. I'm going to my room to finish this damned letter. And there's about fifty yards of chicken wire in the kitchen that some freak dropped off. Said he's a cousin of Judy's though I wouldn't claim him too loud if I were you, girl. Someone should get it out of there. I don't have time for any more of this crap, damn it."

In the end an ambulance takes the sorry Mrs. Miflin away, Eve and Ginny Mustard following on foot to sit with her until she's seen to. By the time they find her in the maze of halls she has been wrapped in a cast from thigh to toe and is none too happy. The doctor tells her there's no point in even thinking about crutches for a couple of weeks and she'll be in plaster until September. With instructions, "Off to bed with you and stay there, take these for the pain, put this on the burns." but without telling her how to get ointment under a cast, he rushes away to mend someone else. Eve calls a taxi and Ginny Mustard wheels Mrs. Miflin to it, hoping Judy is at home to haul the victim up over the stairs when they get there.

She is and she does and once the poor old soul is settled in her bed Eve calls a meeting of the household to discuss the situation and enlist everyone's help. She has a pen and a notebook and reading glasses perched on the end of her nose and looks for all the world as though she knows what she's doing. Which is more than can be said for the others. Things don't happen around here. For all except Judy, every day, every month, is pretty much like the one that came before and reruns can be expected next year and the year after and the year after that. Each knows what the other will say or do at any given time. Maggie has never spoken and hides in her room if she hears so much as a dog bark. Ginny Mustard eats and wanders and when she does talk she's all over the place and no one remembers the last time she made sense. Ruth is bitchy and scowling when things don't go her way and since they don't know what her way might be, they mostly ignore her. Eve walks softly but apparently carries a bigger stick than they would have known if it weren't for Mrs. Miflin's misfortune. And Judy - well they haven't really taken a good look at that girl yet but at first glance she's trouble. Something hovering about her and shining through her eyes all the time puts them on edge and if it were possible Maggie would clutch her shoebox even tighter when she comes around.

With Mrs. Miflin's assistance, Eve has compiled a list of everything that goes into being a success in the landlady department. Ruth must argue for a few minutes that someone should be hired to look after the place - they are paying good money and shouldn't have to work their asses off in the bargain. Ginny Mustard surprises them with " You're on welfare, Ruth. It's not your good money." To which Ruth responds, "Little snip. What the hell do you know about it?" though the fact that she understood an entire sentence from Ginny Mustard keeps her awake later.

Truth is, only Eve is independent of government assistance. The others have, reasons apparent or not, relied on Social Services for a good many years now. While Mrs. Miflin tends to frown on *that welfare crowd,* these people are her bread and butter and she doesn't voice her opinion on the matter aloud. The rest of the world is not exactly beating a path to her door to rent a room, for all that she's a great cook and keeps the cleanest house in the city.

If Mrs. Miflin could get someone to go to Mass for her every day she would but as it is the only items on her list of things that have to be done are basic and according to Judy, "Boring as hell for fuck sake and instead of everyone doing the same thing over and over why can't we take turns and switch around a bit? And how is that one supposed to do anything if she can't put down the friggin' box for a second. What's she going to do? Wash dishes with one hand? Not bloody likely. Tell her Eve. Tell her to put it down. She gives me the creeps. What's in the box Maggie?"

And Judy leaps from her chair and aims for Maggie who hauls off and lets her have it square across the head with the precious shoebox.

"Oh dear," says Eve. "That wasn't very nice Maggie. Judy is going to have a lump on her head and a black eye too from the looks of it."

Judy is hollering blue murder. Ginny Mustard pulls her hair over her face, the better to hide behind, and Ruth, for once, has nothing to say. If anyone were to look closely she might see a twitch at the corner of Maggie's mouth - barely there - not quite a smile but what else would you call it? If she hadn't glanced at Judy as the girl rushed her, none of this would have happened. But there was that something in Judy's eyes daring her - just daring her - to make a move and so she did. And a little voice is urging her up the stairs and into her room as fast as she can go but another is telling her stay and see what happens next and since the latter controls her feet she eases herself back into the old sofa and waits.

From Mrs. Miflin's room comes the sound of pure misery. Judy quits her ranting and they all troop up to see what the devil she wants now. On the bed Mrs. Miflin is a wee, helpless thing. They are surprised. Have never seen her with the wind out of her sails before. Someone must read to her. Everyday. She pulls a battered Bible from her night table. Who will refuse such a request from this wreck of a woman? Ginny Mustard does. She has a reading level of nothing. Maggie as well, by way of Eve, who reminds Mrs. Miflin that if she won't speak she probably won't read either. That leaves Eve, Judy and Ruth and they can take turns in the mornings after breakfast if that's okay with Mrs. Miflin. Eve leaves the room and returns with water. Supports Mrs. Miflin's head and helps her down one of the doctor's painkillers. Tucks her in and ushers the others away.

"She's really out of it," says Ruth when they have settled

again in the sitting room. "Never even mentioned the racket Judy made when Maggie whacked her with the shoebox. Who'd have thought you had it in you, Maggie? Mousing around all the time and turns out you're a bit of a wild one after all." There is something akin to admiration in Ruth's voice, noticed by no one but Judy, scowling.

Maggie is back to her statue self, staring straight ahead and through the others from her perch on the sofa. It might all have been imagined but for the egg-sized lump over Judy's blackening eye. Eve brings a bag of frozen peas from the kitchen, wrapped in a tea towel. Presses it to Judy's forehead. "Here, dear. This will bring the swelling down. I think it might be best not to bother Maggie anymore today if you can help it. Now let's try to get our duties straightened out. Perhaps Judy is right and we should not have assigned tasks. Why don't we write everything on little pieces of paper and then everyone can pick a few in the morning and that way we can all have some variety to our days."

Only Judy cares for variety in any shape or form but no one wants to be stuck with cleaning toilets for the next three months either so Eve goes to the kitchen to find scissors and a nice bowl to put the chores in. All she comes up with are pinking shears and a pickle jar but they will do for now.

Ginny Mustard who doesn't know her ass from her elbow in a kitchen must have Judy's help to read recipes. It's fine and dandy to say let's have pork chops for dinner but if no one can tell her how to cook them they'll surely starve. Judy's prior experience erasing serial numbers from stolen goods makes her one of your better pot scrubbers. Maggie can dust and wax the old furniture with the shoebox tucked safely under an arm. Ruth can sing to her heart's content under the noise of the decrepit vacuum cleaner with no chance that anyone will accuse her of being in a good mood. Eve encourages Ginny Mustard to throw her bit of this and bit of that green things in with dinner but put a plate aside for Mrs. Miflin first since she might not like the taste.

At table they are tired now. Neither has worked this hard in eons and other than the odd, "How does she do this every day?" and, "What's this stuff on the pork chops?" there is little talk. With no Mrs. Miflin to fill the space with her ramblings they will eat in silence until someone stumbles upon the art of conversation.

Within a day or two they are trading chores. Ginny Mustard likes cooking and Judy wants to wax the long front hallway. Wants to slide up and down it in her sock feet until it gleams or she breaks her neck, whichever comes first. Ruth talks Eve into reading again to Mrs. Miflin and in exchange cleans toilets and tubs. Maggie takes what's left and finds herself washing dishes with her shoebox in a plastic bag to keep it dry. When she's feeling brave she puts it on the counter near the sink and only grabs it up again when she hears someone coming.

All goes well. Busy, they keep out of one another's sight for the most part. Mrs. Miflin insists that even the unoccupied rooms be kept clean and tidy and ready for the tenants she dreams of. Judy went out for milk one day and came back with a bag of kittens that some old fellow was dragging to the park. He was going to leave them there and if someone came along and took them home - fine - and if they just crawled around for a day and died - that was fine too and he didn't care one way or the other since he's had his fill of friggin' cats and it's hard enough feeding himself these days with the friggin' prices on everything and if he never saw another friggin' cat in his life it would be too soon. And what's worse, the poor little momma cat was trailing after him and the bag of her babies and no matter how many rocks he threw at her she wouldn't leave and she wouldn't stop her crying. What was the girl to do? She took the bag and, with momma cat close at her heels, brought the whole mess home and plunked it down, though gently, on the kitchen floor.

Ginny Mustard has found a pretty picture of an apple cake in the recipe book and is pleased to see Judy coming. Maggie is putting away the last of the lunch dishes. Eve walks in just as Judy loosens the drawstring of the noisy brown bag.

"Don't anyone go yelling at me. You know you'd have to bring them home too. Well, maybe not Ruth, but the rest of you would. He was just going to leave them there in the park and the dogs'd have them killed in a minute. Look at them. They're so pretty. We have to keep them. No one else is gonna want them. I didn't know what else to do. Stupid old fucker. I'd like to put him in a bag and throw him away. See how he likes it."

And now they are all sitting on the floor. And six kittens waddle every which way on fragile legs, blinking in the sudden light until Ruth comes stomping in and they skitter to Maggie and hide among the folds of her big skirt. Momma cat sits tight. Stares at Ruth with golden eye. Dares her say anything other than welcome.

The cat stares and Ruth stares and before either cracks there's a loud knock at the front door and Ruth leaves to answer it. The sudden collective out-breath is audible above momma cat's wonderful purr. Ruth comes back. "There's someone who says his name is Joe Snake and he wants to see Ginny Mustard. I don't like the looks of him so he's waiting outside."

Eve says, " You didn't invite him in, dear?"

"No I didn't. That cousin of Judy's was here the other day smelling up the place and this one doesn't look much better. Why is it the only people who come around here aren't fit to live? And what the hell are you going to do with those things? You'd better get rid of them before Mrs. Miflin gets a whiff. She hates cats more than I do." And she's gone to her room.

But little cat softness and little cat sounds follow, and the tiny pads of little cat feet - she can feel them on her face as surely as if she had picked one up and pushed her nose into its round belly. Paper thin claws, sharp baby teeth on her fingers. And her kitten ghosts are with her as she falls on her bed, face in the pillow, back to the door. Behind closed eyes she sees her father with yet another brood in a cardboard box and the car running and the hose attached to the tailpipe and in a few minutes kitten bodies in the garbage can. And that last one. The one she loved so much. The one she hid from her father and he had to go and kill the rest of them anyway because he was late. And she prayed hard. If God would only let her keep this one she'd never ask for another thing as long as she lived. She'd go and be a missionary in Africa with the heathens. She'd do anything He wanted if only she could keep this one. And her mother told on her when she found the kitten in the laundry hamper and her father was tired and cranky. Squeezed its sweet neck until there was no life left in it and threw it away. Ruth hasn't touched a cat since she was eight years old. She hates them with a passion pure and harsh.

Ruth refuses supper. When Eve comes to fetch her, says, "Get out of my face you old hag." Turns to the wall again and stays there until the house is quiet and everyone sleeping. Goes to the park and wraps herself around the hyacinth and when she stands up she is all purple and smells of them. And she is them. And she goes to the ocean high up on the rocks and puts her arms in the clouds and she is wave and salt and hyacinth even after she goes back to her room at the very end of the house beyond the linen closet. She turns on a lamp and cuts her hair all the way to the gray and leaves a pool of black curls on the floor surrounding her chair for someone else to clean up.

There are no dreams. Nothing gets her up in darkness and forces her outside for a walk at three in the morning, though when she wakes her pillowcase is wet as if she has been crying in her sleep.

~

Outside and through most of the night, someone watching. Leaning against a tree in front of the old orphanage and staring at the house. He watches Ruth come and go. He watches lights and he watches dark. Before the sun peeps over the hill on the left side of the harbour he is gone and nothing to show for his being there but footprints and the strong scent of something ugly that follows the children who pass by on their way to school. Makes their skin go all shivery. Makes them think of damp places.

Mrs. Miflin smells it when Eve opens her bedroom window and demands that she shut it again. Eve doesn't notice it at all and doesn't understand what Mrs. Miflin is upset about. Judy smells it when she goes outside to work on the compost bin and grins a little fox grin to herself. Maggie just feels cold and piles on a couple of sweaters and Ginny Mustard thinks of nuns. By the time Ruth appears for the day, the sun has warmed the ugliness away and she can't smell it over breakfast.

~

Her hair is a hit, although Judy thinks it too gray and suggests red dye. Eve thinks it softens Ruth. Makes her look almost approachable but she doesn't say that. Smiles her approval. Ginny Mustard memorizes it so she can make a picture later on and Maggie cuts her own thick braid with pinking shears over the garbage can in the kitchen after the table has been cleared.

Mrs. Miflin won't eat. Pushes her eggs around the plate and doesn't drink her tea. The burning has left her legs and she spends much of her time under painkillers. All last night she moaned in fitful dreams of cradles and dark anger. She dug and dug time after time until she found the little bones. Again and again she carried them, washed them, wrapped them. For all her work she woke with empty arms. She has to get out of this bed, this room. She is suffocating under the weight of her helplessness. They won't move her. Follow the doctor's orders. She fears the worst. They are taking over. She heard laughter on the stairs. Someone humming a nothing tune. She hates the noise. She hates the quiet more.

After supper, unrecognizable but certainly edible, the sitting room is fully occupied for the first time since the nuns blew away, and seems pleased with itself. Eve is guiding Maggie through her project. Maggie, feeling brave, has tucked the shoebox under her knees to facilitate a smoother stitch. Ruth is writing her letter. A full notepad gone and she is still on the first page. Judy lies on the floor, her long legs up on the seat of an armchair, her body crawling with kittens, momma cat close by. Ginny Mustard comes in and presents Ruth with a paper place mat, one side advertising events upcoming four years ago, the other showing a likeness of Ruth in her new hair, sketched with colored pencils. Says softly, "I made this."

"Well shit, Ginny Mustard. Is that supposed to be me? I'm flattered, girl, but you really should get your eyes checked."

"Oh no," says Eve. "That looks exactly like you Ruth. You are quite lovely, dear, when you aren't frowning. You are a very good artist, Ginny Mustard."

"No kidding," says Judy. "Do another one but this time make her hair red so she can see how much better it would look. Can you do one of me too? This is way cool."

Ginny Mustard doesn't know what to do with a compliment. She stares at the others for a full thirty seconds before running to her room. Brings back pages and pages of her pictures. And they examine them carefully, with pleasure, surprised. Even Maggie finds the corners of her mouth in a twitch. Second one this week. But after flowers and faces and the river, the hills and the ocean, small bones in a cradle, wrapped in pink blanket, begging touch and feel how soft.

"What the fuck is that Ginny Mustard? What have you got against babies you didn't put any skin on it?" Judy is upset.

"Oh dear," says Eve. "Why would you draw this kind of picture? It is very sad, isn't it? Where would you have seen such a thing?"

Ginny Mustard recoils - a puppy kicked. But they are all looking at her. They all want something of her and she beckons them follow. Leads them to the attic. Around ancient dark furniture. Brushing cobwebs aside. Under dim light shows them the cradle of tiny bones in pink blanket.

"I found this baby when I looked for a lightbulb. Judy said there might be one. So I looked but I didn't find one. I found this baby. She has a pretty blanket and a little rocking bed. I don't think she is sad."

In silence they stare. First at the cradle, then Ginny Mustard, cradle again, Ginny Mustard. There is nothing to say. It is unbearably hot in the attic. A fly buzzes on a dirty window. Eve is the first to head back to the sitting room, the others not far behind. Ginny Mustard closes the attic door ever so gently. They sit wordless for five minutes or more before Ruth speaks.

"I guess we'll have to report this to Her Majesty's finest. I'm sure they have a dead youngster nothing but bones department. Do you think the old nuns did it? I wouldn't put it past them."

"Whatever happened to that poor little baby," says Eve, "someone must have loved it very much to want to keep it for so long. It must be dead forty years or more. There's nothing left on the bones at all."

Judy interrupts. "You're giving me the creeps, you guys. And anyway - it could be dead only last year. You can boil bones in acid, you know, to get all the flesh off. I saw a movie once and the guy had some kind of bugs that could clean bones in a week. He was a cop or something and they use those bugs when they want to get at a skull real fast. It was a true story. Well I'm not sleeping in this house anymore until those friggin' bones are gone out of here."

"Shut up, Judy. I don't know what the hell your problem is," says Ruth. "Nothing ever happened in this place until you showed up. And now here's Maggie hitting people and Mrs. Miflin crippled in her bed and you even managed to talk her into a compost bin. I never would have cut my fucking hair if you weren't stirring things up. I don't know how you do it but you do. You're a pain in the ass. And I, for one, will be only too happy to see the tail end of you heading out. Why don't you leave so we can get back to normal?"

"Normal? You call this normal? Bunch of old bats holed up in a freak house? Sure Eve wasn't in a store for years until I took her out for groceries. You had a good time, didn't you Eve? And if freaky Maggie there can do something besides creep around like a zombie - even if it's just hit someone up side the head - well who cares? It's better than going around half dead all the friggin' time. And if you didn't cut your witch hair Ginny Mustard wouldn't have made that picture of you and if she didn't show us her other pictures we wouldn't know about the bones up there and - oh - right - I see what you mean. Well excuse me for living!"

Eve gets up and stands next to Judy's chair. Reaches to stroke her orange spikes. "There, there, dear. We'll get to the bottom of this. None of it is your fault." She's not sure that's the truth but she did have a grand time shopping and wants to do it again.

Maggie gathers the kittens in her big skirt, pours them on to Judy's lap. "See, dear?" says Eve. "Maggie isn't mad at you.

She's brought the kittens to take your mind off all of this. Your hair looks really nice, Maggie. If you like I can give it a trim around your eyes there so it's not all hanging in your face. Maybe we can do that tomorrow. Now I think we should get ourselves to bed. Why don't you just let me think on this for awhile and we can talk about it again in the morning. There's nothing to be done at this late hour and since the baby has been here for a long time I'm sure it won't be any harder to sleep tonight than it was last night."

The others are skeptical but Ginny Mustard smiles. She likes the singing and the creaking of the cradle and feels much better now that the others know her secret. It's not that it weighed her down, but it did get in the way now and then.

~

Across the road he takes his place under the aspen. Listens to it whisper above him, a greasy frown on his mouth as the fog moves in from the harbour. Up Water Street. Beaton's Row. Caine's Street. Settles thick and gray in his eyes until the house disappears and, nothing to see, he limps back to the river.

In the morning, even before Ginny Mustard begins to prepare breakfast, they gather again in the sitting room, silently, as though the slightest sound will wake whatever else might be sleeping in this crypt of a house. Mrs. Miflin is still dead to the world and Eve's first whisper convinces them to keep her ignorant of the situation. "She's had a rough go of it, poor thing, and there's plenty of time when she's feeling better to let her know what's going on."

"Poor thing, my ass," hisses Ruth. "She probably knows all about it. It's her house. You think she doesn't know what's in the bloody attic? She probably put it there. I'd never have taken her for a killer, though. She doesn't seem the type."

"Fat lot you know about killers, Ruth." This from Judy, who hasn't had much practice whispering and they all jump slightly when she opens her mouth. "You think they run around drooling and knives hanging out of their pockets. Well let me tell you, some of the nicest looking people in the world are bad to the bone. Take my friend Geoff. He'd do in his granny for a dime of hash if he could get away with it. Anyway - I think he did because one day when I went over there was a hearse taking her away and she was okay before that. Just kind of old is all."

Ginny Mustard doesn't like where this conversation is going. She concentrates especially hard to keep up. "Do we have to give it back? The baby? Can we keep it? Judy got to keep the kittens."

"And who the hell would we give it to?" asks Ruth. "Put an ad in the paper and ask if anyone is missing an old dead baby? Check your graves and give us a call? For God's sake, Ginny Mustard, you don't have the sense of a turnip."

"Well, I'm at a loss," says Eve.

From Mrs. Miflin's room comes a weak plea. She needs to get to the bathroom, most likely, and Judy leaps to her duty.

~

Patricia Hartman waits for her plane to board, purse on her lap, ticket in hand. Since the funeral she has debated the wisdom of going and still ponders her decision. Her mother would have disapproved. They had been over it several times in the last two years, each conversation ending with her mother's insistence that in everyone's interest the past was better left alone. Let the lawyers handle it. Her mother died unaware that Patricia had been watching. Never saw the letters written. Never heard the phone calls. Patricia Hartman is not the kind of woman to let go willingly, no matter how calmly she might appear to do so. Her mother never knew that about her. The announcer calls her flight. She leaves her seat and walks tall to the gate.

~

While Judy attends Mrs. Miflin and Ginny Mustard waits with the kittens for a breakfast recipe, Ruth tells Maggie to come with her to the corner store and help her carry back a load of beer. No one has ever brought alcohol into Mrs. Miflin's house. That would be ungodly. But, as Ruth reasons, what the old doll doesn't know won't hurt her. If they can protect her highness from bones in the attic, it shouldn't be too damned difficult to keep a few brews tucked away in back of the fridge.

Shocked by her own willingness to leave the house, but more amazed by Ruth's audacity, Maggie pulls her shoes on and slowly, slowly goes down the front walk with Ruth to break the rules. It's normally a three minute walk but it takes a good ten with Maggie having to step aside whenever anyone comes by, a statue until they pass, with her head down and her shoebox clutched tight against her chest. But she made it. She made it. Spent ten minutes in the world. Didn't fall down. Wasn't struck dead. Nobody hurt her. Only when she hears a transport truck does she realize the extent of her folly, but briefly. Ruth sees the panic and stays close enough to touch if Maggie feels the need.

Breakfast is late. Judy has been waylaid by Mrs. Miflin first and then Eve who thinks it's time to dig another bed in the garden and wants help. She will plant peas and lettuce, just a few of each so no one will get sick of them. Maybe a pumpkin. Tomatoes. There is so much marvelous space crying out for something more than grass. So Ginny Mustard goes ahead without Judy's assistance. Throws eggs and leftovers together with a bit of this and a bit of that green stuff. Cooks it up in the big cast iron pan and pours a bowl of corn flakes for Mrs. Miflin, all the while humming along to the song from the attic.

Maggie can't eat, though she sits through the meal. She has had more excitement than she can recall and is trembling all over with it. Afterwards Eve has a rough time trimming her hair with the constant squirming.

Eve says there is nothing to be done about the bones, they should wait to tell Mrs. Miflin, are they all agreed? Ruth says she doesn't give a damn as long as she can have a beer now and again. Ginny Mustard is pleased they can keep the baby. They take Maggie's movement for affirmation and Judy grumbles, but what the hell. Better than having cops asking questions all over the place with their big old boots on and just her luck they'd think she did it anyway.

Ginny Mustard wants to clean the attic now. It's too dusty for a little baby and before anyone can think of a good reason not to, she's off with a mop and a bucket of water. Scrub brush. No one else will go with her so she puts a couple of kittens in her pocket for company. Quietly past Mrs. Miflin's door, up the stairs.

"That girl is a loon if ever there was one," says Ruth. "And what's with her and the cooking? Does anyone else want a beer?" She goes to the kitchen. Finds one of the kittens has climbed into the fridge. Freezes in mid-reach. It looks dead. It looks so little, tiny paws tucked under its belly. She calls for someone to come but her words have no sound. Slowly puts her hand on the baby cat. The small head moves and the mouth opens to squeak. Grabbing a beer she carries the kitten to Maggie and dumps it in her lap on the way to her room.

~

Patricia Hartman settles herself comfortable in the back seat of a taxi, gives her driver the address of Mrs. Miflin's house, reads it from the slip of paper she holds in her long pink fingers. Deciding that the woman with the best luggage he has ever seen - and he's seen plenty - is probably good for a few dollars more than flat rate, Billy Ralph flips on the meter and takes the scenic route into town. From the airport he turns left and heads through Torbay, Flatrock and all the way into Pouch Cove telling stories and reciting history until his passenger asks him to please shut up she's not interested. He turns around and heads back to the city. If she notices that he has taken her 30 miles in the wrong direction, she doesn't say. He makes a quick run around Quidi Vidi Lake and through The Battery before stopping on Bishop's Road. That'll teach the bitch. Patricia takes off her sunglasses and stares him in the eye before paying the fare. No tip.

~

Mrs. Miflin asks Eve why none of her friends have come to visit. Why Mrs. Hennessey hasn't called. "And they call themselves Christians. There's not one of them cares if I'm dead or living." Eve doesn't have an answer but says she'll be happy to invite them over if Mrs. Miflin will tell her their phone numbers. She doesn't point out that she wasn't aware of any friends, never having seen one around. For all Mrs. Miflin's talk about the people in the neighborhood, most of her conversations with them seem to be in passing, on her way to the market or Mass. And it is rare to hear her speak well of them, confining her reports to the sad state of the clothes on their lines or the godawful colors they choose to paint their homes. With no phone numbers forthcoming, Eve tucks a blanket round Mrs. Miflin and leaves her to her misery.

Judy has had enough of hard labour for one day. Lately

she's been eyeing the ancient swings in the schoolyard. The heavy ropes are frayed but they have thick wooden seats, not like the ones in the park made of plastic that cuts into the sides of your ass when you sit on them. They were earmarked for replacement years ago but the process has been slowed by disinterest and lack of funds. It was simple enough to tell the students and parents that anyone who used them would surely kill themselves. The principal did concede to posting a plexiglass warning sign, though some of the older kids have long since written dirty words all over it in permanent ink and it will probably be removed if anyone notices.

The only way to the swings when the big gates are locked is through a chain link fence. Fortunately there are some good-sized holes in it, plenty of room if you're at all flexible. Judy nags until she finds someone to go with her. She's no fool and if a swing breaks while she's as high off the ground as she plans to be, she wants an extra body around to call an ambulance. So Maggie, nicknamed "good old Maggs" since her trip to the beer store, is enlisted. Puts her shoes on yet again and slowly makes her way to the fence, gets through without much effort, box in one hand, skirt dragging behind.

Judy is swinging up high in the trees, head back and mouth wide open. Maggie takes a chance. Sits down and gives a timid push with her feet. Puts her shoe box on the ground and works the swing a little higher. And a little higher than that and a little higher than that and soon she is flying with Judy, back and forth, back and forth. And then a laugh. Starts off a gasp and leaves like music - like a spring brook - like a happy toddler - and it bubbles through the air and hits Judy square in the face and if that girl were made of lesser stuff she'd have surely fallen. For an hour they swing until their legs can pump no more and they sit on the grass under the leaves until it feels like supper time.

When the taxi pulls up Ginny Mustard doesn't hear it

above her singing in the attic. Her brown skin is covered with dust and cobwebs and there is at least one spider spinning a home in her hair. Within a few minutes of the start of her cleaning project she had stripped to her underpants and between the heat and the dirt she is not looking much like her old self at all. She has scratches on her ankles from kittens thinking they've come to play and a nasty cut on her right arm from when she knocked over an old lamp. Once she shivered furiously but just assumed that someone was walking over her grave. If she had looked through the window at that very moment she would have seen the taxi, would have seen Patricia Hartman staring up at the house, seen her walk to the door and knock.

Eve is flustered. She can't find Maggie or Judy, Ruth won't come out of her room, and now here's the most elegant woman who looks vaguely familiar, claiming she has a reservation. Eve has explained that Mrs. Miflin is not well. Resting. Not to be disturbed. There's no one taking care of the house right now and the tenants are on their own. Mrs. Miflin must have forgotten all about Ms Hartman and it would be best under the circumstances if she take a hotel room. The woman is persistent and asks Eve to speak to the landlady. She doesn't want to stay in a hotel. Mrs. Miflin will be more than happy to have her if Eve will only give her name. So Eve tells Mrs. Miflin that Patricia Hartman is here. Watches as a little light goes on in the landlady's head but whether it's the thought of money making her eyes glow suddenly or the chance for new company or something altogether different, Eve doesn't know. And while she shows Miss Hartman to the sitting room she wonders how much good a woman with fingernails like that will be around here. Wonders if she'll like the others. Wonders how much she paid for her dress. Mutters, "Just when we have a little elbow room at the table, too." and is quickly ashamed of her pettiness.

While Eve checks to see that Miss Hartman's room is in

perfect condition, Maggie and Judy return from their swing in the park to find Patricia examining the wedding photographs. She introduces herself and holds out a hand. Maggie hangs her head and does nothing. Judy grabs the hand and shakes it fiercely. "Well fuck me gently. You've got to be something to Ginny Mustard. Except for she's brown and you're not, you two could be sisters." To which Patricia responds, "Yes. We are sisters. She is unaware of my existence. Is she at home?"

"Shit. This is a riot. I don't know where she is. Last going off she was heading for the attic to clean up. But wait now. You don't want to go up there. I'll get her and bring her down." And Judy races the stairs three at a time thinking how interesting this day has become all of a sudden.

Ginny Mustard is still up to her ears in dust. She found an unlocked trunk and curiosity got the better of her. She's been examining its contents for a few minutes, old clothes and a plaster horse with a clock in its side, a teapot, a christening gown of white silk, a rifle. When Judy comes tearing into the attic, Ginny Mustard drops the gun and leaps to her dirty feet. "Shit, Ginny Mustard, what are you doing with no clothes on? Mrs. Miflin might find that ungodly, you know. You're filthy. Get yourself together and come down. You've got a visitor." Ginny Mustard dresses. Doesn't stop to wash her face or pick the cobwebs off her arms, follows Judy to the sitting room, stands face to face with a whiter, cleaner version of herself.

"Hello, Virginia. I realize this is a shock. Perhaps we should sit down and I will attempt to explain."

"Well she can't sit on anything with that attic crud all over her. Mrs. Miflin will have a fit. Ginny Mustard, don't you move until I get a towel or something to put under you. Wait." And Judy disappears in the direction of the linen closet.

Maggie has been stone since she entered the room. On Judy's return she backs herself into a far corner, lifting her eyes now and then to take a small peek. Judy places a ragged blanket on the sofa and drags Ginny Mustard to sit, guides Patricia to sit near her and claims a place across the room where she can see the action.

Patricia says, "Perhaps it's best if we have privacy." Judy says, "Well there isn't any in this house." And Ginny Mustard says, "Stay here."

"If that's the way you want it, fine. There's no point in dragging this out so I'll get straight to the bottom line. My name is Patricia Hartman. We are sisters. I knew nothing about you until two years ago when our mother was diagnosed with cancer. She suffered an uncharacteristic attack of conscience and confided that she had left you in the hospital where she gave birth. Had, in fact, known there was some possibility of her doing just that, hence the trip to this city. She had been in the process of divorcing our father. He is African, from Nairobi, a professor of Anthropology. It seems that your pigment kept you behind. If you had been white enough she could have brought you home and no one would have been the wiser. As long as she could ignore our parentage, everything was fine, but obviously in your case that was impossible. Our mother was a racist but her parents even more so. She married him to escape their clutches, to defy them and eliminate them from her life permanently. Her strategy worked for several years. I was well into my teens before I met our maternal grandparents. They were unpleasant people although it is difficult to understand how she could resort to such extreme measures to upset them. Before she died I began the search for you. So, here I am. Mother left you approximately $300,000 which will be deposited into your bank account as soon as I inform her lawyers where you are. Those fools might have taken years to find you."

Throughout the monologue, Ginny Mustard stares at her sister's face. Now she reaches to touch Patricia's hair. She looks at her hands, and then her own, brown and dirty, nails ragged. She rises, takes the blanket and climbs the stairs to shower and change her clothes. Judy and Maggie follow close. "Holy shit Ginny Mustard," says Judy. "What are you going to do? You're rich, girl. Can we get cable? What do you think of that sister of yours? She looks a bit snotty if you want my opinion." But Ginny Mustard has nothing to say. They sit on the floor outside the bathroom door while she washes up and follow her to the kitchen when she's done.

Eve shows Patricia to her room and makes a beeline to the others for some catching up. An excited Judy fills her in while Maggie sets the table. "Oh my," says Eve. "How nice for you, Ginny Mustard, to have so much money after all you've been through. And such a lovely sister now when you never had any family before. You probably have aunts and uncles and cousins too. I am so happy for you, dear."

But Ginny Mustard is concentrating on chicken and potatoes and has no room to think about anything else. Judy is beside herself with excitement and can barely read out the recipe for gravy. She has never known anyone with money and Ginny Mustard has been elevated several notches in her estimation.

"God almighty Ginny Mustard. I can't believe you aren't jumping up and down all over the place. I tell you, I'd be making a list of stuff to buy if I had all that friggin' money, that's what I'd be doing. But you don't know how to make a list. I forgot. If you want I can make one for you. I'll get some paper and you just tell me what you want me to write. Back in a minute." And she's gone, almost knocking over the tipsy Ruth as she makes her careful way to the fridge for another beer.

"Do you think you should drink any more of that now, dear?" asks Eve. "Come and have supper. You haven't eaten a thing all day. Ginny Mustard has a visitor, you know. Her long lost sister she never knew she had has come to stay for a while and she's brought lots of money for Ginny Mustard. We'll tell you all about it at the table."

"Well isn't that great," mumbles Ruth. Trips to the dining room. Rests her spinning head on a place mat.

Thinks Patricia as she squeezes into her seat, "How could Mother have left Virginia to this?"

"So where did your mother get so much money?" asks Judy, through a mouthful of mashed potatoes. "I never met anyone that rich and I've been around, you know."

"Yes, I imagine you have. Our mother was an artist of some fame, though chances are that you haven't heard of her, in spite of your having *been around*."

Her insult is not lost on Judy. "Well I wonder was she as good as Ginny Mustard? Probably not. Ginny Mustard is a real good artist. Show her your pictures Ginny Mustard. All except those last ones. Show her the pictures of the trees and the river and stuff. I bet your old bitch mother never drew that good."

Ruth moans that she is about to be sick but can't get up. Eve dips a paper napkin in her water glass and wets Ruth's ghastly face, eliciting faint sounds of relief or protest, difficult to tell. Ginny Mustard has something to say finally, and no one dares leave to take care of Ruth if it means missing anything. "I wouldn't leave my baby. I would take my baby with me and love her all to pieces. And I would sing to her and hug her all the time. I wouldn't let my baby go to the orphan house. You can kill me but I won't let my baby go to the orphan house."

Patricia is puzzled. What is Virginia talking about? Judy is ready to strike back. "Oh Patricia. You didn't know that Ginny Mustard is simple, did you? That's a shock for you, I'll bet. Ginny Mustard is a retard. She can't read or write. The only thing she knows how to do is cook and we didn't find that out until Mrs. Miflin took sick. And she can make art too. But that's all. She used to be a hooker, did you know that? Since she was about twelve years old. Sad that your own flesh and blood turns out to be a friggin' loser, eh? Too bad. Guess you won't be telling your friends about her now, will you? Probably won't throw a party for her and invite your boyfriend will you? Sure hope Ginny Mustard doesn't decide to move in next door to you. But now that she's got some money to her name I suppose she can live wherever she friggin' well wants, can't she?"

Ginny Mustard is pleased by Judy's revelations. She doesn't even wonder how she knows so much. Just puts it down to her being more clever than other people. Looks at Judy with thank you on her face.

Patricia is not easily off-balanced but it had not occurred to her that she might find her sister anything less than she is. She was prepared for the skin color. She was prepared for the affects of a disadvantaged upbringing. She was not ready to claim an idiot as her closest living relative.

Excusing herself she goes to her room, sits at the window and watches a man limp along the road to stand among the trees, stare at the house. She shivers for a minute before closing the curtains. What is to be done? Surely her sister cannot be left on her own to handle her share of Mother's money. But does Patricia really want to be burdened with the responsibility? She will have to consult a lawyer, someone local who can administer the funds, hand over enough to keep Virginia in a reasonable manner of living, make investments on her behalf. Properly handled, it should serve her well for quite some time.

The next morning, after several phone calls she concludes that the only way anyone will do her bidding is if a psychiatrist declares Virginia incompetent. Makes an appointment Ginny Mustard is none too happy with the prospect of getting tested as Judy puts it. "She just wants all your money for herself. Those doctors pick inside your brain to see what's there, you know. My mother had that done once and they shoved electricity into her head and she was real weird after that."

Terrified as she is Ginny Mustard allows herself to be guided through a series of tests, talks to a doctor for hours and then another and another. After two days under their microscopes she is exhausted and when she runs away to hear the music, falls asleep under the rhododendron, wakes surrounded by fat crimson blossoms, a puppy licking her face. Pulling his golden body to her she snuggles close until the music man comes out of the big house. Calls, "Harvey, Harvey, where are you?" and whistles. But the puppy is more interested in being with Ginny Mustard. The man finds both of them under the flowers next to the marble Buddha and stares for a long time at Ginny Mustard's beautiful brown face and long thin arms wrapped around the puppy before speaking. "And who are you?" he asks.

"I think his name is Harvey?"

"No - not the dog, you. Who are you and why are you in my garden at seven in the morning?"

"I came to hear the music. I fell asleep. My name is Ginny Mustard. You have nice music and I had to go to the doctor for two days and I'm tired. They want me to be retarded so Patricia can have my money."

Instead of, "What the hell are you talking about?" his mouth forms, "Would you like some breakfast?"

"Yes. Can Harvey have some too? He's hungry. He chewed my hair."

In the kitchen of the big house, the man cooks an omelette with mushrooms and cheese, makes coffee in a pot. Ginny Mustard watches from her chair at the table, the puppy on her lap. The man puts food on thin blue plates, gives Ginny Mustard a white, white cloth napkin, asks if she would like cream in her coffee, sugar. Serves her first and then himself. They eat in silence until Ginny Mustard remembers that she should be preparing breakfast at Mrs. Miflin's house for the others.

"I have to make breakfast. I cook now. Mrs. Miflin is sick with her leg."

"Would you like to come back some time? My name is Howard James." And he holds out a large hand. Ginny Mustard shakes it timidly. She has never shaken a hand before.

"You have two first names. Will Harvey be here when I come back?"

"Yes. I am usually away during the day, but home by six. I look forward to seeing you again."

Ginny Mustard has met two proper people in three days. Her sister and now the music man with two first names. Her life has been abruptly altered and she ponders the change as much as she ponders anything, on her way along the river toward home.

Howard James tidies his spotless kitchen, waters an orchid, leaves a note reminding the cleaning woman, whose name he can't recall, to dust the paintings, puts a leash on Harvey and walks with the dog along the river to Water Street and his office. Thinks about Ginny Mustard. Asks himself why on earth he brought such a person into his home, ate with her, and invited her to come back. What in God's name was he thinking? He should have had her arrested for trespassing.

Patricia has been given the results of Ginny Mustard's assessment and is shocked to learn that her sister is intelligent. Dyslexic, mistreated, abused, and probably malnourished for much of her life, but smart enough that no one recommends she be deprived of her inheritance. The bright idea that Patricia would find a kindred spirit in her sister has gone the sad way of most bright ideas and she is only too pleased to leave the city and never look at that face again. She contacts her mother's lawyers, arranging the transfer of funds to a local bank. When Virginia returns she will accompany her to open an account.

Ginny Mustard has other ideas. If she can't even write her own name there's no point in having her money in a bank. She would like to keep it in her chest of drawers with the rest of her savings. Wrapped in a huge pair of hockey socks, bound tightly with elastic bands. She shows Patricia her treasure - $967. She will put her new money with the old. Patricia doesn't care. Doesn't wonder how Ginny Mustard has managed to accumulate $967. Ignores the banker's arguments. Calls a taxi while Ginny Mustard sits on her bed, puts her money in order, tucks it neatly in hockey socks.

~

Judy's wish list is complete. She has been working diligently ever since she discovered that her new best friend is rich. She has filled two sheets of paper with television sets, sound systems, clothes, even a few tattoos and some new earrings. Prices. Tax included. A car would be nice but Judy doesn't think anyone in the house can drive, though her friend Leo could take them around anywhere they want to go. She adds car but puts a question mark next to it.

Ruth has been drinking for days. She has slept little and eaten less. There is nothing left in her stomach to throw up. She is eight pounds lighter and even her leggings are baggy. Her eyes are red and her face a pasty white. She hasn't spoken more than two sentences to anyone since the binge began. She hasn't bathed or washed her hair and she stinks. The others have taken to holding their noses and rushing to pass when they meet her, which isn't often since she decided warm beer is not so bad and keeps a case in her closet.

Mrs. Miflin's nagging got to be too much for Eve, what with everything else going on around here, so the landlady has been moved from her bed for the day and lies on one of the sofas in the sitting room. She is extremely upset by the hasty departure of her new tenant, and even more irritated by the news that Ginny Mustard is a woman of means. She supposes the silly thing will move out now, probably buy her own house and, if the last few weeks are any indication of how Mrs. Miflin's luck is going, take the rest of that crowd with her. She can smell alcohol, she just knows it, and there's a strange aroma coming from the kitchen. No one is paying any attention to her or answering her questions. They whisper when they talk to each other. She is no less miserable downstairs than she was in her bedroom. And all over her skin is a crawling sensation, a feeling that something else is going on that has nothing to do with them and everything to do with her.

Mrs. Miflin's fear is real enough. It sleeps by the river, under a bridge, by day. Watches her house by night. Waits for the right moment to make its appearance. After forty-odd years in her carefully constructed cocoon, Mrs. Miflin will have to fly, and she can't even walk. It's just as well she doesn't know. If she did she'd have to shoot herself.

No one is the least bit concerned with Mrs. Miflin's woes. Ruth has gone to the dogs. Judy has glued herself to Ginny Mustard. The poor girl can't even go to the bathroom alone. Maggie would like to swing in the playground but unable to drag Judy from her prey, busies herself by counting her letters and putting them in careful order, avoids Eve and the never ending embroidery.

Ginny Mustard wants to go back to the big house to hear the music. Has to wait until Judy is asleep to escape. By then it's very late but she knocks on Howard James' door anyway and he answers in a bathrobe. She has brought her pot roast from supper for Harvey and a picture of the dog for Howard. He barely glances at her offerings as she moves past him into the kitchen.

"You could have used the front door," he says, wondering again what the hell he has done and how to undo it. She is sitting at the kitchen table, an expectant look on her face. How did he think she was beautiful? She is unkempt, uncouth and clearly lacking in grey matter.

"I'm not stupid. The doctors looked at my brain and I'm not stupid. I have what you call a disorder and I can't read or do my numbers but I'm not stupid."

"You can obviously read minds though," he says, not nicely, regretting the words when he sees her confusion. Then gently, "Would you like something to drink?"

"No. I want to hear the music."

She follows him to the library. He motions her to a chair while he makes a selection. Sits and watches her face while the music fills her, while her hands move with the sound, gracefully, delicately. She is beautiful again and if he had the energy to pull a Henry Higgins he might have a little fun. But no. He has to get her out of here once and for all. He leaves the room and rummages about for a while, returns with a small compact disc player, grabs a few of his favorites and presents her with the lot.

"Here you are. Any time you want music you can play it yourself. You don't have to come all the way over here any more. In fact, I think it's best that you stay away. You can take this wherever you go."

He might as well tell it to the wind. Ginny Mustard is drowning in Bach. She wouldn't hear him if he shouted at the top of his lungs. He pushes a button and the music is over. He makes his presentation one more time, shows her how to work the little machine and hustles her out the back door. Watches while she climbs the fence behind the rhododendron. It isn't until the next morning that he sees what she brought, throws the pitiful package of meat in the garbage along with her picture, in pieces.

You can't expect to get away with treating God's creatures like that Mr. James, even when they look odd and don't speak your language. Such a lovely gift was that Ginny Mustard and now you've thrown her back in His face. Better you crawl into a hole in the ground, pull the earth over your head. Better to spit in His eye than to do what you have done. Looked Him square in the face and turned away, you did. And even if you hadn't pissed God off, you should know enough in your fancy house with your fancy music and your fancy paintings, not to mess with Judy's new best friend.

~

Watching, watching, he has seen Ginny Mustard come and go. Has waited for her outside the big house, followed her home, taken his place under the aspen, its leaves curling to die, choking with the strain of his company.

Mrs. Miflin is curling as well. Though she can't be considered paranoid in clinical terms she is rapidly approaching that state of mind. The tenants, free of her grasp, have taken on lives of their own. Like those little ones you see sometimes when the bell rings for recess in October, like birds freed suddenly, startled by release, but leaping and running, pushing, grabbing at the morning in their brightly colored sweaters and their hair moving with the wind as feathers do. Or the ones whose mommy is too far gone, who cannot reach to swat the backside, the ones who find they can cook their own macaroni and cheese, butter bread, make a tuna fish sandwich, race mad in the moonlight while she sleeps it off. Turn somersaults in the park in their pyjamas. Steal ice cream from the corner store at midnight.

If Mother were wicked. If Mother were clutching. If Mother did not allow room for growth. If Mrs. Miflin were Mother and Mother fell off a cliff, down a deep well, under a truck, her child would mourn briefly but no more than Ruth, Judy, Ginny Mustard, Maggie, Eve. Would mourn no more than anyone who discovered the death knell disguised as life force.

And no one wonders why or how they found her. Moved from another to the same. But time. It's time that works the magic. Not the reason or the sensibilities. And the stars were in on it, and the moon, of course. And said, "These belong. Let's put them here. Here in this place." And time said, "Yes." Examined each and found her wanting. Wanting Bishop's Road, this house, now. And set about shuffling the order. Placed them here to become.

One corner turned left, not right. One person spoken to, "Do you know a cheap place to stay around here?" One mistake too many, one stone flung through the wrong window, one night in the wrong arms. And time said, "Well done."

And Mrs. Miflin knows, as sure as she knows he has returned, that her solid grasp has weakened. That her fingers are old now and cannot hold fast the things she must control.

Ruth has had enough of her shit. She is hungry and tired. Wants food and company. When Judy says, "You smell to high heaven, Ruth, take a shower, for God's sake." she does. Clean and thin she returns to the kitchen where the others are hiding from Mrs. Miflin and her moaning ways. The talk is confusing but eventually she puts it all together. The bones are still in the attic, Ginny Mustard is rich, Mrs. Miflin is in the sitting room, and the kittens are all over the place.

"So what else is new?" asks Ruth. "Is there anything to eat? If I had any money left I'd order a pizza. That's what I need. Fucking pizza."

Ginny Mustard to the rescue. "I have money."

Judy volunteers to order the food. No one has ever had take-out in Mrs. Miflin's house. It's ungodly.

Ginny Mustard brings a $100 bill to the kitchen.

"It's gonna be fun watching the guy make change out of that," says Judy.

They sit around the kitchen waiting for pizza, Eve in the

armchair, Ginny Mustard and Judy on the daybed, Ruth and Maggie on the floor. Anyone looking through the window might think there was a party going on. Ruth contributes the last case of beer that she ever wants to see. She is thinking of switching to gin if the mood hits her again.

Maggie doesn't remember the taste of alcohol but she accepts Ruth's offer with a small smile. Judy takes two bottles on the first go-around but likes hers cold and fills a glass with ice cubes. Eve has one too. Shares with Ruth who, for all her good intentions, says, "What the hell."

Five women laughing through the night. Eating. Drinking. Laughing. Even Maggie laughing. And a person listening through the window might think their laughter obscene. Might think, that is not funny, when Judy talks about her life and Ruth talks about hers. Might think, There's something sick about these women that they laugh at such things. They should not be doing that. But a person listening through the window would be very wrong.

He hears the laughter, smells the food and drink. Hunger and thirst take hold of him. A craving for warmth. A longing such as only one outside the circle feels. He wills it away. Forces it back beneath his hatred. Locks it down.

Mrs. Miflin hears the laughter too. Her lips vanish in disapproval. Her eyes are hard lights. Calls to Judy to come and help her to her room. Calls again. Louder. They won't get away with this. That girl has been drinking and the authorities will know all about it in the morning. She'll have them back in their place before too long. Mrs. Miflin has worked her tongue overtime making sure that they never touch. Has kept them well apart with her, for your own good, and, be careful of that one, she's not right in the head, and I wouldn't trust her, my dear, you know what they say about her kind. All for nothing. She hears the laughter and it is making her sick. Late into the night she lies awake plotting revenge.

~

Summer is in full blossom on Bishop's Road. On this heavy bee morning while her tenants sleep, Mrs. Miflin makes a call to Judy's probation officer. And if he hadn't decided to stop for a cup of coffee on his way, if he hadn't backed his car into another as he was fastening his seat belt, if he hadn't struck his head on the steering wheel and spent two hours waiting for stitches at the hospital, he might have been here. But by the time someone else takes over his case load and gets around to Judy, the girl's drinking will be the least of Mrs. Miflin's worries.

Howard James is having a rough day as well. His secretary is late - assistant, she likes to call herself - and he hasn't a clue where she buys his coffee. He needs copies of some important papers immediately but has no idea where she keeps them. To make matters worse, he stepped in dog shit on his way to the office and the smell is still on his shoe, though he scraped it well. There are tell tale signs on the rich carpet all the way to his desk. He is trapped in the office. Alone. With no coffee. Can't let anyone in until the mess has been dealt with and that won't happen until Ms Know It All shows up and calls a cleaner. His computer is down. The air conditioning is on the fritz. A pretty crappy day all around.

If Dorothy Blake hadn't stopped for his coffee just when she did, and that fool hadn't backed into her car just when he did, she would have been there by now, would have filled Mr. James' porcelain mug with take-out coffee (he likes to think he knows the difference between gourmet blend and Tim Hortons but he doesn't) and be on her knees scrubbing shit off his carpet. But life is no longer going as smoothly as was planned. Everyone within a mile's radius of Mrs. Miflin's house had that figured out before they planted their feet on the floor this morning.

When the knock comes at the front door, it is loud and serious. Mrs. Miflin hears it first and screams to the others to answer it, hoping Judy will be the one to greet the probation officer. Wishing she could see her face. And his when he smells old beer on her breath. But it isn't Judy who opens the door. Eve, still in her dressing gown, but faced washed, hair brushed, is the one to let the man in.

Pushing her aside he demands to see Mrs. Miflin. Takes his filthy self into the sitting room to wait. "I know she's hurt. Tell that tall one to bring her downstairs. Tell Mrs. Jessie Miflin that her husband is home and wants to see her right now."

No one need tell Jessie Miflin any such thing. She can feel his fists. She can feel his feet kicking at her full belly. She screams as the bloody water gushes from between her legs. She cradles the infant forced from her womb. Holds its precious body to her heart while he tears their home to pieces. Hears him snore. Rocks her cold baby for hours until the woman next door comes to visit.

She tried to kill him after that. Pretty Jessie Miflin stole a gun from her friend's husband down the street when no one was looking. October. Cool and bright. Followed him to the hills where he was shooting rabbits. Walked for hours until she saw the blue of his jacket. Came as close as she dared. Looked him in the eye before she pulled the trigger but aimed lower than she wanted. Stood over him while he bled, the ground around him wet, the bones of his pelvis showing sharp through the flesh, through the skin. Stayed there until she heard voices and fled.

No one believed him when he told what she had done. It must have been another hunter. It must have been an accident. Pretty Jessie Miflin wouldn't hurt a fly. Look how unhappy she was with her baby being stillborn and all. She was so frail and sad. Pretty Jessie Miflin didn't shoot her husband. Pretty Jessie Miflin worked two jobs for years, to overcome her grief, they said. By the time she had saved enough money to buy her house there was no pretty left in Jessie Miflin except in deepest sleep. And even if someone had said 'and that's the God's truth!' with one hand on a Bible, still no one would have believed that she could dig up her baby's grave and steal the little bones away. Carefully wash and wrap those bones in the lovely pink blanket she had made and place them in the cradle in the attic. They put it down to vandalism. There's a lot of that on the go these days.

Mrs. Miflin has thrown up all over herself. Eve washes her face and changes the bedding. The others are awake now and wandering about. Judy alone has ventured to the sitting room. Stares at Mr. Miflin. Thinks to herself, I could take him in a second, scrawny little bastard. He'd better not be trying anything around here. But he sees doubt in her face. Cocky as she is, this girl won't be a problem.

Eve doesn't understand why Mrs. Miflin is not pleased that her husband is back, for all that he is rather dirty and seems to have fallen on hard times. She can't reconcile the wedding pictures, the dried bouquet, the place so lovingly set at the table, with Mrs. Miflin's attitude.

"Well maybe," says Ruth, "things are not as they appear. It happens, Eve. All the time. Perhaps our Mrs. Miflin is not who we think she is. What's the story Mrs. Miflin? You spend years yammering on and on about that wonderful husband of yours and now here he is finally home from wherever the hell he was and you're puking your guts up. A little shy all of a sudden?"

"Leave her alone," says Ginny Mustard. "She's sick. Don't you talk to her like that. Make him go away Ruth."

"She's the one who has to make him go away. She did it once and I'm sure she can do it again. How did you get rid of him last time Mrs. Miflin?"

"Please stop this Ruth," says Eve. "Why don't you get Mr. Miflin a cup of coffee and ask him to wait a little longer? Would you like that Mrs. Miflin? If we just make him feel at home until you get over the shock? I'm sure you'll be feeling better in a few minutes."

"No!" Mrs. Miflin screams. "I want him gone! He kicked me and kicked me until he killed my baby and I shot him! I want him gone!"

"Well now," says Ruth. "This is a fine kettle of fish."

Ginny Mustard goes to the attic and returns with the rifle. "I found this in a trunk. We can shoot him again. He killed the baby and we can kill him." Before the others can stop her she is standing in front of Mr. Miflin. By the time they reach the sitting room she has pulled the trigger. By the time Judy turns from the window she has been looking through, before the curtain falls back into place, Mr. Miflin's life is colouring the yellow carpet to rust.

The blast of the old gun was deafening. Maggie is screaming. Hands to her ears and letters all over the floor. Ruth slaps her hard across the face. Tells her to be quiet for God's sake. "What the hell have you done, Ginny Mustard? Are you completely out of your mind?"

"I had to, Ruth. He hurt Mrs. Miflin and he killed her baby."

"That's it? You just decide to kill him? Did you even know the gun was loaded? He could have taken it from you. He could have wiped out the whole lot of us. God you are so friggin' stupid, girl."

"I'm not stupid anymore. The doctor said I am not stupid, Ruth."

Eve takes the gun from Ginny Mustard's hands and places it on the floor near Mr. Miflin's body. Sits on the sofa and says a quiet prayer. Mrs. Miflin is calling from her room. "What was that noise?"

"As if she doesn't know," Ruth is laughing. "Well, this is just great. I'm going to the store for beer. Don't either of you move a muscle until I get back. Don't call the cops. Don't do anything. And for Christ's sake don't let anyone through that door." She nudges the bloody Mr. Miflin with her foot. Nothing. "Well, he's dead, that's for sure. I'll be back in a minute. Don't budge."

But they do, of course. Ginny Mustard wants breakfast. Eve pulls herself together and goes to tell Mrs. Miflin what happened. Maggie shakes in her shoes for awhile but even she decides to get out of the sitting room and gathers up her letters, wanders to the kitchen to play with the kittens until Ruth comes home. Only Judy stays where she's told. But turns again to look out the window. Across the street the aspen has lost all of her leaves. The other trees are laughing.

When Father Delaney hears the noise he jumps. Having been through at least one war, he has never quite forgotten the sound of gunfire. Finishes his breakfast and pulls on his shoes. Runs on his old spindle legs to Mrs. Miflin's house. Meets Ruth on her way back from the store. Frowns at her purchase. The Jezebel didn't even have the decency to ask for a bag. The likes of her - buying beer at this hour.

"What brings you over, Father? Checking up on your parishioners this fine day?"

"I heard a noise. It sounded like a gun. Do you women have a gun in that house?"

"Not that I know of. What you heard was probably the stove. The pilot light went out and it gave a bang when Ginny Mustard lit it. Blew her and the oven door right across the kitchen. I keep telling the missus it's not safe to have something that old in the house but she's a bit tight with the dollars. Don't concern yourself with Ginny Mustard. It'll take more than a minor explosion to kill that one."

"Well. I guess I should see how Mrs. Miflin is doing now that I'm all the way over here."

"No. You shouldn't. She needs her rest and we're just

about to have breakfast."

"How are you cooking breakfast if the stove is broken?"

"It's not broken, Father. It exploded. We put the oven door back on and it's as good as it ever was. Which isn't to say it won't blow us all to kingdom come tomorrow but it will do for the likes of us. Why don't you run along, now, and change your shirt? You've got egg all down the front of it."

"I'm home," sings Ruth. "Be it ever so humble. Pity about the body in the sitting room - but hey."

"What has gotten into you Ruth?" asks Eve. "Ginny Mustard has done a dreadful thing and you are treating it like a joke. It's not funny Ruth. A man is dead. And Ginny Mustard will end up going to jail for the rest of her life."

"Yes. Well I thought about that while I was out. You're right, of course. She'll have to go to jail. It's too bad she turned out to be smart. A few days ago she could have pled stupidity and got away with a few months in the nuthouse. The girl's got lousy timing - that's for sure. I think we'd best call a meeting of the tenant's association. I'm going to put this beer away. Let's have breakfast and discuss the matter at hand. What do you say, old Eve? Think we can work our way out of this mess? And we thought bones in the attic was a problem."

Again Ruth is laughing. "Someone bring food to the grieving widow. I can hear her moaning and groaning all the way down here. And then let's eat before Mister starts to go bad. We'll have to work fast or we'll never get the smell out."

Breakfast is leftovers. Everything from night before last and some vegetables slightly past their prime. Ruth says, "Ginny Mustard you have found your calling. You're not a half bad cook. And you're a pretty good shot too. There may be a place in the world for you yet, girl." And the others smile at that. Cautiously. Unsure of the etiquette of doing so with one newly deceased in the next room.

After the plate scraping and dishwashing have been done, things put back the way they were, Ruth calls them to Mrs. Miflin's room to discuss their latest dilemma. They are in agreement that Ginny Mustard did the right thing. Mrs. Miflin provides vivid details of her married life. The more she talks the less she whimpers. The less she whimpers the clearer her focus. She is more like her old self but without the fuzzy edges that had never made sense. They can see that the man was scum. And that's all he was. Didn't matter that he had been a sweet baby once upon a time, that someone had taken the trouble to name him, maybe played with him. In their minds he was never anything other than what he had become.

If Mrs. Miflin had mentioned the flowers he brought her. Or the way he rubbed her back when she had been sewing for too long. Or the times they walked to the river and threw pennies in to buy a wish, or sat up late at night watching out for falling stars. If she had told them that he cried when their first baby died so soon after he felt it kick, gentle hand on her belly. Oh how he had cried. She had never known a man could cry. If she had told them anything at all, other than what she did, then things might have been different. They might have felt something for the man, some sadness for the waste of life. Might have questioned his fall from saint to monster. Not exactly blissful in their ignorance but, free of pain and regret, they plot to save Ginny Mustard and conceal her wrongdoing.

"What we need," says Ruth, "is a freezer. That's a bit cliché to be sure but I can't think of anything else at the moment. It will have to be big enough so we can store him in one piece. I am not about to start hacking him up."

"Oh, Ruth, no. The man needs a proper burial no matter what he has done. We can't just freeze him."

"Oh for God's sake, Eve. Stop it. You can't run around burying people without someone finding out. Next you'll want an obituary in the fucking papers. Forget it Eve. We have to put him on ice. Ginny Mustard is the only one with any money and since she's the one who killed the bastard in the first place, she's going to have to buy a freezer. We'll put it in the basement and throw some casseroles on top of him so if anyone comes snooping they won't see he's there. Though I can't imagine who'd be looking for the likes of him. Ginny Mustard you'll have to make a lot of casseroles."

"Judy will have to find them in the cookbook. I never made any before."

"They don't have to be edible so don't be getting all fancy on us. It's not like anyone will ever eat them. They're just for show."

Judy volunteers to go with Ginny Mustard to pick out a freezer. "We should go now and maybe we can have it delivered this afternoon."

Eve is still upset. "He should be buried. This isn't right."

"Well Eve. How about we just dig up the backyard and shove him in? What part of your precious garden do you want to contribute for his grave? How about your roses or those beans you've got growing? And what's to stop a dog from hauling him up once we plant him? It's not like we can call up the undertaker and order a fucking coffin, is it now? He's got to be frozen and unless there's a power outage one of these days, we're in the clear and that fool Ginny Mustard won't have to go to jail for the rest of her silly life. God, woman, think."

And Eve relents. Knows that Ruth is right. The thought of Ginny Mustard behind bars is terrible, and just when she found out she can cook so well, too.

"Ginny Mustard," says Ruth. "While you're gone for the freezer, you might consider a carpet as well. That one he's bleeding all over is ruined. I always thought blue would be nice in that room. Something with a pattern if you can find it."

~

Mr. Miflin was laid to rest in the new freezer, covered with enough casseroles to feed a high school as well as some rainbow trout that Eve found on sale and couldn't pass up. And then a giant-sized carton of popsicles with summer here and it's so warm out, and what the hell, a rump roast and a few chickens. Shopping is fun and all but it takes a lot of time from Eve's gardening chores. Now that the blue rug is down in the sitting room it seems only natural to put a fresh coat of paint on the walls and buy slip-covers. Judy decides that the old fireplace will work and sets about removing boards that the frugal Mrs. Miflin jammed in there to cut heat loss. Ginny Mustard has added a microwave oven to her list of recent acquisitions and a new television set with a built-in video tape recorder. She watches cooking shows when she's not preparing meals. Wanders farther afield than usual shopping for ingredients she has never heard tell of before.

She hasn't returned to the big house since the music man gave her the little disc player. She remembers him sometimes, thinks about the puppy. The puppy thinks about her as well. Ever since their first meeting he has been annoying the neighbourhood with his incessant yowling. When he goes to the garden he lies under the rhododendron and it's all Howard James can do to get him back in the house. He wants Ginny Mustard and he doesn't like his owner. He has dug up most of the flowers near the fence in his attempt to escape.

~

When the report of Judy's drinking finally makes it to the top of the stack on Patrick Fahey's desk, Mrs. Miflin has forgot-ten all about her nasty phone call that morning when Mister showed up and had himself killed. No one but the odd delivery man has come to the door since then. Not expecting anyone, they all freeze momentarily before Eve answers the loud knocking. They were not aware that each had been fearing discovery of the secret in the basement. They had not spoken of Mr. Miflin since they covered him with casseroles. The official look about the man who enters the house keeps them all on edge until he tells them why he's here.

He wants to see Judy. There has been a report that she was drinking one night back in June and being underage as well as on probation, she is in a lot of trouble. It's been a good three weeks since anyone has heard from her. He is a police officer, one who has had the dubious pleasure of having arrested Judy on a number of occasions.

"Well, Sergeant Fahey," says Ruth. "Why don't you come in and have a seat and Judy can explain everything. Ginny Mustard, why don't you get a cup of tea for Sergeant Fahey and set another place at the table. We're just about ready to have our supper and we'd be pleased if you can join us. Judy, tell Sergeant Fahey about that night. Remember how Mrs. Miflin was really sick? Remember how she was delirious from the drugs the doctor gave her for the pain in her leg? She was seeing things all over the place. She's okay now but she got it in her head that you were drinking beer in the kitchen. She even accused us of ordering pizza, which we would never do since she doesn't approve of take-out food. It's not good for us, you know and Mrs. Miflin is very concerned about our health. She's like a mother to us. Tell him, Judy, about how Mrs. Miflin thought you were drinking. You probably don't recall what happened, Mrs. Miflin, since you were pretty much out of it. You tell him Judy."

"Yeah. That's what happened Sergeant Fahey. Just like Ruth said. Mrs. Miflin is fucking crazy sometimes. Friggin'. I meant friggin' crazy. But she really looks after us good and we dearly love her."

The landlady is a pitiful heap on the sofa and doesn't have much to say. Ruth forgot to tell Eve that she had given the poor woman her painkillers already and Eve helped her to a second dose an hour ago. Mrs. Miflin is fading to dreamland.

Patrick Fahey knows they are all lying and doing a pretty pathetic job of it too. He's tired, though. He spends twelve hours a day tracking down, calming down, holding down unlucky people who don't have a clue what's wrong and what's right, too stunned to figure it out on their own and nobody bothered to teach them. Patrick Fahey was on his way home to beer and a pizza himself after he made this last stop. But that Ruth woman did invite him to stay for supper and the aroma from the kitchen is interesting. His duty to Queen and country can wait. There's no way he wants to be bothered with Judy right now. And he can't prove a thing either. Everyone in the house has heard Ruth's story and he'll bet dollars to doughnuts they'd repeat it word for word if he were to question them. And this Ruth is not bad looking either. Smart. He could do worse than to sit down with her and have a bite to eat.

Ruth's sentiments are similar. There's something about Patrick Fahey that appeals to her. He's easy on the eyes. Broad shouldered. Thin but strong looking and tall. A woman could lean on him if she ever felt the need and Ruth has been feeling the need lately. He hasn't smiled since he came through the front door but the lines around his eyes indicate that he knows how. He has nice teeth and a good mouth. Ruth is not all that surprised at the direction her thoughts have taken. Very few of the goings-on around here come as a shock these days and if she's attracted to Sergeant Patrick Fahey, well, so what?

"Ginny Mustard is on a Thai kick this week, Sergeant Fahey. So God only knows what she's got cooked up for us. We've all been practicing with chop sticks but you can have a fork if you like. Maggie there has got the hang of it but the rest of us make a bit of a mess still. Are you staying for supper, or what?"

What the hell. Patrick Fahey has had beer and pizza enough to last a lifetime. Against his better judgement he says, "Yes. I can file my report in the morning. Judy, there is still the matter of your not seeing your probation officer regularly. Last chance girl. You get over there tomorrow or we take you away for good this time." With his tie loose and jacket off he looks less threatening but the women are still a little nervous, all except Ruth, who has decided she likes this man very much.

They eat in silence for a while. Judy is not pleased that the law decided to stick around. He's got his eye on Ruth that's for sure - it's almost funny to see the way she keeps looking over at him and being all weird when he notices. Looking away. You'd think she never saw a fellow before the way she's turning all pink in the cheeks. Wouldn't figure Ruth to be nervous like that. He's watching her too. Judy finds the whole thing a bit gross but it might be good for a laugh later on.

Eve makes chit chat and they learn that Patrick Fahey is not married, has a house over on Morris Street and an old dog, visits his mother in the nursing home three times a week. She has Alzheimer's disease and doesn't know him any more but he goes anyway. His father died a few years ago. He has two sisters, three nephews and a niece and spends holidays with them, Christmas and Easter mostly. When his mother wasn't so far gone they used to celebrate with her but one year when she forgot to cook the turkey they gave it up. Soon after that she stopped bathing and when they found her wandering around Water Street in her night-gown they knew she was beyond their help and put her in the home.

Maggie pipes up. "That's where I was. A home. I was bad so my mother put me in a home."

"Interesting," says Ruth. "Patrick - I hope you don't mind

if I call you Patrick while you're off duty - Maggie hasn't spoken to any of us. Ever. And now here you mention home and she opens her mouth. We heard her scream once. And she laughs now and then." She directs her attention to Maggie. "What kind of home? How long were you there?"

"I don't know anything else. Just that there was a home and my mother. I guess she was my mother." Maggie's throat hurts all of a sudden. She puts her hand to her neck and makes little hacking noises, as though she's choking on something sharp. Judy smacks her across the back and Maggie resumes eating, gracefully, with her chopsticks.

"Well now," says Eve. "That was a good start, Maggie. You just rest your voice and if you ever want to talk again you go right ahead." Maggie smiles and nods.

Judy says, "I think that it's time to take a look at those old letters you got there, Maggie. I bet there's all kinds of stuff in them that'll tell us where you've been, even if you can't remember it yourself. And if you read them you won't have to carry them around all over the place. Maggie has letters in her box, Sergeant Fahey. Can I call you Patrick too?" Seeing his frown, "I guess not. That's okay. You can call me Ms Hagen. I can be just as uppity as the rest of you friggers. Never mind. I don't want to talk to you either. Come on Maggs. Let's go for a swing. Leave the old folks alone." Maggie smiles. Lifts her plate to her mouth and licks it, shocking Eve. Takes her shoe box and follows Judy to the playground, giggling.

"They think they're so friggin' smart. Old bats. Good move with the plate, Maggs. I thought I was going to piss my pants with the look on their faces. And did you check out the way old Ruth was looking at buddy? I could've gagged on it." And they laugh all the way up into the trees.

"At the station we call her the mouth," says Patrick, comfortable in the sitting room, his long legs stretched out in front of him, kittens climbing all over them. When they installed the freezer, Ruth had discovered a cache of ancient wine. Fifty or more bottles of wonderful red. They have been sipping it ever since with supper. Just a glass each. Tonight being special, Ruth cracks another bottle. Brings a clean glass to Patrick and pours. Thinks wicked thoughts. Patrick Fahey can see them in her eyes. He wants this woman. He hasn't wanted anyone in a very long time but he wants this woman. It's all he can do to keep from reaching out and touching her thick curls. None of this is making sense to him. He is not the kind of man who shirks his duty and before he entered this house, no one could have convinced him that he would sit around with someone he was investigating and actually have a meal. Wine. And let the little snip go traipsing out the door saucy as she was without saying anything. Patrick Fahey is a cop's cop. But when Ruth started throwing her lies all around the place that sad thing that eats away at the pit of his stomach just kind of up and disappeared. He felt it leave. And noted its absence. And realizes that now, when it comes back, it will be so much harder to ignore. He asks Ruth if she would like to go out sometime. Maybe dinner and a movie. She answers, "Yes. But I have to warn you, I'm a bit of a bitch."

True, he thinks. And you tell lies. And I don't care. Aloud he says, "How about tomorrow night. Are you free?"

"Patrick Fahey, I've been free for about a month now. Why don't you pick me up at seven?"

~

Mrs. Miflin is so angry she could spit. It's all bad enough what with her mister dead in the freezer and that crowd all seeing the bones in the attic and knowing that she dug them up. It's all bad enough they've got company coming and going and she can't sit at the table with that cast on, and the smell of paint is all through the house and she knows they aren't doing the laundry when they should. It's all bad enough but now she finds out from Eve that Ginny Mustard has been designing a nursery. Staying up late and drawing pictures of a baby's room. First she thought the silly thing might be pregnant but Eve corrected her. Ginny Mustard wants a nursery for Mrs. Miflin's baby. She screams out for Ginny Mustard to get up here as fast as her two legs can carry her. "What are you doing? You can't make a room for a dead baby. It's ungodly. Sinful."

"Well, it's not any more sinful than digging up the poor little baby in the first place. Or her being kicked to death before she was even born. She needs a pretty room with pictures on the wall and a little warm rug on the floor. It's not nice in the attic. And she wants a rocking chair."

"You are a raving lunatic, Ginny Mustard. That's what you are. You can't do things like that."

"Why not?"

"Because the baby is dead!"

"Well I'm not dead and I never had a pretty room and a little warm rug. What about if I make one for me and the baby can stay there too. I got lots of money from my sister now and I can buy all the things. It's no skin off your nose."

And Mrs. Miflin can't think of a good argument. Ginny Mustard is making her nervous. She has never spoken like this before. That's what comes of having money. It makes you rude to people. She lies back on her pillow. Asks Ginny Mustard to close the curtains and turn off the light. She thinks she might be getting one of her really sick headaches. When that doesn't sway the girl she gives up. This place is going to hell in a handbasket.

Hell it may be but everyone is coming over. Harvey is still digging a hole under the rhododendron. The dahlias from the yard next door are climbing through and over the fence. The scarlet runner beans have made their way up the lilac and are leaning toward the kitchen window. Zucchini and carrots that someone planted down the street are growing among Eve's zinnias. There are tomato plants crawling out through the chicken wire of the compost bin. Flowering. And if there's a scarcity of earthworms elsewhere it's only because they heard there is a party going on at the old convent. Hedgehogs return from wherever they've been. Birds follow Judy and Maggie home from the playground and they have to shake them away before they go into the house. Eve sits in the middle of her small paradise and marvels at the glory of it all. Hell indeed.

~

Maggie brings her letters to the sitting room and Judy. Checks to make sure they are all in order. Thinks that Judy may be right. Perhaps it's time to read them, perhaps it's okay to read them but not alone. Her hand is shaking as she passes the first one to Judy, indicates that she would like to hear her letter. But now Judy doubts the wisdom of her original idea. Says, "Are you sure, Maggs, cause you might not like what's in this. Who are they from anyway?"

"I don't know. They gave them to me the day I was leaving. But I want you to read them to me now. Please. I don't want to read them by myself."

"Well okay then. But it might be real weird, you know."

Maggie settles herself on the carpet at Judy's feet. Stares at her friend's face as she begins to read. The letters are from her mother. Each a page long and those pages cold. But if the words are empty, the memories they rouse are not. Maggie cries. No sobs. No sound. No change of expression on her pretty face. Just six year's worth of tears and the front of her dress is soaking before Judy opens the fifth envelope.

~

Mrs. Eldridge was amazed to find herself pregnant at the ripe old age of forty-five. She and Mr. Eldridge had decided long ago that she was barren and there was simply nothing to be done about it. After the first three years of their marriage, and before they gave up on the idea of ever having a family, Mrs. Eldridge cried most of the time. Especially when she ovulated or bled. Every twinge and the slightest discharge reminded her that she was not complete, for all that her internal organs seemed to be in working order.

There were times when Mr. Eldridge was sure he would have to leave her. The disappointment of having no children, he could handle, but the constant weeping and wringing of hands almost drove him mad. Every day they went to their work like normal people. They ate lunch with their colleagues. They chatted with friends. Attended all of the obligatory cocktail parties and company dinners. Sometimes they even went out for a drink on Friday evening and a movie just the two of them. But as soon as they were home, it started. Mrs. Eldridge would get that look in her eye and Mr. Eldridge would brace himself for the waterworks. She would cry and walk back and forth through the house, from the basement to the kitchen to the dining room, to the living room and the window to stare outside, up and down the hall a few times, upstairs to each bedroom and the bathrooms. Back to the basement to begin again. She would stop to eat when Mr. Eldridge put a meal in front of her. She would stop when he gently took her hand and led her to bed. The few times they made love, she sniffled her way through most of it.

For years she didn't buy groceries, prepare meals or wash

a dish. She went to work and earned her keep and suffered. Weekends were especially difficult. It never occurred to them to see a doctor, to try to adopt, to hire a surrogate. One day, shortly after Mrs. Eldridge turned thirty-eight, she called Mr. Eldridge at his office and said, "I don't think we're ever going to have a baby." She stopped crying and they bought a few bonsai trees and a Great Dane. For the next seven years they lived happily enough. They bought more bonsai trees and another Great Dane. In the evenings they would walk the dogs and chat about their days. They invested wisely and dreamed of early retirement and trips to exotic places. They bought books about Cuba and the Galapagos, Egypt and South America. They began to tell people that they never wanted children anyway. There were so many other things to do with one's life.

Mrs. Eldridge was a good four months pregnant before she noticed anything amiss. Her skirts were tight. Her bras were not as comfortable as they had been and they were the expensive ones too. For years she hadn't noticed her cycle at all. When she couldn't remember her last period, she went to see her doctor. She told Mr. Eldridge the news and he smiled which made her very angry indeed.

"Do you think?" she said, "that I'm going to be dragging a youngster to kindergarten when I'm fifty? That's what I'll be, you know, fifty years old. I could be a grandmother by now for God's sake. There's no way I want a baby at this stage of the game. I'll have an abortion, there's no more to it than that."

Mr. Eldridge was not happy with her decision but there was little he could do about it. Her mind was made up. The doctor had other ideas. "You're too far along for an abortion. It's against the law to have one now. You'll have to have the baby." And so she did. Gained the appropriate amount of weight and not an ounce more. Bought baby clothes and furnished a nursery. Worked right up to the last minute of her pregnancy and was back at it as soon as she delivered. She told Mr. Eldridge that since he was the only one interested in having a child around, he could look after it himself.

He named the baby Margaret for his favorite sister who had died. He doted on her but only when Mrs. Eldridge wasn't looking - which was quite often when she was given a promotion at work and usually came home late after that. He and the old dogs would walk with the baby every evening. He held her in his arms until she was big enough to sit in a carrier on his back. When she learned to toddle they went ever so slowly, at her pace, he holding her little hand and bending over as far as he could to hear her every word. He fired babysitters as fast as he hired them, rushing home from the office more than once if he sensed the slightest anxiety in her voice during his daily phone calls. He took her to school, joined the PTA, volunteered to haul kids to field trips, signed her report cards and helped her with her homework. He was a dear dad.

Life was grand until Margaret was fifteen and her father developed heart trouble. Surgery was scheduled and during his recovery the world came to an end. Margaret sat by his bed and held his hand until her mother shooed her away. The time for having fun, just Mr. and Mrs. Eldridge, had come and gone and the only one who had gained anything from it was Margaret. Jealousy reared its head and Margaret's mother devoted her days to destruction. She picked and picked and nagged and bitched until Margaret could take no more. Retaliation came in the form of drugs and boys - the ones who like to play with lonely girls.

In a one-hour session, Mrs. Eldridge convinced a psychiatrist that the only recourse was to have Margaret committed to a private mental institution, the kind where bad kids go to straighten out when there's nothing else to be done. They came for her in the middle of the night and dragged her, kicking and screaming for her father, into the dark. Strapped down and terrified, drugged and finally oblivious to life, she sat still for the next six years. Until the insurance ran out. Until the final diagnosis that this young woman was never going anywhere again, but harmless, could be boarded out and her room assigned to someone else.

None of this is in the letters that Judy reads to Maggie. A page a month to Margaret from Mother described her father's ill health, the stroke he suffered after Margaret ran away so abruptly, their latest dinner party, trips to visit relatives. A twenty dollar bill in each envelope *for a little something*. That was it.

And Maggie remembers everything now. His good face and the smell of his aftershave. His bedtime songs and piggyback rides. The fun they had when mother wasn't home. And she puts her head back and howls. Frightens Judy who runs to fetch someone. Ruth. It should be Ruth. And Ruth comes to see what the fuss is. Looks at Maggie in a hollow heap on the sofa and knows enough to do little. Sits close by and touches her hair for awhile. Sends Judy to bring tissue, hands them over two by two until the box is empty. Coaxes Maggie to the kitchen. Makes tea.

~

Harvey has managed to dig his way out of the backyard and makes a beeline for Bishop's Road. Whines at the front door but nobody hears him. Scratches until the mud from his feet is well embedded in the paint. Lies down and takes a dog nap. Ruth falls over him when she goes out for beer, curses, but remembers she is happy and lets him in the house. He snuffles all over the place for a minute and then heads up the stairs to the attic and Ginny Mustard who is delighted to see him. She decides that a nice basket on the floor near the cradle would be a lovely place for the puppy to sleep. He can keep an eye on the baby when she is cooking, since no one likes her idea of bringing the bones to the kitchen, yelled at her, in fact, when she broached the subject. It doesn't occur to Ginny Mustard that Harvey will have to go home. If this is where he is then this is where he should be.

~

Maggie has been talking a blue streak. For hours. About her dad and her mother. Six years of silence and now the lid is off. When Maggie was carted away she kicked and screamed until someone jabbed her with sedation. When that wore off she cried for a day and a night. No one cared. There was no comfort. She stopped talking. Laughing. Smiling. Crying. And now she's spilling out all over the place, following the others from room to room, yelling through closed doors, not caring if they listen. Enough that they are present. She won't shut up, though Ruth asked her to, nicely, several times. All night long she talks and in the morning she is slowing down a little but far from empty. They go about their business and still she follows. They don't bother to hide. By unspoken consensus they let her rip. Eventually she'll have to fall asleep, they reason, and then someone else can get a word in.

Judy is less patient than the others. By her calculation, Maggie has a good $1440 from all those twenty-dollar bills her mother put in the letters and she's eager to get out and help her spend it.

Ruth is busy finding something to wear for her date. She has had a shower and a long bath. Shampooed her hair twice and done four lots of make-up. Pickings are slim in this house. Judy has some garish eye shadow and pure white powder, blue mascara, nasty looking lipstick. The others have nothing at all. Having spent every cent she had on beer, there was no option but to head out to the drug store and sample their wares. On her last visit the sales clerks decided she was never going to buy anything and asked her not to come back. But she looked pretty good by then and told them to stuff it, gave herself a liberal dose of Poison on the way out and went home to wait for Sergeant Patrick Fahey.

~

There is no place in the world more wonderful than this city at the height of summer. Winter has its moments. When the fog is in but the snow falls anyway - at night - and they compete to be the prettiest thing in front of the street lights, watched from windows or wandered about in when you're alone and everything is hushed so sweetly there might be no one else in the world. Or on a freezing morning after the rain paints everything, every tree, bush, leftover weed, rickety fence, the most brilliant silver. And the sun comes out and blinds you silly and there's no safe place to put your foot until the salt trucks get out around so you might as well stay put and have a coffee and stare. And the spring, when the earth thaws and smells so deliciously sexy and there's rain and more fog and it seems there'll never be anything green again until that day when it turns, overnight, to summer and the old ladies come out of hiding and sit with their cats on the front steps and the boys wear tee-shirts and the girls find their short dresses and they all drive around with car windows open and the music is loud when they pass by. And you put on your lipstick and think you might like new earrings one of these days and if your hair is still wet when you go out, no matter, it'll dry soon enough in the warm wind. And the park fills with children and moms and dads and there's music on the downtown corners and open guitar cases lying on the sidewalk for your offerings. And someone decides to head out for England in a small sailing boat and everyone goes to see him off and if he's coming from the other direction, to cheer him home. And people walk the hills again, mind the gullies because you don't see them until you're almost over the edge and gone for good. And the flowers bloom and in a good year the cold fog stays out far - you can just see it on the horizon - and maybe it won't come ashore until the Folk Festival is over and the Youth For Social Justice might get a weekend of sunshine to spread the message. Summer here is magic. It doesn't strut its stuff so much as melt its way into your being. There is no hurry. No one cares if service is slow. The work day ends on time and you can waltz your way through the rest of it. The streets are full of merriment long after the moon is down and only the honestly sad can feel the *blue horror of dawn.*

Ruth and Patrick eat and drink and wander. They talk all night and when Patrick puts his hand on the back of her neck as they walk along Water Street she feels that's right where it should be and their steps match and in a few minutes she can't tell where her skin stops and his begins, the heat and the touch blend so nicely. They watch the sun come up over the water from Ruth's favorite perch on the hill among the bracken and the blueberry bushes. A dozen times one or the other says, "We have to go - it's really late", but they can't seem to take it seriously and Patrick ends up going to work without changing his clothes and Ruth doesn't even brush her teeth before falling into bed.

The others let her be for most of the morning so she can sleep but when the flowers arrive curiosity gets the better of them and, en masse, they present themselves at her door to hear about the big date. And the flowers, unwrapped, are the prettiest anyone has ever seen, enthusiastic flowers, happy to meet you flowers. The old plaster walls perk themselves up, suck in the yellows, pinks and violets and throw them back, even to the deepest corners of the shabby closet, into worn slippers and empty pockets. Someone finds a big old pretend crystal vase and it overflows and Ruth says, "Take some. Everyone have some flowers." And they do. Carry to their rooms, jam jars and drinking glasses of flowers.

And when the second bouquet arrives they fill the sitting room and the kitchen. With the third, the house starts humming and Ruth calls Patrick at work and tells him to stop it or he won't have any money left and she isn't interested in going out with a pauper.

~

Ms. Know it All, whose real name is Dorothy Blake, Dorrie to her friends, Ms. Blake to Howard James, is knocking at Mrs. Miflin's front door. She has come to find Harvey, missing for several days. When Howard remembered that Ginny Mustard said she lived at a Mrs. Miflin's house, he tracked down the address and sent Dorrie over on the off chance the stupid animal might have shown up there. Dorrie has had just about enough of working for H. James and Company. She spends her time fighting with a photocopier when she's not running around picking up laundry and coffee for his nibs or scraping shit off his carpet and, during her most recent bout of PMS, wrote up her letter of resignation. She is waiting for the right time to present it. Thinks, as she stands in the rain banging on the front door, any damned second now.

Judy towers over the tiny Dorrie, says she never heard tell of any dog around here and if she wants to look she had better get a search warrant. From somewhere in the house comes the sound of barking and laughter. This is not a good day to be pissing off Dorrie Blake. "Listen you big freak, if that goddamned dog is here I want it and I think you're lying through your teeth. I've put notices all over the city and I spend more time looking for that bloody animal than I do sleeping. Bring him out here. Now!"

"Well. Why don't you come right on in and take him if you're so friggin' tough. Good luck getting him away from Ginny Mustard."

That's the name Mr. James couldn't remember. Came up

with Jane and some sort of condiment. All he could think of was chutney. "Jane Chutney," he said. "Something like that. She's black with long yellow hair. You'll know her when you see her."

Judy marches out of the house and down the road to the playground. Dorrie stares after her for a minute before going inside. Calls out hello and when no one answers takes herself from room to room, listening for barking and laughter. But the house is quiet now. As she walks to the third floor she can hear movement and goes to the attic. To Ginny Mustard in her new rocking chair, in her pretty nursery, eyes closed and singing to a cradle of bones. *Hush little baby, don't say a word.* Close by, the dog raises his head, smiles at Dorrie and goes back to sleep.

The sound of Dorrie hitting the floor when she faints is exactly the same as the sound in Ruth's dream. Of her father hitting the wall with his fist, punching a hole so that her mother would have to hang a picture over it, too low to see comfortably but at least no one would know. No one ever knew. She is startled from her sleep and thankful that it's over before it really got out of hand. Hears the dog barking. Runs to the attic to see what's going on now for God's sake.

Ginny Mustard knows for sure that Dorrie is a thief. Wealth does not come without its share of worries and it's hard enough keeping Judy out of her room. She looks around for something to tie up the little woman until she can get the police to come and arrest her. Ruth is more concerned that one of their secrets is out. "For God's sake, Ginny Mustard, how could you not hear her coming up the stairs? Are you deaf?"

"I was singing the baby to sleep."

"That baby's been asleep for decades. You sure as hell don't have to sing to it. What the hell are we going to do? She had to see it or she wouldn't have fainted. Though anyone wearing a skirt like that might keel over. She must have it painted on."

The captive is coming to her senses, staring up at the

women standing over her. She readies herself to let out a good scream. Ruth claps a strong hand across Dorrie's mouth and tells her not to make a sound. "Get something to tie her up with. We might as well gag her too. Give me that thing you've got around your head. Quick. We have to figure out what to do."

But once poor Dorrie has been bound and shuffled to the rocking chair, Ruth is fully awake and approaching the realization that they may well have complicated matters for, in addition to bones in the attic and a body in the freezer, it seems kidnapping is on their growing list of crimes. What are they doing? What was she thinking? No - she wasn't thinking at all. A bliss hangover. No less than she deserves, either. Muddle-headed and then there are those damned flowers to keep you like that until you're weak and can't think straight. "Damn it all to hell, anyway. This is just great, Ginny Mustard. Once people notice that she's missing they'll be all over the place."

From downstairs comes the sound of Judy stomping about. She's in a mood and no amount of swinging in the rain has helped. She's wet to the bone. Hungry. "Where's everybody gone around here? Are we having anything to eat or what?"

Ruth tells Ginny Mustard to go down and get that one to shut up. She's loud enough to wake the dead. And she laughs, leading Ginny Mustard to believe that everything will be all right now so she goes to fetch Judy, who tells them that Dorrie has only come to get the dog and what did they have to go and tie her to the rocking chair for anyway, lunatics.

Maggie comes in then, to say that she wants to go and see her father and Judy has to come with her, right away. "Can't Maggs. These two fools got this tiny little woman all tied up and I want to see what happens next. Fine mess you've got us in now, Ruth."

"For the love of God shut up Judy. I can't think with your tongue wagging. I guess the best thing is to find out who she is."

She removes the scarf from Dorrie's face, telling her to be quiet, that they are not going to hurt her. Dorrie doesn't believe her for a minute, but now there are four of them staring at her and she's smart enough to know she should follow orders. "My name is Dorothy Blake and I came to get the dog for my boss."

"Well, this is Ginny Mustard and Judy and Maggie and I'm Ruth. We're sorry that we had to tie you up but we've got this problem with the bones. Mrs. Miflin dug up her dead baby and Ginny Mustard has taken a liking to it. Made this room all nice and clean and sits up here rocking and singing. We're afraid that if anyone finds out about it there'll be trouble and the cops will come around and who knows what will happen. Ginny Mustard never had much to do before and now she's happy and we'd just as soon keep her that way. If we thought you wouldn't tell we'd be glad to let you leave but we're going to have to think about that for a while yet. Okay?"

"What the hell difference does she make?" demands Judy. "You're screwin' a friggin' cop. You think he's not going to find out? They've got noses like bloodhounds. You mark my words, Ruth. Any minute now the shit is gonna hit the fan."

"Shut up Judy. So listen Dorothy, do you have your make-up with you? I'm going out tonight and I sure could use some of that lipstick you're wearing."

"You people are nuts. Why should I let you wear my lip-stick? Besides it's not really your color. If you put some powder on top of it, it could work."

Dorrie Blake has had few adventures in her life. Now that she thinks these crazies are not going to rape her or sell her into slavery, or cut her up into little pieces and cook her, she relaxes a little. "You can untie me, you know. It's not like I could get away with you crowd chasing after me. I'm really hungry. Do you think I can have something to eat. I get cranky when my blood sugar drops. If you like I can do something with your hair. A bit of gel would get that frizz out."

"Well okay then. Ginny Mustard have you got supper started yet? Judy you stay with Dorothy here while I take a quick shower. Should I dry my hair or leave it wet for the gel? I've never used it before."

"Wet is best. We can blow it dry after."

Maggie has her heart set on finding her father this evening. Gets a bit of a whine in her voice when she asks Judy again to please come with her.

"Let's go in the morning. It's been six years already. Another night isn't going to make that much difference. I don't feel much like doing anything right now if it's all the same to you. I'm going to my room." And Maggie resigns herself to waiting. Sits on the floor. Stares at Dorrie until Ruth comes back to have her hair done.

Mrs. Miflin has been banging on things with her crutches for a good fifteen minutes and no one can be bothered to go see what she wants. Since the doctor checked her out and told her to get moving, that's about all she uses them for, other than the time she threw one through her window, just missing old Father Delaney as he was walking by. She won't even try them out - too many stairs - and Judy has given up lugging her around so she stays in her room and mopes. They had to tape a piece of cardboard over the broken glass because she won't have anyone in to fix it until the weather turns cold and the rain has made a soggy mess all over her carpet.

Usually it's Eve who answers Mrs. Miflin's demands but Eve's bones are cold today and she fell asleep in her chair, watching the ocean churn in the wind, thinking it's almost time to leave. It's not that anything hurts. Her heart beats as beautifully as it ever did. Her breath comes and goes, smoothly, surely as it always has. But the warmth is fading and the big striped afghan pulled to her chin is useless, can't retain what isn't there to begin with.

Judy lies on her bed and lets her anger subside until the sadness underneath can get a grip. Winds the music box over and over again, listens to the tinny sound until she starts to cry, such quiet small tears for one so bold.

Grammy Hagen gave her the music box and it was real pretty until Alfred ripped the ballerina off. And Mike threw it in a bucket of water and she couldn't get it dried properly before the rust set in. Judy never had very many nice things and the box was special. When Grammy Hagen died her mother wouldn't let Judy go to the funeral. Made her stay home by herself and she just cried and listened to the song over and over for about two hours until she went to the corner store and ripped off a few chocolate bars to feel better.

And this is just the kind of day that makes a person remember things they'd rather forget. All rainy and windy, not a break anywhere. Is it summer still or have we stepped backwards into spring? There's a chill but it's early for fall. Whatever. Things have been a little too comfortable around here lately if you don't count Mrs. Miflin's woes. The gods are jealous, or bored perhaps, their palms itching with the urge to smack someone up side the head.

Judy would go out and steal something if the weather weren't so damned lousy. Instead she makes her way to Eve, dear Eve, and sits on the floor by her chair, with her head practically in the old woman's lap, hoping she'll reach out and stroke her hair like she did before. Of course, Eve does but is silent, barely says hello and Judy asks what's wrong. "It's almost time for me to go, sweetheart. I can feel it in my bones. I won't be able to stay much longer."

"What are you talking about. Eve? Where are you going? It's pissing down rain out there. Not fit for a dog. You can't go out in this. You'll catch your death."

Eve smiles. "That's where I'm going. I am dying."

"Don't be so foolish Eve," says Judy, suddenly afraid. "You're not sick. You got to be sick to die, Eve. Everybody knows that. Don't talk crazy. If you up and die now who's going to look after the garden? I don't know how to grow things. And you were going to help me name the kittens. That's not fair Eve, to say things like that just when we're having such a good time around here." And she runs to the door. Hollers for Ruth to come quick. Eve is dying.

Ruth's hair is only halfway dry but she and Dorrie hurry to Judy. "What are you talking about? Eve looks fine to me. You're okay, aren't you Eve?"

Eve looks up. "You're so pretty, Ruth. Are you going out with that nice Patrick again?"

Ruth smiles. "Yes. In about an hour. What's the matter?"

"I'm going to die and I was just telling Judy. I hate to go but it's almost time. Who's this, then?" she asks of Dorrie, and Ruth makes introductions.

Judy is crying again but louder than she did earlier. Big tears all over her face and she wipes her nose with the tail of her tee-shirt.

Ruth says, "It's okay Judy. When you gotta go you gotta go. Except in Eve's case she'll be back soon. Right Eve? Tell Judy how many times you've lived already. God. Must be dozens. Eve is the original. Mother of us all. It's called reincarnation, Judy. Mrs. Miflin won't let Eve talk about it anymore, it being ungodly and all, but she used to tell us about her other lives and all those sons she had who kept on killing each other. Tell Judy that you'll be back one of these days, Eve."

"I hope I will but it's different this time. I'm really tired. Oh I will miss this place. It's so lovely. So many beautiful things I've seen. And the people. I really enjoyed the people."

Judy screams, "You guys are freaking me out. What is she talking about? You can't come back if you're dead."

"Sure you can," says Ruth. "Why not? You just show up as someone else and pick up where you left off. That's what the Buddhists believe."

"What the fuck is a Buddhist? Do you really think that could happen? Do you think my Grammy could come back? I really liked her a lot. She was nice to me sometimes. Used to come over when Mom was out of it and she'd take me to her place for the night. And that time Mom was in the hospital I stayed with her a full month and she never once let my brothers pound on me. I'd like it if she came back."

"But she wouldn't be your Grammy. She'd be someone else and you wouldn't know her."

"Well, that sucks. What's the point of people coming back if they got to be someone else?"

"I don't know. I think I have a book about it somewhere. I'll let you read it if you promise to give it back when you're finished. Eve, do you need to go to the hospital?"

"Oh no. I'll be here for a little while yet. I just wanted to prepare Judy for my passing. She's so young and she hurts so much."

"I don't friggin' hurt. I just can't stand all this talk about dying, is all. And coming back. You're all crazy. And we sure as hell don't need any more bodies around here. Oops."

But Dorrie doesn't hear plural. Is wondering how much a room in this house would cost, supposing, of course, that they don't decide to keep her locked up here but if that's the case she probably won't have to pay anything at all. Dorrie has plenty of friends but none of them interesting. Mostly hold-overs from secretarial school where she never wanted to go in the first place but her parents wouldn't pay for anything else. She had her heart set on being a flight attendant but she was too short. Some of the girls she grew up with went off to universities to be teachers and doctors, but on Dorrie's side of the tracks that was considered a waste of money and you couldn't go wrong with typing. Dorrie hates typing. Even on her fancy computer. She's thirty years old. Has given up hope of ever finding a man, though she's still pretty and keeps her hair as blond as it ever was but she's five foot nothing in two inch heels and most of the fellows she meets treat her like a six-year-old. And she never wanted children first nor last after looking out for brothers and sisters since she could walk. Her life revolves around working for that jerk, Howard James, and saving money for her old age. She visits her parents now and then, listens to them whine about what so and so said to what's his name, goes out with "the girls" every other Wednesday for a couple of drinks. Listens to them go on and on about their homes and husbands and kids until she could scream. Dorrie is sick of listening.

In her spare time she makes clothes for the Barbie dolls she has been collecting since she was seven years old. Her favorite is dressed like Scarlet O'Hara. She wonders if Ruth will let her go to her apartment and get them and the pretty glass cases that she polishes once a week. She wants to live here. These women don't have shoes on, half of them, and she'd like to go barefoot now and then.

By the time Patrick arrives for Ruth dinner is just about over and Dorrie's fate decided. She has called Howard James and left a message saying that she can't find the dog, it's not at Mrs. Miflin's house, and she is never coming back to his office again. Don't bother to call because she doesn't want to talk to him. She told her parents and a few of her friends that she is leaving her apartment tonight. The others are pleased that Dorrie is moving in, but secretly agree that she must never go to the basement, concoct a story about rats so big and hungry they'd eat the face off you in a minute.

It's not like Dorrie to do anything rash and spontaneous. She has always been old reliable, the first one to sell tickets to the church raffle, or go door to door collecting for the Heart Foundation and Cancer Research. Her friends are burning up the telephone wires all over town wondering what the heck has gotten into her.

Mrs. Miflin is tickled pink when she finds she has a new boarder, almost gushes as she accepts Dorrie's cheques, tells her she can have any room in the house and hurries Ginny Mustard off to make it up real nice. Says the Joyful Mysteries. Sings a few rounds of Amazing Grace before nodding off.

Dorrie has a car. Judy volunteers to go with her to gather her things. Almost weeps when she sees the pretty clothes, about six sizes too small to borrow. Is fascinated by the Barbie collection. Judy never had a doll of her own that survived more than two days of her brothers' abuse, no matter how clever her hiding places. She and Dorrie dismantle the shelves, wrap the dolls in pink tissue paper and special boxes. Three trips later and it's almost midnight, they are finished, a note on Dorrie's door to tell the landlord he can keep the furniture, she's out of there, after ten years of being his star tenant, the cleanest, quietest he's ever known. He'll be grumpy for days.

Ruth is home at a civil hour tonight. She and Patrick are too tired to do much of anything, fell asleep at the movie, barely spoke, held hands. They arrive as Judy and Dorrie are lugging the last of their loads into the house. Ruth wonders how the hell it's all going to fit, suggests that the dolls be given a room of their own since there are so many vacancies. They enlist the exhausted Patrick to help out and he stumbles back and forth over the stairs until Ruth takes pity and sends him on his way.

"Wait until Ginny Mustard gets a look at these dolls." says Judy. "There must be a hundred of them. Did you ever see anything so pretty in your life, Ruth? And Dorrie's got little tiny dresses and boots and shoes for all of them to change into. Even underwear. And catalogues if she wants to buy more. I never saw anything so nice before. And she's got dresses for herself to match the little ones exactly. She made them on her sewing machine."

Ruth agrees that yes they're nice enough and goes to bed. Sleeps through the sounds of construction as Dorrie puts her shelves together, scrubs the Barbie room spotless and arranges the dolls just like they were at the old place, thinks about going out tomorrow for a nice piece of lacy fabric to make new curtains. Maybe some paper for the dingy walls. Perhaps she'll even buy a starter Barbie for Judy so she can begin her own collection. Dorrie has never met anyone who didn't mock her passion, didn't ask if she wasn't just a bit old to be playing with dolls, imply she had shit for brains, wasting good money on toys, what's wrong with you Dorrie?

All through the night she works and when Ginny Mustard wanders in at six to see what's going on, the smile on her face is well worth the effort. "You know," says Dorrie, "they make black Barbies too. The same color as you but they don't have blond hair. We could go and see if there's some in the stores, if you want one. I don't have any myself, but I know they're out there." Ginny Mustard doesn't respond. The dolls are like her music, so pretty that they hurt, but it's a good hurt and she nods. There has never been such a marvelous sight in Mrs. Miflin's house if you don't count the flowers that Ruth got.

Mrs. Miflin isn't happy to be giving Dorrie two rooms for the price of one but she's pleased enough to have another tenant, and a nice dresser too, different than some she could name who go around like streels half the time. And besides, she reasons, it won't do any harm to have a classy-looking woman out and about telling people where she lives now and what a lovely boarding house it is. Clean. Who knows? She might end up with more just like her and be able to tell the rest of them to take a leap and go find somewhere else to hang their sorry hats. So when Ruth asks if it will be all right for Dorrie to set up her sewing machine and dress forms in yet another spare room, she is feeling magnanimous, envisioning her future glory as the landlady of all landladies and says yes without batting an eyelash. She shoots a 'Your days are numbered, Missy' look in Ruth's direction making her wonder what the old bat is up to now, but who cares anyway.

Patrick is off today. He arrives early to see Ruth. Judy finds them hugging in the sitting room when she comes downstairs. "Oh, gross, you guys. That's really gross." And they stop, though they'd rather not.

"Don't you have anything better to do than hang around here, Judy? We could stand a little privacy, you know," says Ruth.

"No I don't. Not until Dorrie is ready and then we're going out to look at wallpaper and material for curtains. Ginny Mustard is coming with us. We're bringing Maggie over to her father's house first cause she hasn't seen him in six years. She found Lester Eldridge in the phone book at the address where she used to live so we figure it's got to be him. Right Maggs?"

Maggie is nervous. Nods her head.

Ginny Mustard has never been in a car that she knows of. Is excited about going to the mall. Asks Ruth if she'll mind the baby while she's gone.

Patrick says, "I didn't know you had a baby, Ginny Mustard." Ruth starts up about the imaginary baby that poor Ginny Mustard conjured in her warped little brain, that she thinks is real, how she rocks it to sleep and sings to it all the time. And Patrick's nice blue cop eyes narrow a bit while he listens to the lies but he doesn't say anything else. Ruth hurries the others into the kitchen for a little talk. "Watch what you're saying Ginny Mustard. And the rest of you too when Patrick is here. I'm not going to let anything screw things up for me. I really like him and if he finds out what's been going on in this house, I might as well kiss him good-bye, that's for sure. He's a cop, for God's sake."

Dorrie doesn't understand what the all the fuss is about. "Couldn't you just tell him what you told me? I mean, it's not like any of you killed the baby, is it now."

"Ha," says Judy. "You don't know the half of it, Dorrie. We'll all be up to our necks in it if old Patrick starts snooping around."

"That's enough Judy. Now you crowd take off and do whatever it is you're doing. Patrick and I are going out for the day. Where's Eve? Did anyone remember to feed Mrs. Miflin?"

"She had some corn flakes but she wouldn't eat them. Says they're stale and we're not closing the box right. Eve is in the Barbie room. I brought in her chair so she could sit and look at them. She thinks they're pretty too."

"This place is turning into a regular looney bin. I'll say goodbye to Eve. Make sure you're not gone too long and check on her when you get back." Ruth ushers them out the front door and goes to see Eve who is pleased to stay right where she is with her cup of tea.

Anyone knows that if you allow yourself too much happiness you court disaster. If you dare to relax and assume life is grand, well then, it simply has to up and prove otherwise. That's all there is to it. Ruth knows this is true but she seems to have forgotten the teachings, though Heaven knows how. Mrs. Miflin knows, which is why she takes her pleasure in small doses and even then is not too swift to recognize one. Dorrie knows and has Barbie insurance to her eyeballs. Ginny Mustard can be forgiven since she never quite caught on. Judy and Maggie, well they're what you might call heathens, not having been born into the one true church. And Eve, dear Eve, never believed it anyway since she has always found evidence to the contrary. But there's no excuse for Ruth. She knows better.

~

The man who opens the door to Maggie bears little resemblance to the father she remembers. He has folded considerably in six years.

His voice is low and gentle. "Margaret? Is that you my Margaret?" Maggie nods yes. He puts out his arms. She steps into him and holds on, laughing and crying all mixed up together. He needs to know why she ran away. Needs to know how she could have hurt him like that. That she has been all right. That she is back to stay. He can hardly believe what she tells him about the home and her mother's face hard, turning away while Maggie screamed and screamed. He thought he had dreamed that night. For years he's been dreaming that night.

The house is the same as it always was. Still neat as a pin with bonsai trees all over but no dogs. They sit close on the sofa and talk. Smile and cry some more until Dorrie's car pulls up and they all troop in. Maggie wants to stay until her mother comes home but her father says she should go. That he wants to talk to his wife about all of this before Maggie sees her again. Perhaps that will be best. Maggie is reluctant to leave. Writes her address and Mrs. Miflin's phone number for him, laughs and cries again through a long good-bye until Judy leans on the car horn. Mr. Eldridge watches them pull away, waving even after they've turned the corner, out of sight.

Ruth is still out when they get back to the house. Once they dry off from the rain that shows no sign of ever wanting to quit, Dorrie asks if they'd like to have a tea party in the Barbie room. She and Judy set up a big round table and some chairs from the attic with Ginny Mustard's blessing; she needs space for a playpen. Dorrie makes another trip, brings home little cakes with pink and yellow frosting and a poppy seed loaf. They dig out the good cups and saucers. No one can tell Mrs. Miflin, though, Judy says. "She only uses them when the Pope is visiting." Dorrie has lace-edged napkins and a matching tablecloth and in a few minutes the room is fit to entertain royalty. And now they must dress up pretty as well. No problem for Dorrie but the rest of them have to make do with odds and ends. Judy shares her junk jewelry and Eve has some old hats with lace that falls down over their eyes and makes everything look soft and blurry. Gloves that come all the way past their elbows, even Judy's, accessories that haven't seen the light of day for fifty years.

It's this picture of elegance that greets Ruth when she comes looking for them and she wishes to God she had a camera. Accepts Ginny Mustard's offer of tea and cake and they all sip together, quietly.

The pounding rain is louder than the sound of Mrs. Eldridge banging away at the front door but they certainly hear the crutches on the floor below and Mrs. Miflin yelling to see who's there. Eve goes to the door and the others follow. Maggie's mother is fit to be tied. When she sees her daughter her face opens into a scream. Eyes popping. Mouth spitting. "I told them to find you a place away from this city. What are you doing coming back and upsetting your father. He's sick. I wouldn't be surprised if he had another heart attack with you crawling out of the woodwork now. I'm going to sue those bastards for moving you in here. What the hell were they thinking? You had no right to go to my home."

Her hands are raised to strike and Maggie is about to crumble. Judy steps between them, tucks Maggie safely behind her. "I think it's Maggie's home too Missus. She's got as much of a right to be there as you do. And if she wants to visit her dad then you can't say anything about it."

"Like hell I can't! She's insane and I can get papers to prove it. And if I have to take out a restraining order to keep her away from my husband, I will. Do you understand that Margaret? If you come anywhere near him again I'll report you to the police so fast it will make your head spin. They'll lock you up again and believe you me, it won't be as pleasant a place as the last one. I'll make sure of that." And she's gone, nothing but a puddle of rain water on the floor to prove she was ever there. Maggie sits right down in that puddle and shakes all over. Rocks back and forth and doesn't make a peep. Picks up a passing kitten and holds on tight until it starts to cry and Judy has to pry the struggling creature from her shaking hands to keep Maggie from squeezing it to death.

The rain will not let up. All night and the next day it beats on the house. Eve's garden is a shambles. Gladiola are flat on the ground and the morning glory trellis has blown over, pulling the plants with it. Ugly toadstools sprout everywhere among the ruins and the slugs are having a field day. It's all doom and gloom and if Judy hadn't decided to bring up a casserole from the freezer, Ginny Mustard having wandered away into the fog before she made breakfast, they wouldn't have known that Mr. Miflin is well into thaw mode, popsicle juice soaking all the way through the rug they wrapped him in.

Tearing into the Barbie room, soaked to the knees, Judy practically screams her news. Dorrie says they just have to call a plumber and get him to pump it out, it's not that big a deal. The others are a little more agitated than the situation warrants as far as she's concerned and she tells them so. "Well," screams Judy "That just goes to show what you know, Dorrie Blake. Mr. Miflin is thawing out faster than May snow down there and we'll all be fucked if we don't do something about it. Where's Ruth? We have to find Ruth."

But Ruth is waiting for Patrick at the station, staring at a picture on the bulletin board. Leaping to her feet and out the door with no explanation to anyone when she recognizes the missing person. Racing into the house minutes later, yelling to the others to get down here right now we've got troubles like you wouldn't believe, ripping photographs out of frames, off walls, flushing little pieces down the toilet fast as you want. In Mrs. Miflin's room looking for more. "Do you have any other pictures, Mrs. Miflin? We have to get rid of them now!" Oh God. Prays Patrick never makes the same connection. Prays please God. Please. Please. And Mrs. Miflin is howling from her bed. "Ruth. Stop it. What are you doing? What will I say when Mr. Miflin comes home and there's none of our wedding pictures around? He'll think I don't love him."

Ruth is stunned. "What are you talking about? Ginny Mustard killed him. He's frozen solid in the basement. In the freezer. Don't you remember?"

"Well actually," says Judy. "He's not all that solid anymore, Ruth. The basement flooded and the freezer stopped working. The casseroles are ruined too and all those chickens that Eve bought. What are we going to do Ruth? Won't it start to smell bad soon?"

"Well yes, Judy. It's going to stink to high heaven, just like everything else in this Godforsaken place right now." And Ruth sits on Mrs. Miflin's bed. Puts her head in her hands and feels very small until Mrs. Miflin whacks her across the back with a crutch and tells them all to get the hell out of her room.

Think. Think. Think. Ruth pulls herself together. Tells Maggie to look up a plumber in the phone book and ask him to get over here as fast as he can. Goes to the basement to survey the damage. It's not so bad. No smell yet, anyway.

"Judy. When he gets here you stay in the basement with him while he drains the water out. Sit on the freezer and make small talk."

"What about the rats?" asks Dorrie. "You should take a stick or something with you for the rats."

"There are no rats, Dorrie," says Ruth. "We made that up so you wouldn't find out about Mr. Miflin. Fat lot of good that did."

Since Ginny Mustard can never be sure she won't tell secrets, she hasn't said anything at all lately to Joe Snake but when she runs into him at the Sea View Tavern, decides to fill him in on the summer's events. Tells him all about her baby and the kittens. How she shot Mr. Miflin. About Dorrie and the Barbie room. About Maggie's mother coming and upsetting everybody being so mean when they were having such a nice tea party. Tells him about her money and the doctors saying she isn't stupid anymore. Invites Joe Snake to come home and have some supper with them because she feels like cooking and thinks he could use some fattening up, being so thin. He accepts her invitation, thanks her for her generosity. They pick up a case of beer on the way.

"Well this is just what we need," moans Ruth when they arrive but she accepts a beer and sets another place at the table. Patrick calls to see why she hightailed it out of the station so fast and she has to tell him another lie about having a nasty stomach flu and she'll be in bed, most likely, until tomorrow and it's best if he not come over since she'd hate for him to pick up the germs too.

If the friggin' sun doesn't come out soon I'll hang myself," says Judy and Ruth tells her to go right ahead, she's sure there's rope in the basement and if not she will personally go out and buy some for her.

Eve wants them to come clean. This problem is way out of hand. "You can never go wrong telling the truth," she says. "Though it will be hard on Ginny Mustard, I suppose."

Joe Snake speaks up. "You're probably better off just getting rid of the body. You'll all be considered accessories to the crime. Why don't you bury him in the back yard? Plant a few bushes over him. As long as everybody can keep a secret, it should work."

"Well, it seems to me there are already too many people in on this secret. We'll have to live in each other's pockets to make sure no one tells. Look what happens when Ginny Mustard goes out alone. She spills her guts to the first person she sees."

"Joe Snake is my friend. He can know. He won't tell."

"We can't start digging until the rain stops. Dorrie, tomorrow you and Maggie buy some kind of bushes or trees or something that we can plant over him. Ginny Mustard you'll have to pay for them. Tell them what to get, Eve. You're the only one around here who knows about growing things."

"But I really wish we could tell the police what happened, Ruth. It is starting to wear on my conscience."

"You didn't do anything, Eve. Stop fretting. Unless someone has a better idea, we'll stick him in the ground and that will be that."

When Joe Snake says that he wasn't really serious about burying the body, Ruth ignores him.

It's a sorry lot that greets Patrick when he comes to see how Ruth is feeling. Glum and nervous in the sitting room. Quiet. Kittens racing up and down the heavy curtains and no one telling them to stop. Dishes still on the table, and pots dirty in the kitchen. Ruth doesn't care that he ignored her warning to stay away but does nothing to make him feel welcome either and he leaves after a quick beer. Gives Joe Snake a ride to his rooming house.

Finally sunshine but there's autumn all over it. Everything green looks tired, ready to quit this party and rest up for the next one. Judy sniffs the air like a cat when she steps outside to help decide where the new trees will go. A weeping birch is what Eve wants and a blue spruce. They take turns digging. There's only one shovel and it's too late to tell Dorrie and Maggie, off in search of trees, to buy another. The going is tough and muddy. Huge rocks have to be removed before the hole is deep enough. They wait until dark to fill it. Cover their secret. Father Delaney is up all night with his rheumatism, sitting out back at the rectory with his glasses on. Watching.

When Patrick comes to the door next morning they are still sleeping. If Ruth hadn't flushed all the pictures away he might never have put two and two together. But the missing pictures and pictures of the missing got into his dreams and, as he likes to put it, his spidey senses are tingling. In his hand is the photo of an odd-looking fellow, a vagrant, the kind few will admit to knowing. But someone in the world has reported his disappearance. No one who cares much mind, just another odd fellow who claims this one owes him money and filed a report. When he woke, Patrick added forty years to the newly-wed face in Mrs. Miflin's photographs and came up with the unknown hangashore on his office wall. When he got to work, old Father Delaney was waiting to report some strange happenings last night on Bishop's Road.

Those women buried something and it looked like an old rug but it was heavier. And that Indian was hanging around yesterday so he thinks they might be up to something which doesn't surprise him at all since no good ever comes of letting a crowd of women live together without a man around to keep things normal.

Ruth doesn't know Patrick all that well yet but she's in love for sure. Tuned in. She knows what's wrong before he says hello. Knows that whatever they have begun is over. Can't make up her mind whether to cry or scream so she just sits and does nothing for a minute before calling to the others.

"The arse is out of her now, ladies. The arse is out of her now." And she laughs. Bitterly. "Sergeant Fahey is here on official police business. Tell them, Patrick."

"I think this missing person is Mr. Miflin. He looks a lot like the man in Mrs. Miflin's wedding pictures. No one has seen him for a month or more. Has he come around at all? If it is Mr. Miflin, it makes sense that he would show up here. Does he look familiar, Eve?"

"You would have to pick on Eve first. Nice going, Patrick. It's okay Eve. You don't have to lie. Go ahead and tell Sergeant Fahey everything you know about Mr. Miflin."

One by one they tell him the story but when it comes time to take Mrs. Miflin's statement things get confusing. There's no way her dear husband is dead. It can't be true. He just went out and he'll be back any minute. She doesn't know who the man in the picture is but it's not her husband.

"She's out of it," says Ruth. "She knew all about this until he thawed. I guess she just kind of snapped, lucky bitch."

"Are you going to arrest me?" asks Ginny Mustard.

"Yes," says Patrick. "You'll have to come to the station with me now. There'll be other policemen here in a few minutes to dig up the body and take it away."

"Well that was a friggin' waste of time!" yells Judy. "What are we supposed to do with those friggin' trees? I'm not touching another shovel as long as I live so someone else is going to have to plant them next time."

"You'd best keep a civil tongue in your head, young lady," says Patrick. "Neither of you is in the clear. Ginny Mustard is not the only one in trouble." He calls the station and in no time there are a good dozen officers all over the place, who haven't investigated a murder for years and can't wait to get their hands on a real crime. Sirens blaring and brakes screeching they come tearing up the road. Important. Cool. Digging out their spiffy sunglasses even though it's a drab day and looks like more rain. They take their own sweet time wrapping Mrs. Miflin's house in yellow tape. Block the street to traffic but not pedestrians and they're everywhere, rumors flying so thick and furious you need a swatter to get through them.

With promises to take care of her little baby the others wave Ginny Mustard goodbye. Watch the police car inch its way around neighbours they never knew they had. Mrs. Hennessey rushes home to bake up her famous tuna casserole for the bereaved. That's what you do when someone dies no matter how they meet their end but when she brings it over she doesn't get a peep inside the house, has to give it to the policeman standing at the front door. Several of the other women on the street do the same. By the time they figure out that a satisfying meal is no ticket to the inner sanctum and give it up the tenants have enough to keep themselves fed for a month.

Aside from missing the baby and Dorrie's dolls, things on the inside aren't much different than anywhere else for Ginny Mustard. Patrick lets her bring along the little CD player and one of the hookers takes a liking to her so nobody steals it. She has her music and plenty to eat. And if she can't walk to the river whenever she wants, well, it is still better than going hungry and having people yell at you all the time, listening to children crying and being beaten for no reason at all every time you turn around. As long as she never has to be a little girl again, life is grand for Ginny Mustard.

Under the assumption that she is as poor as a church mouse the courts award Ginny Mustard legal counsel free of charge. The young woman assigned the case is having a hard time making heads or tales of the story. Asks that Ginny Mustard be freed on her own recognizance until the trial date. If Mr. Miflin had been a person of any importance she might have been held forever, but he wasn't, and after a few days in the lock-up she is sent home to wait it out.

~

Judy is going back to school. Her probation officer and Patrick have worked it out. If there's any chance of her getting away with aiding and abetting the criminal, Ginny Mustard, those men will see that she takes it. She's not thrilled with the idea. School has always been a pain for her. Not that she isn't smart. She surely is. But it's just so difficult to sit still and listen to some deadhead teacher drone on and on about wars and kings and the economy of Brazil and where to put your commas and who really cares about the square root of anything when you get right down to it.

Maggie wants to go as well. She never did finish up, what with being dragged away and all. When Patrick comes to deliver the news to Judy he says that since this particular school takes just about anybody that no one else will, he'll talk to them. It might help to have Maggie on board. At least she'll get Judy out of bed in the morning. Maybe even out the door.

"That's what we can spend all my money on, Judy. We can buy some new school clothes. My dad used to do that every first of September and we'd have lunch too. He would take the whole day off. Do you want to do that?"

"When can we go? Do you want to get some tattoos while we're at it? I know a guy who does them dirt cheap down the end of Water Street. It's really a video shop but he has all the gear in the back room."

~

Ruth doesn't want to see Patrick and he's been asking for her. Eve has tried to get her to come downstairs but she won't budge. She has locked her door and no one is allowed in. Late at night when the house is asleep she wanders about. Stares at the streetlights from the sitting room window. All of the hurt she has ever swallowed is a monster that she cannot get around. She doesn't even try. She is as flat as if someone had run her down with a steam roller. Raw. There is nothing but the pain. She slows her existence to a series of deliberate movements. Says to herself, "Now I am walking down the stairs. One stair, two stairs, three," all the way. "Now I am turning on the tap. I am filling a glass with water. I am drinking water. I am rinsing the glass." Nothing more. She does not think. She cannot think. She can only hurt all over. One foot in front of the other. Carefully. Carefully. Slowly. She is broken. There is nothing anyone can do to help. Her agony fills the house. Dorrie opens every door, every window, but there's not enough sunlight in all of creation to dispel the darkness.

Eve says they must stop trying. Says that when Ruth is ready and able she'll come back. Eve tends poor Mrs. Miflin, assures her that her dear husband will be here soon, helps her fix up her hair and holds the mirror to show her how pretty she looks. Mrs. Miflin won't go back to the hospital to have her cast removed, she doesn't want to chance not being home when he arrives, so Judy carries her to the tub and they soak it off. She still won't walk though, no matter how Eve coaxes. Sits at her bedroom window and watches the road. Waits.

The school that Judy and Maggie attend is just like a real one except it's not crowded and the teachers treat them like human beings. Judy says, "This is a nice friggin' change from the last place I was." Everyday they walk home past Maggie's old house and if the car is gone they go in to visit her dad. When he knows that Mrs. Eldridge will be out for the day he makes cookies and they all sit at the kitchen table and talk about what's happening at school and he helps Judy with her math. When they leave he makes sure they take the leftover cookies with them so his wife won't know and she can't figure out why there's never any flour or sugar around when she needs them. They don't acknowledge the existence of Maggie's mother except for one day when she came home early and they had to hide in the backyard until Mr. Eldridge signaled that it was okay to run around front and disappear.

Fall is much too soon this year but pretty enough anyway that most people don't care. Along the river the leaves are changing to yellow gold and burgundy. Now is the time to stake out a blueberry patch on the hills; it's so easy to find the bushes when they turn flame red. Draw a little map for yourself and keep it tucked away until next year. Some nights there's a dusting of frost and only the calendula and marigold, the marguerite daisies, alyssum, malva have the tenacity to hang on, wait for the sun to warm their cold petals and then they're as nice as you'd want. In Eve's garden the zinnias and poppies are blooming over and over as though to please her one last time. She washes her pots and wheelbarrow but the flowers keep on growing.

~

Ruth has gone away. She borrowed Dorrie's car and some money from Ginny Mustard. Judy made sandwiches for the trip. She put a few things in a small suitcase and no one knows the wherefore and the why, just that she'll be back and they should keep their chins up. The darkness went with her or maybe it got off at the overpass as she was heading out of town. Either way the house is bright again except when Patrick comes by, which he does a couple of times a day to ask if anyone has heard from Ruth and to see if they need any heavy lifting done or walls painted. Their answer at first was no but now each tries to think of a little something to keep him busy since he doesn't seem to want to go home. They feed him and get him to change a lightbulb or move a dresser or take a look in the basement to find out what the strange sounds might be coming from the water heater. He's easy enough to have in the house even as gloomy as he is all the time and they tolerate him the way they do the kittens, stepping around him when he's underfoot and shooing him to another room when he takes up too much space in the kitchen. They send him outside to rake leaves or spread compost. He's building a potting shed and replacing some of the rotting boards on the back step. But he doesn't whistle while he works or smile very often.

Ruth has gone home. Home to the place she was born. Home that is empty now, but for the sad thing that haunts the landing at the top of the stairs just outside her old bedroom door, sits and listens in cold bare feet and flannelette nightgown. Blue. Frayed at the edges. Much like Ruth herself. She has come to do penance in the only place cruel enough and hard enough to grant her absolution.

Ruth's mother despised this village. The rocks and the cliffs and the pathetic scraps of earth around the clapboard houses that hang on for dear life and at first glance seem fragile but are as tough as the coltsfoot sticking out of the pebbles at their feet. She hated all of it. The people were ignorant and dull as dishwater, she used to say. She wanted more than this. Nagged her husband to move away to a real town with a decent school and social opportunities but he never would. The fishing was fine. His family had been here for generations and besides, they owned their home. They would never find better than this anywhere else. He had been through the war. Had seen as much of the rest of the world as he cared to and would live and die here thank you very much. What was he thinking to marry a teacher? He might have known she'd get fancy notions one of these days. Grand ideas about what was proper and what wasn't and how to dress and sit and eat and speak and she drove him right up the wall with her picking all the time. When she took to drinking it got worse. The fights lasted long into the night and Ruth wouldn't sleep until they were finished. Listened from her perch on the landing at the top of the stairs.

The house stands back from rock a few hundred feet or so. Nasty cruel vertical layers razor sharp and a million years from Africa or wherever they were before the earth shifted and the waters rose. From a distance they look inviting. You think, I'll sit here with my sandwich and apple and watch clouds and dream awhile but up close you can see that the only place comfortable is underwater where the waves have beaten the stone to submission. So you must have your lunch on the grass at the land's edge with the seagulls that scream if you take too long to fling your scraps.

Behind and to the sides of the house are rose bushes gone mad. They push hard against the walls and might crush if they ever felt the need. Among them, stunted pine and alder and way at the back aspen to keep you awake at night with their gossip. Lonely looking from the rocks. Derelict. There's a wind blowing through the rooms and the roof makes heavy sighs like something in very old pain.

The village was abandoned thirty-five years ago. Resettled. Its inhabitants moved a few miles down the road where there was more of what Ruth's mother wanted in her life. Forty houses, once yellow, red, green against the fog, boat launches, the wharf, church, school, all lonely grey and crumbling with nobody home except the feral cats. If Ruth had ever wanted kittens she has them now. And they are about as friendly as she feels, snarling when she comes upon them, backs arched and tails puffed three times normal size.

Gardens abandoned went wild. Everywhere the remnants of a summer that must have been beautiful. Hollyhock, delphinium, foxglove grow year after year wherever they damn well please. Mint, rhubarb and lavender. Ivy, unchecked, filled ditches, climbed over fences and down the road, in through broken windows and rotting doors.

The house is cold. Ruth wants to light a fire but doesn't know if the chimney is safe. She fills a bucket with water from the well and drags it to the living room, just in case. It's all the care she feels like taking now. She hauls wood from the shed. She peels paper from the walls of her parents' bedroom. It has been there for a hundred years and comes away easily once she gets a corner pulled up. She feeds her fire faded flowers and it works. Her toes are warm. She falls asleep on the rug and the sad thing is crying, shivering, on the landing at the top of the stairs.

Ruth wakes to sunshine through dirty, cracked windows and a brown mouse just beyond her reach, staring with black eyes. "You're the fool. There are cats everywhere. It's a good thing the old man is not around - he'd have you mashed to nothing with a broom and flung in the trash before you could blink."

The house is cold again, the fire long dead. Ruth finds rags in the kitchen, wipes a circle clean in the living room window, stares at the ocean for a few minutes before washing her face, brushing her teeth. She walks the village one end to the other again and again. Sits in the old church for hours with the cats that lie about the altar and leap over pews, fight in the aisle. She closes her eyes and hears Father Murphy sing the mass, preach eternal damnation, salvation, take your pick. *I believe in one God, the Father Almighty, Creator of Heaven and Earth and of all things visible and invisible.* She can smell incense.

At the house she scrubs with cold water, no soap, the living room. Windows. Floor. Furniture deemed unacceptable for the new home, what will people think if they see us dragging that garbage along. Job's Landing is not like this place you know, it's going to be hard enough fitting in anyway, I won't have them taking us for a crowd of peasants. And they had gone, her mother thrilled with the idea, her father grumbling all the way, her brother ready for his own place with his new bride and Ruth not caring one way or the other.

She scrubs the walls higher and higher as far as she can reach and that's not good enough so she stands on a rotting chair and by the time she is done even the ceiling gleams and the light fixture. She takes the rug she slept on outside to the fence and beats it with a stick and the dust is in her eyes and ears and nose and she is crying. She goes to the ocean. Stands on the rocks too close for comfort. Thinks she might let the waves take her but knows they don't want her, will throw her back bloodied and broken. She is no longer part of water and water knows that. Even a lake would tell her float. Her toes curl in her shoes to grip the slippery rock. She is not brave. She does not want to die.

For days she wanders the house. Takes her rug and a bucket of water, scrubs her parents' room and sleeps where their bed was, her brother's room and sleeps where his bed was, her room and sleeps a while, sits at the top of the stairs and listens, sleeps a while, sits and the top of the stairs and listens, sleeps a while. She has eaten all of her sandwiches and is down to water when the house is finished, clean as it can be with no soap. She gathers lavender and branches of rose hips, fills the bucket and puts the arrangement in the middle of the living room floor. Tells the sad thing at the top of the stairs in bare feet and shivering to get in the car, you might as well come with me, and drives to Job's Landing.

It is late and dark when she arrives at her brother's house but she knocks at the door anyway. When Matthew answers he does not recognize her until she speaks. He makes coffee. Joanna wakes and prepares the guest room. They are happy to see her, to know that she is alive after all this time. They sit quietly at the kitchen table. Ruth showers and sleeps. Time enough tomorrow to find out why she's here.

~

"I've been to the old place. Spent three days there. Or four. Hard to tell. I cleaned it top to bottom. The village looks so much prettier with no people. Nature just kind of moved in and grew all over it. The gardens have gone wild. I met a man. The first one worth knowing for as far back as I can remember. But I've been unbelievably stupid. Fed him a pack of lies. He's come to see me but I can't even look at him. Knowing I lied. I've been feeling like crap so I went to the old place. Considered throwing myself into the ocean but I'm too much a wimp."

Matthew and Joanna take the day off. Listen to Ruth. "We didn't know what had become of you. The last letter was twenty-five years ago. From Jamaica. Where have you been all this time?"

"Around. You can't go wrong being a great waitress. Especially if you don't care how seedy the bar. If you stay one step ahead of immigration. Not all that difficult, really. But when you start looking your age it's not so easy. They like the young ones with perky tits. Once your ass starts to fall down around the back of your knees you're pretty much washed up. I got tired. Now I do nothing. Your taxes have been feeding me for a good six years now. I have a room in a nuthouse and I pretty much do fuck all."

Joanna says, "Peter is fine. Do you want to see some pictures?"

Ruth starts to cry. "Yes. Where is he? His birthdays are the hardest times. Usually I just get very drunk the night before so I can feel like shit all day."

"He's in the city, now. Teaching at the university. Married to a really wonderful woman. Sarah. They have two children. A boy and a girl. Joseph and Eleanor. Eleanor looks so much like you it's eerie, Ruth."

"Does he know? Did you tell him?"

"We did what you wanted. As far as he's concerned you're his aunt, long missing, but his aunt anyway. We've always talked about you. I have all the pictures that Mom and Dad took. We used to go through them now and then when he was young. You can be proud, Ruthie. He's a great father and husband."

"I can't take any pride in that. You raised him."

"But he's strong, Ruth. Stronger than I ever have been. That came from you," says Matthew.

"Hell. I can't even fling myself into the ocean when I want to. No. Whatever he is he got from you two. I want to see him. I won't give away our secret. No matter what. I have to get back soon. A crazy old lady is threatening to die and I should be there I guess, or the others will fall apart and I'd hate to have to clean up that mess. Besides, I may have a date with the courts."

~

Ginny Mustard is planning her wedding. Well, she's not doing all that much really, but Maggie and Judy are having a great time. The guest list is a little ragged what with so many of the invited having no known address but Ginny Mustard has an idea where most of them are hanging out and Joe Snake, the groom, stuck up a notice at the Ocean Bar and Grill for anyone they might have forgotten. The reason Ginny Mustard has decided to marry is that she likes Joe Snake a lot and she wants to have a baby since the police took her pink blanket of little bones and arranged a burial after they determined that there had been no foul play in its death. Mrs. Miflin had become suddenly lucid one day and told Patrick all about the secret in the attic and what she had done. And for some reason that no one can fathom it's okay to have a jar of ashes kicking around your house but if a body hasn't been burned beyond recognition it has to go into the ground no matter how clean the remains, unless it's a million years old and then it can go in a museum.

Patrick has worn himself out trying to keep Ginny Mustard from marrying. She is about to be tried for murder, after all. He is especially adamant that she not get herself pregnant since she'll have to give the baby up if the jury finds her guilty anyway. But Joe Snake says he'll look after the little one if there happens to be a little one and Ginny Mustard can see it on visiting days and forever after when her sentence has been served. Ginny Mustard listened politely to Patrick's arguments against her plans and went ahead anyway. She likes him but he doesn't make a lot of sense sometimes.

Joe Snake convinces Ginny Mustard that she should get her money out of her hockey socks and into a bank and she opens an account, insisting that it be joint so Joe Snake can withdraw money to take care of the baby and buy oranges and bananas to bring to the jail since Judy told her there is always a shortage of fruit there. He says that he can look after a family on his own wages, thank you, but succumbs to reason when she says he'd have to find something with decent hours when the baby comes if she is found guilty.

Everyone is happy that Ruth is back and in a better mood. Dorrie is especially pleased to have her car since there is so much running around to do. Ginny Mustard has to be in court on December first. They're all in a mad rush to hold the wedding on November fifteenth so there can be a honeymoon and a few laughs before the season gets serious.

Ginny Mustard wants a formal wedding with a long white dress and she finds the perfect one at the second-hand store down the road. It is very old and has a good twenty pounds of tiny beads, just like pearls, on the bodice, and a veil with pretend satin flowers and blue ribbons that hang long. Dorrie thinks that unless it belonged to your mother or grandmother, it's probably unlucky to wear someone else's wedding dress but since Ginny Mustard seems to have such lousy luck anyway she doesn't bother to air her views.

~

At first old Father Delaney is unwilling to perform the marriage ceremony but is persuaded after only a few minutes with Joe Snake. Father Delaney has always been afraid of tall men but until now has managed to counter his feelings of intimidation with the white collar. Joe Snake can see the priest's fear and stays his ground until he receives the answer he wants. Joe Snake will do anything for Ginny Mustard. If she wants him and babies and Father Delaney he is happy to oblige.

The reception will take place at Mrs. Miflin's house. Walls and floors have been scrubbed to within an inch of their lives. Ginny Mustard will make all of the food herself with help from Judy who found a book about weddings with all kinds of recipes for fancy morsels. They have cleaned out the corner fish store of scallops and shrimp and crab and are working on finding enough large mushrooms to stuff for the hoards who don't eat as often as they might in a perfect world. With the freezer no longer occupied, and back in working order, much of the preparation is being done ahead of time and stored.

Since one wedding menu seems paltry, they are doing three and a few extra odds and ends. "Just in case," says Ginny Mustard, "they don't like fishy things and want a bit of roast beef and potato salad." There is liquor stored from stem to stern. Since many of the guests have no telephones and few know what RSVP means - Dorrie had to translate for Ginny Mustard - they have no idea how many to expect and there's nothing worse in this part of the world than leaving a party hungry and sober unless you are on a serious diet.

When Ruth arrives the smell of Murphy's Oil Soap is enough to knock you over. It doesn't take long to fill her in on the details of what she has missed, all of them talking at once. Judy got her first ever 'A', in math of all things, Eve is embroidering pillow cases, Mrs. Miflin is still nuts but she told about the baby,

Maggie is alive and kicking, and Ginny Mustard is getting married.

"Well," says Ruth. "I can't beat that. I cleaned a house. Has Patrick come around?" Yes. Patrick came around. It's a wonder he didn't just move on in. You have to talk to him Ruth. He's as miserable as a cut dog and he's driving us all crazy. Call him for God's sake. But Ruth waits. He'll come around again and she'll see him then.

She does have a call to make though, and has been trying hard on the drive home not to rehearse the conversation, not to think about her son, married to a real nice woman and with children of his own. She can't imagine him grown. Even after looking at all of those photographs she only sees the tiny being he was when she met him, can still smell the sweet baby scent of him, can feel his soft hair on her cheek when she held him to her face and cried so hard. And he just blinked with his dear eyes all out of focus but he did look at her and he knew what she had to do.

Her brother was a gentle person. Good enough to attract another like him. Childless and longing for babies. Better than she could ever be to raise her son. And so she had bundled up the one who'd grown under her heart and said to Matthew, "Take him. He's yours. Because I am our father and you aren't. Don't tell him about me. Don't hurt him. Don't call him names. If you ever raise a hand to him I'll make sure that you don't have a minute's peace for as long as you live. If even once he sits at the top of the stairs and shivers and listens, I'll know and I'll be back." And she had left him there. Had run as fast as she could through the years and now she will see the baby who is a man and say hello, I am your Aunt Ruth come back from the dead.

~

Ginny Mustard asks Eve if she can borrow all her pretty

hats and gloves for some of the people who won't have anything nice to wear to the wedding reception because once they see how fancy she looks they might like to dress up themselves. The clothesline is a rainbow of finery as the cold breeze distributes the scent of mothballs to the rest of Bishop's Road.

Patrick has a handful of invitations for the policeman who spent time at the house when they dug up Mr. Miflin. Dorrie especially likes the one with blond hair and hopes he might be free that evening, writes a personal note saying so. When Patrick sees the guest list he shudders. Tells them he'll drag along as many cops as he can find. Wonders if they should carry arms. Bring outstanding warrants. Back-up.

Throughout downtown you can almost taste the excitement. In the alleyway just beyond the Sailors' Inn, Mabel Porter has happened upon Dim Dinn and they are wondering what Ginny Mustard might like for a wedding present. Over at The Crossing are a few of the girls on the way to their corners for the evening, stopping to chat about what to wear and who would have thought that Ginny Mustard could do something so smart as marry Joe Snake, almost coming to blows when Betty Parsons wonders aloud if maybe he's only in it for the money since Ginny Mustard is not that good a catch heading off to jail most likely. Betty is new to these streets and doesn't know that Joe Snake can do no wrong so they let her off with a stern warning.

There never was such a time as Ginny Mustard's wedding is shaping up to be. Celebration of the century, no doubt, and there is little else to talk about. The immediate neighbors get wind of it and are none too pleased that the dregs of humanity will congregate on Bishop's Road so Ginny Mustard posts an invitation at the corner store and they stop complaining. Dig out their best clothes. Go shopping for gifts.

Mrs. Miflin gets in a real snit when she floats into reality for a minute here and there. Thinks about the mess her house will be when that crowd gets finished with it if they don't burn it down with their cigarettes first. But she still refuses to get out of her chair by the window. Can't seem to walk and is getting as big as the broad side of a barn just eating and sitting all the time. Eve has given up on her and it's only when she starts banging on the floor with her crutches that anyone remembers she's alive and brings her food or takes her to the bathroom.

~

When Ruth called Peter he was delighted to hear from her. Asked if he could come and get her, bring her to his home for a visit. But Ruth said, "No. Tell me where you live and I'll get there on my own steam." Turns out that his house is just a walk along the river, his back garden gate opening off the boardwalk, a path of brick leading to his kitchen and Ruth sets out in the crisp leafy air to see him. Passes Howard James with his new puppy who doesn't look much happier than Harvey did.

Peter hugs Ruth when he answers his door, brings her inside. Introduces Sarah. Eleanor. Joseph who doesn't like to be called Joey because he knows someone else named Joey who is mean at school. Ruth barely hears him, staring as she is at the little Eleanor who might be Ruth's seven-year-old self, same dark eyes, same smile, same head of corkscrew curls.

Her son is beautiful. She searches his face again and again for clues that she did the wrong thing leaving him but there is nothing sad in him at all. He breathes affection. Peace. Acceptance. The way Ruth looks at Peter is not lost on Sarah. Ruth is Peter's mother, she says to herself, and he doesn't even know it. And that makes her the grandmother of my children - not a great-aunt at all - and she smiles. Asks if Ruth would like to come to Sunday dinner and says she'll walk her back along the river when she's ready to go since she has to pick up a few things at the grocery store anyway. Eleanor and Joseph want to come too but Sarah tells them no. She wants some time of her own with Ruth and they can see as much of her as they want tomorrow. Sarah is not one to mince words. Tells Ruth that she suspects Peter is her son and not her nephew at all. No long lost aunt looks at a person that way. They stop walking. Stand silent for a few minutes by the cold water while Ruth ponders her next move. And she might have denied the truth forever if Sarah hadn't put her hand gently on Ruth's arm and looked at her as though she liked her and could forgive anything. So there was no choice, really.

"For three days after he was born I cried. Every time I looked at him so helpless in that silly plastic cot. Every time I picked him up and fed him or changed him, I cried. All I could think of was hurting him. I was so fucking afraid that I would hurt him. I didn't sleep. I thought that I might strangle him in my dreams. I didn't know what else to do so I gave him to Matthew. I don't regret it. I wanted him so badly but I was too afraid that I was my father. He thought that if you smacked a three-month-old hard enough it would stop crying. My mother wasn't much better. She stayed in her bed while he disciplined. Handed him the belt when he came in from the boats so he could teach us to mind her. She never hit us. Her specialty was emotional torture. And I bought it all. But Matthew - it's as though it rolled right off him. I don't understand how but it did. Something good got through to him in spite of all that went on."

By now Sarah is crying and Ruth starts too and they have their arms around one another and Sarah whispers, "You poor, poor thing to have suffered so."

Ruth sobs. "What a load of crap we mortals must endure. Hardly seems worth it sometimes. If the alternative weren't so friggin' much scarier we'd probably all hang ourselves before we hit kindergarten."

Sarah laughs. Ruth laughs. And Sarah kisses Ruth on the cheek and tells her she's happy to meet her. "And now you have to come around as often as you can. And get to know your grandchildren and your son."

But Ruth says, "Are you sure you want that? You don't know where I'm coming from at all."

"Well yes I do," says Sarah. "You loved your baby enough to give him up. You might have done fine with him you know, but you really thought you couldn't so you gave him up. That tells me more about you than anything else you will ever say or do. I want you to be part of our lives. My parents have seen Eleanor and Joseph once. They live on the other end of the country and find it difficult to get away. They've always been busy. I don't remember a time when they weren't rushing off to some event or other. I have no brothers or sisters. They didn't even have time for that. And, of course, Peter is an only child as well. Perhaps that's why we connected. We grew up lonely. I want my children to have people who matter in their lives. And here you are out of the blue. In my mind I'm setting a place for you at the Christmas table."

"You know Sarah, you're a bit too trusting. Not very realistic if you ask me. Why don't you come to my home and see how Ruth lives. Tell me after you meet my family, if you want me within a hundred feet of yours."

"You're on," says Sarah and they walk arm-in-arm to Bishop's Road.

~

Dorrie's surprise bridal shower is in full swing. A number of the guests are three sheets to the wind. There's a game of strip Go Fish on in the Barbie room with several of the losers, hookers by the looks of them, down to their bras and thongs and Mrs.

Miflin in their midst, fully clothed and winning. Seems that no one was going to sit at a window during this party and when Sassy Connors came upon the landlady in her search for a bathroom she rounded up a few of her friends and they carried the old woman chair and all to the card game. After the place had been eaten down to a shambles Ginny Mustard checked her supplies and will have to spend the next four days cooking if she's to have enough for the wedding reception.

"Well?" says Ruth. "What do you think, Sarah? What do you think of my family? Did I happen to mention that I have obstructed justice? Do you really want your children hanging out with a woman who knows people like this crowd?"

"I wouldn't mind staying if it's all the same to you. I know I wasn't invited but I doubt that anyone will notice an extra body. Before I had the children I worked at a halfway house. I'm pretty sure I recognize a couple of the guests. Why don't you offer me a drink? And if you show me where the phone is I'll call Peter and tell him I'll be home later on."

"These people are losers, Sarah."

"I know who they are, Ruth. And there but for the Grace of God go you or I."

"I'm already one of them. Don't think for a minute I'm not."

"Right. I don't consider that a problem. I'd love to meet the bride-to-be. Is that her over there?"

"That's her. Come on. I'll introduce you."

The party winds down around midnight. Sarah stays to help clean up and is invited to the wedding for her troubles. Before they leave the ladies help themselves to gloves and hats and Betty Parsons takes two of the kittens. Many of the guests will spend Monday at the thrift shops digging through old dresses and shoes to find something to match. The rest of the country upped the prices of relics from the forties some time ago but here in this city you can still pick up a good formal gown for a couple of dollars whenever some old woman passes on to her heavenly reward and her own daughters don't want her tatty clothes, send them to the poor unfortunate.

In the morning Ginny Mustard and Judy take stock of the remaining food and make a list of essentials so they can begin again tomorrow. But this is a day of rest and hangovers and the list is a long time growing. "They ate all the shrimp and roast beef," says Judy, "but I think the turkey is still there and they didn't touch the scallops or the cookies. That's good. I don't think it's as bad as all that and if you like, me and Maggs can help after school."

Patrick is waiting when Ruth finally emerges from sleep. Since Ginny Mustard has decided to take full responsibility for the murder, freezing and eventual burying of Mr. Miflin, no one else will be charged in the case, leaving Ruth and the others off the hook.

"Well. That hardly seems right, does it? I'm the one who suggested we freeze him in the first place so the silly thing wouldn't have to go to prison for the rest of her life. I'm the one who told the others to go out and get trees to plant over the body."

"Yes. Everyone in this house knows that. But nobody else does except for Joe Snake and he'll say whatever Ginny Mustard asks him to," says Patrick. "Ginny Mustard is claiming that she forced all of you to go along with her. Said she was prepared to shoot the lot of you if you didn't. And if she wants to say that in court to clear you - well - who's to say she's lying?"

"We wrapped the gun in the rug with him for God's sake. How the hell was she going to shoot us if she had to dig him up to do it?"

"That's her story and she's sticking to it. I don't know why but there you have it."

"Seems strange that a woman who can barely string two

words together on a good day managed to come up with that. Are you sure you didn't talk her into it?"

"I would never do that. As far as I'm concerned you're all guilty of something but it's hard to say what. Gross stupidity or aiding and abetting or just concern for a friend. Take your pick. In the meantime would you like to go for a walk with me?"

"Sure," says Ruth. "You can see me to my nephew's house. Peter is his name. I'm spending the evening at his place."

The walk along the river is not exactly close. No hand holding. No indication that Ruth and Patrick even like each other very much. Ruth's neck is prickly for want of touch, a stone's weight heavy on her heart, Patrick's blue eyes clouded and he finds it hard to swallow. When they reach the garden gate to Peter's house the children are waiting and Sarah is raking the last of summer's leaves. When she sees Ruth she walks quickly to greet her, is introduced to Patrick and invites him to dinner. Tells Joseph to run and ask his daddy to set another place before Patrick even accepts. Whispers to Ruth, "I hope you don't mind but I like the look of him."

~

Dorrie has to wash all of the clothes her Barbies were wearing during the bridal shower to get the smell of smoke out.

"I don't know why you're bothering with that now," says Judy. "They'll stink worse after the reception. Might as well do it next week."

"I will but I'd like it to smell nice in here in the meantime." And she sprays another dose of air freshener.

When Eve goes to put her stockings out to dry there is no room on the line with all the little dresses hanging there.

Ginny Mustard and Joe Snake have not decided where

they will live as husband and wife. His place is only one room with a kitchenette and bathroom but he doesn't like the idea of moving in here with so many women. A man could lose himself in Mrs. Miflin's house.

~

Ginny Mustard wants to stay with the others. She's been here so long now it would seem odd to move out. She doesn't know if her feet would ever get used to it. Thinks they might keep coming back no matter where she wanted them to go. And the nursery is just right. Painted so pretty and cozy. Neither of them will ever raise a voice to the other but it's easy enough to stop talking since they've never done much of that anyway. They are still making wedding preparations, though. There is no question of their calling it off. They will just have to work out the sleeping arrangements another time.

Judy thinks they're crazy. "How can you two not know where you're going to live? That's the dumbest thing I ever heard tell of. Why don't you get a nice apartment somewhere close? Then you could visit us whenever you want. It's not like you can't afford it. Though if you're going to be in jail anyway I guess it doesn't matter where Joe Snake lives. Never mind."

~

Sometimes Ginny Mustard thinks about jail. Imagines how it will be. Not just a couple of days like before - that was easy - but a really really long time. Imagines never being allowed to go for a walk by the river or down to the ocean and as busy as she is, every chance she gets she's out the door and off by herself to look at the wind on the waves or stand on a bridge under the bare trees and she pulls the cold air as far into her self as she is able, feeds like a person starved who knows she will be hungry again soon and forever.

Eve's old heart aches for the girl who needs such freedom. Sees her face light when she plays with the kittens and Harvey, when she talks about the baby she will have with Joe Snake, when she buys a recording of lullabies and plays it over and over, memorizes the words. And Eve thinks hard. Remembers the morning of the murder. Comes up with a plan. Walks down to Water Street and the police station to look for Patrick.

Sergeant Patrick Fahey is in a better mood than he has been in weeks. His dinner with Ruth and her family still warms his belly. They like him and he likes them and Ruth has said she'll see him when his shift is over today. He is surprised to find Eve waiting for him. More surprised by what she has to say.

"I am here to confess to the murder of one Mr. Miflin on Bishop's Road. I was upset and angry because he killed Mrs. Miflin's baby so I took a gun from the attic and I shot him."

"Eve," says Patrick. "You can't confess. Ginny Mustard has already admitted that she killed Mr. Miflin."

"I can confess if I want to. I just did. If you aren't going to take this seriously then I will have to confess to one of the other policemen. I think you should just arrest me now and let Ginny Mustard go."

"It's a fine thing you're trying to do, Eve, but it won't work. Ginny Mustard's trial begins in a couple of weeks and that's all there is to it."

"Well maybe you should check the gun because my fingerprints are all over it. Just check. You'll find them there. In fact, why don't you take my fingerprints now so we can get this over with? I'm confessing to the crime and I want to see justice done."

Patrick sighs. He was hoping to knock off early today but

it looks like that's out the window. Excuses himself and consults with his captain for a few minutes who tells him that if Eve says she killed the bastard and her prints are on the gun he'll have to investigate. He doesn't give a damn who did it but it does complicate matters if every old goat in the city decides to confess. Patrick arranges to have Eve fingerprinted and sends her home. There's no way she's guilty but he has to go through the motions, is surprised to be told that apparently she did handle the murder weapon and wonders what the hell those women are up to now.

When Eve tells the others what she has done there's quite a fuss in the house. Ginny Mustard is upset. Wants Eve to go back and say she was just fooling. Ruth, on the other hand, is ready to have fun with this new development. "In fact," she says, "I'm pretty sure it was me who killed Mr. Miflin. I just forgot. Doesn't anyone remember how I was so pissed off that I just grabbed the gun from Ginny Mustard and shot the bugger?"

"But they won't find any fingerprints of yours on the gun, Ruth," says Eve. "Mine are on it for sure because I took the gun from Ginny Mustard after she shot him. Remember? I put it on the carpet next to Mr. Miflin's body. I forgot that until this afternoon and that's why I went to the police. See? I even have ink on my fingers still."

"The only reason they won't find my prints is because I had the good sense to put gloves on before I shot him. Blue wool gloves that I happened to have in my room. Remember how I ran upstairs and got them before I took the gun from Ginny Mustard? And how I burned them in the fireplace a couple of days later when Judy got it working again? Cut them up in tiny pieces and burned them and then put the ashes in the compost bin? Come on. You must remember that."

Maggie says, "I think I must have shot him. I was pretty crazy back then. All anyone would have to do is go to that place I was in and ask the doctors. I'm sure they'll tell you I'd kill someone if I got upset enough. I could say I did it anyway."

Judy can't stand it. "You're all nutcases if you ask me. But, you know, maybe Mrs. Miflin did it. She had plenty of reason and why else would she be so friggin' out of it now? Because she feels so guilty, that's why. What do you think of that?"

"For one thing," answers Ruth, "she had a cast on her leg and couldn't get out of the bed. You might as well say Dorrie did it."

"I didn't even live here then. You can't say I did it," cries Dorrie.

"No one is saying you did Dorrie. We're just trying to figure it out since it's obvious no one wants Ginny Mustard to go to jail."

"Did you ever think," asks Judy, "that maybe they won't find her guilty anyway?"

"Not bloody likely," says Ruth. "Her goose is cooked and ready to serve. It's well and good to pretend we can change things but we can't and that's all there is to it."

~

Lights from the north are dancing over Bishop's Road. Streaking blue and pink and rose, green and yellow, as far as anyone can see. The air is right and the temperature cold but if God has a hand and if it is as big as it must surely be, then this is His work and atmospheric conditions be damned, as far as the people watching are concerned there's no other reason for the show that covers the city now, than His feeling good about something or other.

And mothers in the midst of yelling one more time to hang up your coats when you come home for goodness sake and fathers raging because the garbage hasn't been taken out and why the hell can't anyone do anything I ask around here for a change, stop in mid-sentence when someone says geez, come look at the sky. And every door is open letting the heat out but no one cares. You never know when you'll see the likes again and someone is whistling because they say the lights will dance if you do and when it's all over they are a touch more gentle with their world for the rest of the night. Some of them on into the next morning.

~

When Joe Snake began his studies at the university his name was Joseph Benoit, changed quickly to Snake because he was long and lean, and Joe because it sounded better, at least to the other fellows in the residence. They liked him. Enough to hang out and cut class and do a bit of drinking with, but not enough to invite him to their homes for long weekends and study breaks. He was born too late for that. If it had been the sixties they would have been falling over themselves to be cool enough to have an Indian friend but in the eighties he would have dragged them down. Bummer. So Joseph Benoit, aka Joe Snake, went his own way, moved into a boarding house, studied hard and graduated with an honors degree in Chemistry. Ready to teach. But the only school wanting his services at the time was on a reservation and he'd had enough of small town living. He found that he was an excellent bartender. Quiet, patrons thought him a good listener. The better bars loved him but bored him senseless. He prefers the less desirable establishments where drinkers are more interested in beer and a few laughs than philosophizing over wine spritzers.

Joe Snake's needs are minimal. His room is tidy, clean. His prayers are honest. He has his computer and a bed, two armchairs, subscribes to *Scientific American* and *Discover*, and over his desk is a framed poster of the Periodic Table of the Elements. The rest of the wall space is taken up with pictures of bears. He banks one half of his pay and sends the other to his family. Lives on his tips mostly, which were better when he worked uptown but are still enough to keep him.

Into his life all manner of women have come and gone. The only permanent fixture, the only one whose company he values, is Ginny Mustard. It was Joe Snake who found her in the back pool room of the bar when a couple of college boys out slumming had hit on her, literally, because she said she was tired and had finished work for the night. He took her to the hospital to be patched up and while she was being tended, searched out the boys. He promised them ever so gently that they'd never get it up again if he found them anywhere near her, went back and took her home. Fed her and read to her until she was well enough to leave. He convinced her she could give up the streets, took her to Social Services and helped her find a better place to live. They are the best of friends. There have been times when he hasn't seen her for days on end. After her first few retreats he stopped worrying. Knows that she is sitting by the river, or listening to the music, walking the waterfront night after night after night. When she told him she wanted to have a baby or six or seven would he please marry her so she could, he said, "Yes." Wrote to his family. Invited them to the wedding. Sent bus fare.

Ginny Mustard has arranged for his people to stay at Mrs. Miflin's house. Rented two rooms for a week. Mrs. Miflin doesn't like Indians - drunks the lot of them and they'll have feathers from hell to breakfast most likely - but the money keeps her mouth shut. Joe Snake's parents and sister are surprised when they meet Ginny Mustard. He is their pride and joy and they trust his judgement but a black-skinned girl with yellow hair is an unlikely choice as far as they're concerned and they can only imagine what the children will look like.

Joe Snake's mom and sister speak in unison, confusing Ginny Mustard, since she doesn't know how to listen to both and has to make a decision each time they start. Joe Snake points out that they are basically saying the same thing so it doesn't matter, just nod and smile back and forth and it's fine. She's not going to get a word in edgewise so there's no dilemma really, of whom to answer when a question is flung her way. They don't need a response. His father is a quiet man. Sits on the sofa and looks inward, goes outside to smoke his pipe once in a while, takes himself for a walk. Joe Snake says he has to do that or perish with those two yammering all the time. They can't live without each other, his parents, but they are like chalk and cheese, they have that much in common.

Joe Snake's mother has brought along a wedding suit for her son. Of deerskin, beaded and ribboned, as well as her own wedding dress just in case Ginny Mustard wants to wear it. And Ginny Mustard is torn between the gown she bought and this one. Lays them both out on her bed and calls the others in for a consultation. Since long white gowns are a dime a dozen and no one has ever seen anything as exotic as Joe Snake's mother's dress the vote is unanimous in favor of the latter with its tiny beads in bright colors and the softest boots.

~

Mrs. Miflin is waking from her madness or perhaps scraping the bottom of it but no matter. There is a fury boiling in her. Memory is alive in vivid colour of each wrong done her for the last few months beginning with that damned Judy coming here to live and then Ginny Mustard singing that horrible song and making her drop the water and ending up with her crippled for the rest of her life. This is her home for God's sake and they have taken over. Filled it with noise and wretched people who ought not to be allowed near a good woman such as herself. This is the work of the devil, of that you can be sure, and Mrs. Miflin isn't going to have any more of it. She's up and off on legs none too pleased to be carrying the extra weight she's accumulated but the will is strong and she only has to stop and lean once in awhile on her way to the sitting room to give them a piece of her mind.

But the room is empty. Neat as a pin and decorated with candles and crepe paper streamers - purple, red, blue, yellow, green, orange - as though a particularly bright rainbow had found its way in and exploded. "Well," says Mrs. Miflin as loud as she can. "They think they can do whatever they want, now, do they? We'll see about that. Yes. We'll see about that all right." She stumbles about on protesting legs, stands on a chair and now a sofa and an end table to reach the pretty paper, tears it from the walls. Exhausted she goes to the kitchen, crawls back with a garbage bag, fills it with broken candles. The pantry is floor to ceiling alcohol and she carries bottle after bottle to the sink, pours it all away.

"There's your heathen wedding, Ginny Mustard, down the drain. You won't be marrying no Indian in my house and that you won't." And she sits on the floor with her back to the stove to rest from carnage. That's where Ginny Mustard and Judy find her when they come back from the wedding cake shop with Ruth not far behind them.

"I'm selling this house, do you hear me? I am calling a real estate company and putting it on the market right now." And Mrs. Miflin gets up from her break. Grabs the phone book yellow pages and dials the first agency that catches her eye. "Someone is coming over this afternoon to look at the place so they can sell it. I'll get a pretty penny for it too and you'll be out on the street, the lot of you. What do you think of that?" And for good measure she pushes the wedding cake off the counter and stomps on it with all the strength remaining in her fat, tired body. Collapses in a sugar heap.

"Judy," says Ruth. "Carry her upstairs to her bed, will you?"

"Why? Didn't you hear what she just said Ruth? She's selling the house and we all have to get out and what are we going to do? Oh Ginny Mustard! Your beautiful cake is all ruined. Where can we get another one now? The wedding is tomorrow. And she tore down all the decorations."

"Just take Mrs. Miflin upstairs, Judy. Then come back and we'll try to figure it out. I'm not talking about it while she's in the room and it appears she wore herself out wrecking things so you'll have to help her. I was gone for an hour and she wasn't moving when I left. She must have worked like a house on fire to do this much damage in that length of time. It's a wonder she didn't have a heart attack."

"I don't think she's got one to be attacked. What a friggin' Grinch. Can't stand to see anyone having a good time," grumbles Judy as she half drags, half carries Mrs. Miflin upstairs.

Ginny Mustard is cleaning up the remains of her pretty cake when Joe Snake comes in with his family. His mom and sister don't miss a beat, start in together about the terrible thing happening. This can't be good. What can they do? Joe Snake helps Ginny Mustard, watching her face for some sign of feeling about the mess things have become. But there is nothing. He asks if she'd like to take a walk with him and she nods yes. They leave and the restoration crew goes to work. Joe Snake's dad (Mr. Snake is what they call him though that most certainly is not his name) tells them that he has a light hand for baking. Do they think it would be all right if he makes a new cake for Ginny Mustard. Of course they do. And he sets about finding pans and ingredients. Turns on the oven. Starts measuring flour. Says he'll need some food coloring for the icing. Do they think she'd like flowers on top and all around the sides or something else? Flowers would be good.

"I used to make birthday cakes for the children. They liked flowers all over and I made them with Smarties candy. All colors with yellow centres. But I won't use Smarties for these flowers. It is a wedding, after all. Once Joseph wanted a bear on his cake and I bought a special little contraption that shoots the icing out just right once you get the hang of it. But I don't need it to make flowers. We'll be just fine. This is going to be a nice wedding cake."

~

Ginny Mustard is crying as hard as she ever has and for the first time since she was a little girl. She does not want to go to jail. She wants to have a good time with her babies and Joe Snake and all her money. She has never had anything - ever - and now she has everything and has to give it up. It isn't fair. She had to kill Mr. Miflin. He was a mean man. Other people get to decide all of the time if a person is bad and should be killed or locked away but when she does it she has to pay so dearly. She can't understand why and Joe Snake can't explain it so they walk along the river and there is Sarah who invites them in for a cup of tea.

Sarah and Peter live next door to Howard James. Isn't it strange, thinks Ginny Mustard, how even a small world gets smaller the more time you spend in it. Sarah hears the entire story of Ginny Mustard's wrongdoing and so does Peter when he comes home from work. And the more she talks the more she realizes that she truly will have to go to prison and may be there for a long time and she can't stop crying. Ginny Mustard is having the pity party to end all pity parties.

Eventually she gives it up and then there's just a little whimpering for awhile and soon her eyes are dry and she has a quick game of checkers with Eleanor before she and Joe Snake leave to buy more alcohol for the wedding. By the time they get back to Mrs. Miflin's house the new cake is cooling and supper is ready and there's no sign any more that Ginny Mustard was ever upset. Joe Snake is pleased that she broke since he knows you can't haul pain around for long and the more time you take to let it out the worse it can be for a body. She had as good a howling as he has ever heard and now they can party and start making that baby she wants so badly. And Ginny Mustard has the same notions though not in that order. Whispers to him that she'd like to spend the night at his place if it's okay. And when their meal is done they leave. Quickly. Laughing. Mrs. Miflin watching from her chair by the window sees them pause under the street light. Kiss. She spits as hard as she can at the glass but it sprays back into her face at the very moment Ginny Mustard looks up and waves.

~

The real estate agent is thrilled to list Mrs. Miflin's house. Puts his sign on the front lawn. Says it's probably a waste of time since houses like this one are going like hotcakes right now. Lots of come-from-aways are moving in and they're always looking for a big old place to put another bed and breakfast. In fact, Mrs. Miflin should raise her asking price as far as he's concerned. It's way below the going rate. He measures every inch of the house - no small feat but he has an assistant and now he's off to call some prospective buyers. Of course, it would be easier to show if there weren't so many tenants all over the place. Might Mrs. Miflin ask them to leave when he brings his clients around? She assures him there'll be no problem getting them out. Just say the word and give her an hour's notice.

~

Howard James is invited to the wedding as well and if there were some other way to reach Ms. Blake he would never consider attending such a gathering. But hard as he tries his old secretary will not see him and he has many questions about the running of his operation that only she, it seems, can answer. He hasn't had a decent cup of coffee since she left. If he can just corner her for a few minutes, beg her to come back or at least train the new one, half of his troubles will be over. There's no way he will bring a date though, and the woman he has been seeing lately is pissed to find that they won't be spending Saturday together and he can't tell her why. If he had any sense he would make something up because Rachel is not dealing with a full deck but he can't see around corners, poor man, can't even see what's staring him right in the face. Oh well. Serves him right. He wasn't very nice to Ginny Mustard, after all, and one mustn't spend too much time worrying about him.

~

Ginny Mustard and Joe Snake wake in a delicious tangle of limbs and warm skin. The best sleep, it was. Worn out bone tired honest and now their bodies feel like jelly. If they roll to the edge of the bed they will go over in a heap - none of their extremities will bother to stiffen to catch them, hold them from hitting the floor. So they stay in a knot for as long as they can. Until Ginny Mustard gets hungry. Until Joe Snake says, "Let's go out for a quiet breakfast. This is going to be one hell of a day. We'd best be fortified."

After that it's pretty much a blur, time being what it is, a mad rush, and no hot water after the third or fourth shower, but all are dressed and shining before too long and there's a lot of old furniture piled up outside Mrs. Miflin's bedroom door to keep her from doing any more damage while they are away from the house.

Old Father Delaney is in misery with such a motley crowd filling up his church. Is flustered and impatient throughout the ceremony until Joe Snake fixes him with dark eyes and he slows down. Manages to sound, if not loving and kind, at least respectful and those not used to being treated with more than contempt, which would be the majority present, think it a wonderful wedding altogether.

The reception is more than anyone needs and will keep them cozy until spring. Dorrie Blake is having a good time with her pretty policeman when she can get away from Howard James. The Fagan twins are arguing points of faith, which they had sworn they wouldn't but there are so many statues in that house there is no avoiding the topic. Martha is a true believer and Mary isn't and they have been fighting tooth and nail since Mary discovered quite by accident from a teacher who was fired as soon as the words were out of his mouth, that there is a theory of evolution. They are seventy now and still dress the same so there's no telling them apart until they get started.

Judy is drinking vodka as though her very life depends on it, keeping as much distance between herself and the cops as she can. Eve is serving tray after tray of food. It's loaves and fishes with no sign that the larder will ever be empty. Maggie has latched on to the good-looking son of one of the policemen, who came by to pick up his father's car and decided to stay when Maggie smiled at him which makes Judy jealous so she calls Jimmy to come over and don't bring any dope for fuck sake.

Joe Snake brought the music - mostly Big Bands - loud - everybody dance music - and if the adults for two blocks around weren't already at Mrs. Miflin's house there might be some complaining. The only ones who aren't real happy are the kids who didn't sneak out for the night. The ones stuck babysitting the little ones. Artie Shaw and his ilk aren't their favourites and even with the windows closed they can't hear anything else.

Come midnight someone says wouldn't it be nice if Ginny Mustard and Joe Snake opened their wedding gifts so we can all see what they got. Then someone else says let's play charades and we'll act out our favorite presents and knee deep in wrapping paper and ribbons, they do, and Lulu Crummy pees in her pants she's laughing that hard.

Mrs. Miflin made it to a telephone at one point and called the cops to complain about the noise and when they got there they joined the game for a few minutes because Officer Hutton likes charades more than just about anything and can never find anyone who wants to play since his wife started calling ahead when they go to parties and telling the host to say no to his suggestions. He is very good at guessing and even better at pantomime and does a great job on a very heavy cake platter that no one else picked.

Patrick and the other policeman have given the newlyweds two nights in the fanciest hotel in the city which should delay their discussion of where to live by a few hours anyway and that's where, on the softest sheets, Sweet Polly is conceived, and if love and comfort and good feelings starting out can have any influence on a person as she grows, then surely Sweet Polly is blessed.

Before Crazy Rachel comes in and before she stabs Howard James a few times and before the wonderful party disintegrates, Sweet Polly has a good grip on life that she won't release for a hundred years.

When Crazy Rachel waltzes through the door no one thinks much of it. They are packed in like sardines with overflow dancing in the backyard and on the front porch and another body is hardly cause for notice. Only Patrick pays her any mind. Says to himself, it's not often you see a woman in a floor length fur coat these days, and turns away for a moment before his second thought - she's a loon for sure from the look in her eyes - brings him to attention. By then it is too late. Crazy Rachel asks Judy where Howard James is, who tells her and wishes her good luck with that knife thinking serves him right for sending Ginny Mustard away with a crappy little CD player and never being nice to her again. There is blood all over the place before Patrick moves to follow her. Guests are hollering and a couple spill their drinks. Some get little drops of blood on their clothes which will never come out but will make for fond memories of a good time in later years. Holly Bartlett - who is very large and takes up more than her fair share of space - falls backwards on to a table, crushing Joe Snake's CD player beyond recognition. The sudden silence is huge. Nothing left but Crazy Rachel's laughter and one of the Fagen twins praying. Fifteen of Her Majesty's Constabulary are in attendance and snap to their duty all over the Crazy Rachel except for Constable Brothers who has the good sense to dial 911 and get an ambulance over before Howard James bleeds to death.

Ruth says, "It's good the bride and groom left when they did. This would put a damper on the honeymoon for sure."

The party continues after that but with a little less enthusiasm since several of the good looking policemen leave to file reports on this most recent disaster in Mrs. Miflin's house, though a few of them do come back afterwards. Dorrie does her best to be upset but finds it difficult to feel much for Howard James. Is more bothered by her young man's leaving so suddenly. She watches at the sitting room window until his return. When the police come back with their yellow tape they cordon only the kitchen as a crime scene after the merry makers move the microwave oven and the tasties to the Barbie room along with what remains of the alcohol and some ice.

~

You might suppose that a near murder in the kitchen would make people think twice about buying your house but after the place has been cleaned up there comes an offer that Mrs. Miflin can't refuse. A couple from away who have been looking for just such a mansion in the city with the lowest crime rate in the country, wanting to raise their children where nothing ever happens, buy it sight unseen and start packing before the ink is dry on Mrs. Miflin's signature.

Cheerfully she gathers her tenants and tells them to be out within two weeks, that's all the notice they are getting and there's no use in begging because the house is sold and she doesn't care where they go but they can't stay here. And Eve in her garden with winter just a few degrees away sits under the lilac and that's where they find her late in the day, a smile on her face and her body cold, a hedgehog curled and sleeping in the big pocket of her overalls.

Her quiet passing leaves them lonely but for her gentleness that seems to have remained and shares itself among them in direct proportion to what each needs with enough left over to fill the house. Soften it. Except for Mrs. Miflin's room with a blanket rolled up and stuffed under the door to keep the noise out and her grumbling in.

Judy covers her grave with Eve's favorite plants from the garden. There has been no hard frost yet and the daisies, black-eyed Susan, wallflower, lamb's ears give way easily, happily. Maggie wants to plant some crocuses and so they do. Dozens of little bulbs carefully, gently. They settle over Eve's bones and thrive.

Moving out of Mrs. Miflin's house goes smoothly, as though Eve were still there saying, "Why don't you make two trips with that load, Ruth, it looks so heavy," and "Judy, check and see if Dorrie needs help taking her Barbie cases apart, she seems to be having a hard time with them," and they get through with few mishaps.

Patrick wants Ruth to come live with him but she has other ideas. One day she dresses herself up neat as a pin, takes a bus over to Zellers and gets a job just like that because they are hiring for the Christmas rush and need anyone they can get their hands on. Then she finds an apartment so tiny that no one else wants it, signs a one-year lease and goes to the second-hand furniture store where she buys a bed and a chair and a lamp. She lets Patrick help with delivery. That service is extra.

Judy and Maggie have nagged Children's Aid to please let them live together since Judy has been so good lately and though she is technically a minor and they aren't supposed to allow it, they give in after a visit from Patrick who says he will keep an eye on her. The girls are not having much luck finding a place until Ginny Mustard tells Joe Snake that they will be pregnant soon if they aren't already and must have a real home. Buys an old house on Caine's Street - there is no other kind, really - that needs work but with a ground floor apartment she rents to the girls for next to nothing if they promise to baby-sit when Joe Snake goes back to school because he says he needs his Master's if he's ever to find a teaching position and raise their child properly.

Dorrie alone is lost. No job. No place to live. Plenty of savings to keep her but things could get boring now that she has tasted life. She figures that since Zellers hired Ruth they might take her as well. She is right about that but much too qualified for her dream job in the toy department and they want to stick her in an office at a computer. She puts up a good fight and wins. The Barbie display has never looked better. Mothers ferociously opposed to allowing their daughters to own the little doll find themselves saying, "Yes, I'll take that one and maybe the dress with the sequins and what the heck, throw in a package of those accessories too," when Dorrie works her magic. For the first time in history the store has to re-order supplies twice before the rush is over.

And what of Mrs. Miflin? Truth be told she's not as jolly as she had expected to be. None of the tenants is very upset. In fact, she distinctly heard someone humming outside her bedroom even through the blankets stuffed under the door. She is the only one with nowhere to go and it's two days left before the new owners arrive. Her bank account is full to overflowing and she sits by the window and stares at the empty trees, at their witch finger branches clutching the sky, grey above the cooling earth.

~

Ginny Mustard knows before the jury gives its verdict that she is growing a baby. She feels taller than she really is and as big as all outdoors and has the wonderful sensation that if she stretches her arms just so far and touches finger tips together lightly they will envelop the world and all that's in it. So, of course, she knows and is looking around to tell Joe Snake when she hears guilty and a ruckus behind her as people say no and that's not fair and someone is crying. And the bad news isn't as bad as the good news is good so she just stands there smiling and only Joe Snake guesses why.

~

Fred the real estate agent is upset. Inspecting the house for progress he finds Mrs. Miflin sitting by the window. "You only have a day to move everything out. I thought I made that quite clear. Have you arranged for someone to take your things to your new place?" Mrs. Miflin turns her head to look through him and now he's really worried. She says, "There is no new place. I have nowhere to go. All I ever wanted was this house and I worked hard and saved my money so I could have it. And it's only because of that crowd I had to sell it. I changed my mind. I don't want to go." Exasperated, Fred explains that she must. The house has been sold. "You've done quite well, Mrs. Miflin. If you like I can find you a lovely place right now. Smaller than this one. Easier to look after. We can arrange to auction some of your furniture. You can be in a nice renovated home in this area almost immediately. I can put a rush on everything and you'd only have to be in a hotel for a week or so." But she is not listening. Stares again out the window.

~

Ginny Mustard's prison is comfortable and practically empty of criminals but with guards enough to keep it looking like a going concern. There's a craft room and a library and TV area that a few kind souls contributed through numerous bake sales and raffles and for a few hours a day the inmates are allowed to read or watch the soaps or whip up a potholder for Mom's birthday present.

Ella lives in the cell next door where she recently found Jesus, spends much time on her knees begging forgiveness for poisoning her husband. Across from her is Janey who threw her baby out the window and mostly she rocks back and forth with her head on her arms and cries. Down a way is Becky Norris whom Ginny Mustard remembers from her days on the street, who cut off a customer's private parts but only because he begged her to and paid her a goodly sum for doing it. His wife was pissed as much by the money he spent as by the physical damage and talked him into changing his mind so he said Becky came up with the idea all on her own.

Ginny Mustard faces two years under lock and key with a chance for parole in twelve months. No one knows why the judge was so lenient but it might have had something to do with the length of time it took the jury to come up with a decision which was a full two weeks until they were fed up and life beckoned. Mr. Oldford's son wasn't studying for his exams and Mrs. Lockyer just knew her husband was spending too much on Christmas this year with her not there to keep him in check so one by one they went over to the guilty side though some of them felt real bad about it for years after.

Visiting days are every other Saturday and the big holidays which is just as well with the prison being a two-hour drive from the city. Joe Snake has to buy a car since the bus doesn't get there until late afternoon. Before Ginny Mustard settles in one of the guards brings a list of jobs to see which one she wants so she works in the kitchen, cleaning pots and pans and chopping vegetables for soup. In the library she discovers that Becky can read and for a carton of smokes a week will teach her to do the same. She's having a rough go of it. Nothing makes sense but Becky gets her smokes anyway.

The nurse confirms what Ginny Mustard knows. Says she's healthy as a horse and should have a strong baby. Gives her folic acid and multivitamins. Tells the kitchen staff to let her drink as much milk as she wants and to do the heavy work themselves. That's how Ginny Mustard becomes head chef and while she can't order provisions until she learns to read, she manages to talk the person who does into adding a few more interesting items to the list now and then. Joe Snake brings cookbooks and she passes them around so the other inmates can pick a nice dish and read aloud how to cook it.

She wants to see what the new house looks like since Joe Snake moved in and he takes pictures of the work in progress, brings a new batch every time he visits. Paint samples and a catalogue to choose a couch and kitchen table. Fabric and dimensions so she can make curtains in the craft room with Ella's help when she takes a prayer break. Ella knows how to knit as well and is teaching Ginny Mustard to make a blanket, soft and pink, with hope and dreams set in delicate stitches.

When the guards put Crazy Rachel in the cell across from Ginny Mustard, peace and quiet get up and leave in a flash. For once, her family, rich as they are, cannot bail her out and since she is only mad when she doesn't get her own way, no one is able to convince the courts that she's insane. Attempted murder earns her four years. Her chances of getting out a minute sooner are slim to non-existent. When they take her street clothes and give her prison garb they find half a pound of cocaine and a couple dozen joints in her fur coat pocket. She's pissed and screaming and no one is going to shut her up. They can do as they please, she'll stop when she feels like it and not before. Short of slapping a piece of duct tape over her mouth there's nothing much can be done so the guards hand out ear plugs and let her rip.

~

Joe Snake works hard to make the new house a home. He peels wallpaper, repairs plaster, scrapes old paint off the bannister, gets his friend Alf to help replace the kitchen cupboard doors. And he goes to the university and enrolls for January courses, buys a book about being a dad, reads every word. Ginny Mustard says the baby is a girl but he reads the boy sections too, just in case.

Ruth doesn't find it easy being on her feet all day and with minimum wage she can barely make ends meet but it's okay. She is happy with her independence. She is pleased to pay her rent and buy her groceries with money she earns. If there's nothing left over for new shoes or a watch, so be it; there wasn't any on welfare either. And in a few months, if they keep her after Christmas, there'll be health benefits and a pension plan which you certainly don't get working the bars.

Patrick wants to marry her. The idea of spending her life with him is appealing but she's damned if she's going poor to him, will have her own income, however meager. She's tired at the end of her days and mostly just wants to go to her small home and be alone so they don't see as much of each other as he'd like. And of course, she spends time with Sarah and Peter, and though Patrick is certainly welcome, she doesn't always bring him along, doesn't feel like sharing her family with him every time she visits. He tries not to be hurt but he is.

Judy and Maggie are thrilled with their new place. They have a living room, kitchen, bathroom and a really big bedroom with space enough for two as long as they don't plan on entertaining the young fellows. Patrick told Joe Snake all about the conditions of Judy's probation and he keeps careful watch, takes a good sniff in the air around her when she comes in just in case she's had a bit of pot after school. Days when they don't stop at Maggie's dad's house he asks about homework and tells them to do it upstairs in the dining room where he has installed his computer and where he does his own work, the better to raise a baby.

Ginny Mustard wants Joe Snake's family to come for Christmas. She sends an invitation from prison with Becky doing the writing. There's plenty of space in the new old house. She orders furniture from the catalogue for the guest rooms. Tells Joe Snake where to buy a good turkey - fresh - for dinner. Makes him write down her instructions for gravy and tells him how much cream to put in the mashed potatoes.

Christmas at Mrs. Miflin's house had always been a dreary affair. A little fake tree with blue plastic balls glued all over was set on the coffee table next to a plaster stable with sheep and the Holy Family, lest they forget the true meaning. The tenants drew a name each and gave a gift and there was a turkey and fruitcake but that's as special as it ever managed to be. Ginny Mustard would walk along the river and stare through windows at magic trees and parties for hours and never went home until all the pretty lights had been turned off for the night.

~

Christmas can break the hearts of women in prisons. They mightn't buy princes or the fantasy of the ball or happily ever after but the picture-perfect Christmas with soft snow and candles, rosy-cheeked children and gentle families, keeps vigil, reawakens every year in every Christian as soon as The First Noel hits the airwaves. And they crumble one by one, the women in prisons. And the bars may be steel or poverty or apathy, it makes no difference and no matter what they are saying aloud, if you listen closely you'll hear the desperation of the one dream that might come true but obviously not this year, maybe next.

~

Joe Snake brings home the biggest tree he can find and it takes up the entire living room with only space enough to squeeze past it into the dining room. It touches the ceiling and he has to cut some off to make room for the star. The back of the box of lights says that 200 will be right for a three-foot tree so he buys 4000. He covers the bannister with boughs and the house smells like a forest after warm rain.

Maggie wants her dad to come for Christmas dinner and

he says yes. One way or another he will get away from his wife who thinks they are going to Cuba for the holidays. She bought tickets ages ago because she just knows that Margaret will be causing trouble for them and is surprised that she hasn't heard tell of the girl since the time she threatened her at the house on Bishop's Road.

Dorrie came around the other day and asked if she could spend Christmas at Ginny Mustard's house and since she has such a flair for decorating as well as her own porcelain nativity scene that she will bring along if they want, Joe Snake said sure, the more the merrier. Dorrie hasn't seen her policeman since the wedding reception. Is feeling unloved these days and small lines are beginning to show around her eyes and mouth that weren't there before.

~

Over Eve the earth is working and moving ever so slowly. You won't notice if you aren't a bird. The weather has been warmer than it should but who's to say if that's true or false or if it even matters. Tiny shoots of green appear and then buds and one day a hundred purple crocuses in the fog, in the rain, and a reporter from the Daily News who happened to be covering a story about vandalism in the graveyard noticed the color and at first thought someone had lost a pretty sweater but soon saw the flowers. Called a photographer and a picture appeared on the front page next day.

It didn't matter that other people had crocuses blooming in their own yards and even a few tulips poking their way up through dead leaves to see what's going on with the seasons. Someone needed a miracle. Remembered the northern lights a while back. Connected them with the flowers for some odd reason and asked around about the occupant of the grave.

Judy told all she knew which wasn't much but apparently enough and the rumors began that Eve was who she thought she was - mother of all - and as with most miracles, people figured that getting close to the source would heal them of their woes and the caretaker had the devil's time keeping everyone on the beaten path and not walking all over the dead. Someone decided to make a special headstone for Eve. Fashioned a large fat goddess with breasts and tummy and backside all falling over and plunked it down on top of the crocuses which demolished quite a few of them and pissed off some of the old ladies who come by every day to pray for each other's sick and dying husbands. They gathered up enough strength to push it over and planted more bulbs from their own gardens but they never did bloom as purple as Eve's.

~

Crazy Rachel has decided that Ginny Mustard is the bane of her existence and must pay. Dearly. That baby in her belly is rightfully hers since the father is most definitely Howard James. It all came out in court. How Ginny Mustard used to go to his house at night. How she stole away his dog and how Dorrie came to be living in that old Mrs. Miflin's house. If it hadn't been for her meddling, Rachel and Howard would be happily wed by now and she'd have her own baby on the way. But if she can't have her own, she'll have Ginny Mustard's.

Crazy Rachel's family is scared to death of her. While in her mother's womb she made life miserable for all. Kicked and screamed - her mother swears she screamed and her father is inclined to believe it with the nightmares his wife had from the moment of conception. The boys had never caused a minute's trouble. That's because this is a girl and she's weird, said Crazy Rachel's mother.

Simple folk they were, who made a fortune in packaging materials when Missus complained once that sending a parcel was hit or miss every time and so Mister came up with something better and the world beat a path to his door. They bought the biggest house and the nicest cars and raised their children in the lap of luxury even if they didn't have a clue which fork to use. Rachel didn't bother to speak until she went to school and discovered that merely pointing at an object and yelling was no guarantee that she could have it. Nothing ever changed at home though, and her wish was her family's command. She grew up beautiful on the outside and warty mean on the inside but she was rich so no one cared.

Prison suits her. If she had a metal cup she'd be banging it on the bars of her cell day and night. Instead she elbows people in the side for no reason, trips them when they walk past her, preferably when they are carrying trays of lunch, picks a spot on their bodies to stare at hard for an hour or so, a shoulder, a nose, an ear. She's a bully, pure and simple, but subtle and it's not easy to pinpoint exactly what she's doing wrong. After enough complaints the guards try solitary confinement to teach her a lesson but Crazy Rachel doesn't learn lessons, uses her time alone to fortify herself and is always worse when they let her out.

~

Odd how we get from there to here. How life goes on and we work and play and grow and in a still sudden moment we stop and wonder - how did this come to be? It was just yesterday, wasn't it, when I was that person and now here I am this one and what transpired to make this happen? How did I get to be living in this place and putting my dishes in this cupboard and taking my bath in this tub? How did I come to be looking at these walls and where are the ones that came before?

Ruth stares at her little tree with the white lights and pretty glass balls from the big sale at work. Snuggles down under a quilt and is pondering just such questions when Patrick comes by with champagne and roses and a diamond ring in a blue velvet box. Makes her cry until her nose runs and her eyes are red. And she looks at him long and hard. Says yes she will marry him but not yet. There is something she needs to know and it is in this place alone with her. Alone with no one else around. When she sits in the quiet she has the sense that it is just there. Or there. If she moves her head quickly enough at the right second of time in a certain light she will have it and if she hasn't yet that doesn't mean that tomorrow - or tomorrow - the knowing that is so close will not be in her grasp. "I wouldn't mind dying," she says. "I have a bone to pick with God, and so many questions." She smiles and the knowing skitters away to hide until Patrick leaves.

Downtown is aglow with Christmas except for the empty shops and two or three houses where nobody bothers and the city looks silly all green and red in the fog. Everyone wants snow but it looks like there won't be any in time and after the twenty-fifth it doesn't matter if it never comes. Parents who bought toboggans and skis for the youngsters are thinking they should exchange them for scooters and skateboards but it's probably too late now anyway and they ready themselves for the disappointment. Those who remember the rules make a big deal of putting the shovels and winter boots away, taking out raincoats and pretending that this suits them just fine in hope that the gods are listening and will fling a storm their way just to mess up their plans. Forgetting, of course, that the gods know what's really going on and can recognize a fake-out miles away.

The people who haven't finished their shopping keep putting it off and retail business has come to a standstill with customers poking around half-heartedly and leaving the stores with nothing and no one is thinking of saying Merry Christmas when they stop to chat.

In prison it doesn't matter if it rains or snows and Ginny Mustard is still putting a holiday together for her outside world. She has pictures of the tree full of little cats who find the branches just perfect for napping and tormenting Harvey who can't climb, and has taped them to the wall at eye level all around her cell. Joe Snake takes a roll of film a day and has it developed at the one-hour place, sends the pictures to her by courier and after the guards have finished looking at them she puts them up.

Christmas. Cold now. Earth round and sweet. Worried. A bubble on some giant's tongue who can spit or swallow - makes no difference to him and either way, we fall together and most things land where they began the day. Paper and gifts and some sad some happy same as last year and the one before that except for maybe Uncle Fred didn't get in from the rig or Aunt Floss died in July and is missed or there's a brand new baby who has never seen the pretty lights before and tries to eat any tinsel that the cat didn't get.

Our friends recount the year's blessings and sorrows and make resolutions. Ginny Mustard puts hers to rhyme and sings them to her belly that she has taken to protecting with both hands whenever Crazy Rachel is about for she sees what is on the warped mind and has a sharp kitchen knife tucked away in her mattress just in case. She sings, "Daddy's gonna take you to our pretty house," and "You're gonna be a smart little girl" to the tune of *Hush Little Baby* and never in the same order so her dreams are many different songs. Soft and no one hears.

Mrs. Miflin was in a boarding house on Caine's Street until she took herself to the waterfront and walked off the edge of the wharf leading some to believe that she was a few bricks short of a load and after they fished her out they put her in the hospital for the mentally deficient where she waits. Sometimes quietly and sometimes not so - especially on the days when she tucks her happy pills under her tongue and pretends to swallow and spits them in the toilet when nobody's looking. When the new owners of her house came to move in, she still hadn't moved out and there was quite a to-do until poor Fred the real estate agent dragged her to Caine's Street and signed her up for a month at Mrs. Pretty's house. Even paid with his own money. And put her furniture in storage. He still has the key.

When Mrs. Miflin forgot that she had a fat bank account and couldn't figure out what she'd do when her time was up at Mrs. Pretty's place, she tried to end it all. Not realizing that of the hundred or so people taking a walk on the waterfront there'd be at least a dozen who would try to save her.

Ruth has a lovely Christmas but for the knowing that waits for the quiet and has become a nagging thing lately - pulling her away from wherever she happens to be - calling her to come and find secrets. And so she leaves what she's doing and hurries to her womb. That's what she calls home - it being too small to be a real apartment. Once she told Patrick that she was going to the washroom when they were at a very good movie but when she reached the lobby - well - she just kept going. And halfway through dinner at Peter and Sarah's house she upped herself from the table before dessert and coffee and said, "Good-bye. I have to go now." They worry about her but there's nothing they can do. No more can Ruth. It beckons and she's gone.

~

Judy is in constant pain - she's that angry. Maggie has left her and she hasn't felt this alone since Grammy Hagen died.

When Mrs. Eldridge came back from Cuba without her mister he got it with both barrels - never mind that the man has a bad heart - and was sent packing with half of everything they had accumulated over the years and a yearning to see the world with his daughter. They had their passports in no time flat and were on their way - to Egypt and Belgium and England and Peru - though not necessarily in that order. And if Judy had been around to say good-bye she'd have known that Maggie will send a postcard every week and will miss her and wishes she could come but school is first if Judy is ever to be set free of the watchful eye of the law.

While Maggie awaits her flight arm in arm with her dad, Judy sits on her favourite swing in the schoolyard and won't leave even when the principal comes out and threatens to have her expelled if she isn't back in her classroom by the time he counts to five. She yells at him that she doesn't go to his friggin' school anyway and he can take a flying fuck at the moon for all she cares and he goes inside to call the cops but little Josie Gullage has a nosebleed and he has to take her to the hospital. Between the jigs and the reels, Judy is left swinging until four in the morning when Joe Snake finds her and tells her to get on home out of it.

And Judy has sworn off friends forever and doesn't care if she never sees Maggie again but she cries in her pillow at night and has dark circles under her eyes and a sad droopy way of walking with her text books folded hard against her breasts and holes in her shoes where she drags her toes every slow step.

Joe Snake worries about her and tries to get her to eat vegetables but she is unbearably lonely downstairs and he is unbearably lonely upstairs and even though they watch television together sometimes they don't have much to say and neither is any help to the other. They take the little cats and their momma to be spayed or neutered - depending on which is which - and don't speak a word the whole time going or coming.

Harvey haunts the house on Bishop's Road looking for Ginny Mustard. Joanie Harris keeps shooing him away when he comes crying at the front door so now he's digging a hole under the gate to the backyard. Through the snow and his big paws are raw from working the cold earth. Every time a door is opened at Ginny Mustard's house he's away. Joanie calls Animal Control but they can never catch him in the act. By the time they come around Joe Snake's been out looking and has talked him into going home. And now he's in the house and Joanie finds him in the attic so she says what the hell and leaves him there. When Joe Snake comes to fetch him yet again they reach an agreement. Harvey can go back and forth and live wherever he pleases. Joe Snake explains that Ginny Mustard will be home some day and Harvey will be with her and out of Joanie's hair for good. Joanie says that will be fine with her. She gets lonely in the big house all day when the children are at school and can use company.

Lonely is only one of the things she is feeling of late. Nervous is another but that's nothing new. She tries to convince herself that she's tired and when she gets used to the house she won't be imagining things the way she does now but still, there, out of the corner of her eye the tail of a black dress disappearing. She finds herself humming *hush little baby* when her mind relaxes for a minute and at night when the moon is on the garden someone in a red sweater is moving about. Looking for something.

There is a day in February when the sun is warm and snow melts a little and you can open windows and air the house as long as you remember to close them again when it gets dark. It is reprieve for people in places like this. A short reminder that the season will not last forever. And in March when the rest of the country is shaking off the cold for good and you still can't see over the snow banks to the sidewalk, you remember that day in February when you opened the windows and aired the house and you are strengthened for the duration. Joanie Harris doesn't know this and should be in rough shape by the time May rolls around.

~

Crazy Rachel is staring at Ginny Mustard's hands. Burning holes in them all the way to the belly she tries to protect. All the way to the baby floating, floating. Sweet Polly tries to escape the heat. Thinks cold as hard as she can. Makes her mother hum a song of wind and icy water. Sleeps.

~

Judy sits on the stone wall in front of the old orphanage and stares at the house. Smokes a little pot. Her life has been noisy since day one and the quiet is about to drive her right around the bend. She went to her parents' house the other day but couldn't even get a decent fight started. Her father is in jail again. Her brothers are at home. The oldest is medicated to the eyeballs and lies in bed all day and the others are selling crack from the basement, a relatively silent enterprise with their customers coming and going through the back door, shoes off so mom won't hear. Not much chance of that. She starts the day with rum in her coffee and doesn't stop drinking until she passes out right around supper time.

Judy hasn't seen Ruth since they all moved out of Mrs. Miflin's house. She hasn't heard tell of Dorrie since Christmas day. She has given up shovelling the snow off Eve's grave. And now Maggie has left her and there's no one but Joe Snake. Patrick checking once in a while to see if she's keeping her nose clean. And he doesn't even bother to come round. Just telephones. Well screw the lot of them. She jumps from her perch on the wall and walks to Ginny Mustard's house. Packs a bag of clothes. Searches Joe Snake's desk until she finds his cheque book. Takes the bottom one and heads to Water Street. At the automatic teller she fills it out, giving herself $1,000. Signs Joe Snake's name and deposits the cheque to her own account. Withdraws everything. It takes two transactions because you can only have $500 each time and the fellow waiting is getting irritated. She tells him to piss off - who the hell does he think he is looking at his watch and making impatient sounds. Strolls to a taxi stand and hires a limo to the airport where she buys a one-way ticket to Vancouver, as far as you can go in this country before falling off the edge.

She watches the lights of the city disappear into nothing and curses the place with such venom that she brews an ice storm to keep it immobilized for a week with power lines down and a state of emergency the likes of which no one can recall except for a few really old people and they might be making it up. Shows the flight attendant her fake ID and drinks scotch to the end of the line.

~

Mrs. Miflin wants to go home now. She's had enough of this place with these nurse types smiling ear to ear and asking, "How are we today?" all the time. Holding out their little pills like an offering at some altar. That young pipsqueak of a doctor has been telling her that if she keeps improving the way she has she will be out in no time. Back with her loved ones. She made up a crowd of them just for him. He seemed to need them. Isn't the kind to let her go until he knows she'll have support. So there's Florence, her sister, and Melvin, her nephew, and Malcolm, her dear husband who misses her so much and the only reason they don't come around is they can't bear to see her like this. And Dr. Pipsqueak buys every word of it because he only understands half of what she says - being from away - and won't admit it.

She weaves her web. Works the tangles out. By the time the release forms are signed she has concocted a new life for herself and the only task remaining is to get on over to Bishop's Road and take her house back from whoever the hell is in it now.

~

Dorrie wants her own shop. She has found the perfect place, cashed her RRSPs and discussed her ideas with the small group of Barbie fanatics she met through her work in the toy department at Zellers. Once a week they gather in Dorrie's apartment. She makes tea and pretty cakes and they talk about their dolls. Take turns with show and tell. Jaime Cochrane read the dissertation she presented at the university on the positive aspects of Barbie the night she was ousted from the Women's Studies Program. "Not a minute too soon," she said. "If I had to sit in one more talking circle and listen to the crap they spout I'd be pulling my hair out for sure. I think I'll go into engineering."

Kate Morrison, who has a flair for words, is writing advertisements and designing posters to entice the other Barbie women out of the closet. Dorrie has fabric enough for a thousand little dresses and order forms for all the accessories they will ever need. It's just a matter of signing the lease and decorating the shop and planning the grand opening.

~

When Judy lands in Vancouver she is tired and still a little drunk. She takes the bus downtown and wanders aimlessly for awhile until she happens upon a youth hostel that appears half decent and has finished signing in when she realizes the place has a curfew. Demands her money back. "I can get this shit at home." And leaves. Finds a nasty little room with holes in the sheets and stains on the ceilings. Rusty water in the toilet and no sign that anyone cares what she does. Unpacks her bag and takes a nap. Time enough for adventure when she's rested.

Joe Snake tried to call Patrick as soon as he realized he wasn't going to find Judy but by then her ice storm was in full swing and the phone lines were down. There's no going out in weather like this so he stays inside by the fireplace. Burns old newspapers and cardboard boxes to keep warm after he uses up all the wood when the electricity dies. Wraps himself in blankets and reads his books by flashlight. Listens to tree branches crack and break in the frozen wind.

It takes Judy a full nine hours of sleep to feel fit to venture out into the world. It takes another two minutes to get herself in trouble. She can't help it. When she sees the guy with two little kids on the street and he yelling and calling them stupid fucking idiots and he's going to pound them as soon as he gets them home if they don't stop crying right now, she goes aboard of him. And when he doesn't back down it takes two policemen to keep her from doing to him what he plans to do to the poor little kids. And when she calls him a dirty black bastard everyone decides she is a racist and it looks like game over for Judy because you can still say what you want to a youngster but God forbid you should mention the shade of an adult's skin. When they finally stuff her into a squad car and take her to the station they figure, and rightly, that she is a runaway and from the accent on her they are able to pinpoint the place she has run away from. With technology being what it is these days her description and details of her most recent crime might have reached Patrick in no time. With nature being what she's always been it will take a week or more.

~

Joe Snake is the saddest man alive. He studies more than he needs to and has time on his hands. He has painted every room in the house. Stripped and refinished the floors. Read all the baby books. He moves furniture and takes pictures of the living room every which way so Ginny Mustard can tell him what setting she likes best. He plans a garden. Stares at the back yard from the kitchen window. Climbs over banks of ice. Measures every inch. Goes to the seed store and finds there's nothing on the shelves but last year's stock and the sales lady tells him he wants to wait a few weeks; she can't guarantee a decent germination rate on the old stuff. She talks him into buying grow lights and heating cables but they won't be any good to him until the new seeds arrive. She sells him books about gardening. There's no one else in the store and he stays for three hours. They have coffee and when she's told him all she knows about flowers and trees they talk about weather.

Home is dark and cold. He turns the heat low whenever he leaves to have something to look forward to on return. Waits a long time for warmth. When he wants a cigarette he holds out until he can't stand it any more before lighting up. Same with coffee. Food. The suffering makes every ordinary act a gift. Every puff of smoke. Every sip. Every taste an answer to a prayer. The little cats are sleeping in the bathtub with their momma and he takes them out of it gently. Places them in a heap on his bed. His bed. His and Ginny Mustard's bed. Runs hot water and slides under to thaw his thin body.

~

From behind Ginny Mustard looks the same as she always has. Side on you can see she's pregnant. When Joe Snake comes to visit he brings oranges and they eat them together. Count the seeds. He puts his big hand on her belly to feel their baby move and though it's too early for that, they all three smile anyway. There is nothing to say.

~

Ruth has called the store and told them she can't work tomorrow. Locked her door and won't answer the bell. Unplugged the telephone and pulled the curtains to block out the world. Now it's just her and the secrets and the knowing. And if she can somehow find the right place and time the pieces will meld. She waits. She will not sleep. She stands on a chair. She sits in a corner. And now here's her mother telling her what a dirty filthy creature she is. Cringing each time she must touch her. Rough when she washes her little face, scrubs her hair. Hurting her always hurting her with touch and words. And here's her father. And she's a tiny girl standing in her crib and crying. And she can hear the sound of his shoes on the stairs and he's coming to her and she screams for her mommy who hears but will not move from her bed. And her father is beating her brother. With his fists. With his belt. And her mommy is just standing there. Just standing there.

For two days and a night Ruth is haunted. Now and then she tries to stop it but it's too late. She has to see it through. And she howls into her pillow and hollers at her parents with all the strength she has and when she finally allows them back in their coffins, slams the lids shut, there is some peace. And now she wraps her arms around herself and laughs for a very long time.

"Well, bitch, letting that man at me with his dirty fingers and his ugly mouth. I guess it explains a lot of things. Like my entire fucking life, for instance. And I don't know who is worse off but I'm guessing you two because you're long dead and rotten and I'm still kicking. Okay. Okay. Okay. It's done. It's done. And if I can't make it go away at least I know what it is. Good for you Ruthie girl. Good for you." And she gets up off the kitchen floor where she had landed some time earlier and fries a couple of eggs. Eats them sandwiched between stale bread and watches the watered-down light of the setting sun through her living room window.

~

Eve is restless. Dear God, she is restless. Too long in one place and missing what she's left behind. And she prays for another earth walk. Just one more time around. Wanders her garden but only at night so as not to frighten anyone. And Joanie Harris looks at the footprints in the backyard of the house on Bishop's Road and can't figure out why the grass is green in each one and everything else frozen solid. Thinks the old lady in the red sweater must be wearing some kind of heated boots though she's sure her feet were bare the last time she looked. Walks her own feet through the path of prints and would swear she smells lilacs. She wants to tell someone but she still doesn't know a soul in this place except for that man who used to come around looking for his dog. When Mrs. Miflin shows up at her door she is lonely enough to invite her in and puts the kettle on.

"That old Eve had a garden out back. Used to get a hedgehog every summer to eat the slugs, you know. I told her she was crazy, wasting good money like that but would she listen? Not for a minute. None of them ever listened to me which is how I ended up in this sorry state after all my hard work."

Joanie has no idea what Mrs. Miflin is talking about. She

had assumed that one of her neighbors had finally come by to say hello. Not the Welcome Wagon exactly but better than nothing.

"She got that no-good Judy to build a bin for her garbage compost too. If you don't have rats yet you will soon, mark my word. I wouldn't let them youngsters anywhere near that thing if I was you. What did you take that nice paper off the kitchen walls for? That was there for a long time. I put it up myself, you know. I really liked it with them little roosters and grapes all over it. And now you got it painted blue. And what in God's name possessed you to hang all your pots and pans off the ceiling? Sure they'll collect dust like nothing else and you'll have to be cleaning them every time you want to make a meal."

While Mrs. Miflin tells of her trials and tribulations all because of her wicked tenants, Joanie half listens, half dreams. It's been a long time since she met anyone who strayed over the line that defines normal, unless you count her husband, but she's not ready to do that. The women Mrs. Miflin is describing, the things they did. Joanie's mom used to bring home people like that. She gathers that the man with the dog is the heathen Indian that Ginny Mustard married. She wishes now that he would come back. Perhaps if she keeps the dog long enough, he will.

"Are you after hearing a word I'm saying?" asks Mrs. Miflin, bringing Joanie back to earth. What was she going on about? The house. Something to do with the house.

"I want it back. I've still got all the money. I never spent one penny of it, you know. It's as good as the day I got it. Now what do you say to that?"

And Joanie who hasn't said anything really since she offered Mrs. Miflin a cup of tea and shortbread, looks confused for a minute until her children come running in for lunch and she ushers Mrs. Miflin out the door. Not without difficulty. She doesn't want to go and is sitting on the steps when the children leave for their afternoon classes.

Joanie would call John at work but she is only allowed to do that if something happens to one of the children and even then it had best be a life or death situation. She has a car that she can use if one of them breaks a leg or she has to pick up groceries. John checks to see how much gas is in the tank without warning. She used to walk back and forth to the store, saving up for a secret rendezvous with the highway but he noticed once that she couldn't have driven anywhere because the gauge read full and caught her in the lie.

Joanie has no clothes to speak of. A suit to wear for emergencies - a trip to the hospital perhaps - as if she would actually stop to change when one of the children comes to her broken. Hurting. She has a pair of good pants and a pair of everyday pants and two shirts. She washes her underwear every night. John figures she'll never have an affair if it means stripping down to graying cotton. He buys the cheapest panties for her that he can find - three for five dollars - and keeps two tucked away until she can show him holes and elastic beyond repair. She has evening gowns which John keeps under lock and key. He takes them out when it's time to entertain clients. Always says, "Maybe you should wear the purple one this time." The one with no sleeves that makes her feel so beautiful, and he watches as her eyes light up before saying, "No. I think the gray. We don't want every man in the place staring at you, do we sweetheart?"

Joanie didn't care one way or the other about the move to this place. She stopped caring about most things just after she and John married. What was the point? The only things she wants are her children and the purple gown.

~

You never know the half of it, really. The old woman

shoving to pass you in the grocery check-out line was your mother's kindergarten teacher. The men in hardhats, over there, hanging off the scaffolding, sandblasting that building, grew up in the same town as someone who knows your uncle. If you follow your gut and take the long way home today you'll see the car your brother sold last year in Edmonton and what's it doing here? If you slow down when you pass the school you'll hear little girls singing the same skipping songs you sang once upon a time. But first you have to get that look off your face and let your eyes roam free.

When Judy stepped out of her hotel she sniffed the air and smiled to no one in particular but Artie Mason was testing the new video camera his wife gave him for his birthday and set his sights on the most pleasant thing he's seen yet. When Judy attacked the man with the kids Artie kept right on filming.

He brings his tape to the local television station. They show it on the six o'clock news, further proof that the young people today are totally out of control, but Opal Freeman sees it and calls her friend Jenny Watson up north who has been trying to find her babies for six months.

The cops can't understand why the man with the children doesn't want to press charges and go to see him. When he doesn't answer his door and they hear small crying they break in. The sight of those two little ones dirty and hungry and bruised is enough to make young officer Carter quit the force and take up truck driving.

By the time Jenny Watson's bus arrives her babies are safe and sound and Judy is some kind of hero. And in the flurry of radio interviews and television appearances that naturally follow, everyone forgets that she is a runway and she never is sent back to where she came from.

And Simon Grace of the Simon Grace Model Agency doesn't have to fire any of his staff for their apparent lack of imagination when three of them independently decide that Judy has the next fabulous face, showing up one after another during her most recent talk show appearance and hauling her off to meet the great Simon. All she does is sniff the air and smile. He signs her up on the spot and sets about making her over. Takes the rings out of her ears and nose and eyebrows. Dyes her hair and dresses her up. Teaches her how to walk and declares her beautiful. Puts her on parade. And all of the other pretty girls have to learn not to pout so hard at the camera and work on smiling though they never quite get that look in their eyes that Judy has, that magic fox thing that lurks way back and takes you off guard. Makes you look twice and then again.

~

Joanie Harris finishes her chores for the day. Puts on her flannelette nightgown and washes her panties. The children are asleep and John is away. A business trip to Montreal. She sits at the kitchen table and drinks tea. She would love a glass of wine but John keeps it locked in a cabinet and has taken the key with him. Harvey comes down from the attic. Stares at her a minute before going to the back door. Whimpers to be let out.

"Oh dog. I wish you would stay." She goes to the basement. Returns with a rope that she fastens around Harvey's neck to keep him from leaving. Puts on her old boots and coat. Takes him outside to do what he has to do. The rope reminds Harvey of Howard James and he balks on the stairs. Pulls back. But more interesting than his sad doggy memories is the sight of dear Eve who used to give him snacks from her plate and rub his head whenever he went to her room. He leaps away from Joanie, rope and all. And Eve is just as happy to see Harvey. Bends to pet him and stroke his silken ears. Joanie asks, less bravely than she had hoped, "What are you doing here? This is private property, you know."

Eve extends her hand in greeting. "I will show you where the flowers are. This is my first earthly garden and I am afraid I have taken too much a liking to it. I can't seem to leave. It's all right to come out. The children are fine. They are dreaming now. Just over here there is lily of the valley. You could miss it, tucked away as it is, and never know where the perfume is coming from." Joanie can't help herself. She goes to Eve and follows her to the juniper to see, there, underneath, it's ice and snow now but soon the leaves will appear and then the pure white flowers, so tiny you have to marvel that they can make such perfume. Lily of the valley. And Eve points to the place where the scilla grows brilliant blue against the May snow. Crocuses. And here it looks like dead grass but wait awhile. The most incredible flowers. Cheddar pinks. And you get down on your hands and knees. Push your face as close as you can for surely that scent is God's breath.

"My husband will hire a landscape architect to make it over. He likes things to be just so when he brings people around. We give a lot of dinner parties during the summer and he will need to score points with his garden. There's no sense in telling me all this. I'm sure the flowers would be pretty but unless they are rare or exotic they won't be staying. My husband doesn't care for sweet things unless they make him look good. Like me. I make him look good. Obedient little wife," and immediately regrets her words. Regrets that she has so hastily broken the rule and spoken ill of John. What if this woman were to tell him what she said? But Eve smiles a sad smile and Joanie knows she won't.

"Oh, you poor dear. You are so unhappy. But you must have my garden. It will do you all the good in the world. I don't think we can let John have his way. I must think about this. I'm not supposed to be here, you know. But I miss it so much. Usually this time of year I'm digging and moving things around in my mind. Do you have a sheet of paper? I could draw a little map for you. And show you what I would do this year if you'd like me to. Did any of my seed catalogues arrive? Everyone left in such a hurry they probably didn't have time to cancel them. My, it is nice to have someone to talk to. I'd love a cup of tea if you're thinking of putting the kettle on."

~

When she has exorcised her demons to her satisfaction Ruth goes around to visit Sarah and Peter. Finds they have been wondering about her. "You look rested," says Sarah. "We were worried when you didn't answer the phone. Where did you go?"

"Hell," says Ruth. "That must have been hell but I'm back now and everything is okay. I thought I'd take the children shopping. I have a sudden need for something green in my little womb. Can't say for sure but I think Eve came by last night and all I can think of is flowers. I haven't a clue how to grow one but they probably come with instructions."

"Eve is dead. Are you saying you saw a ghost?"

"I didn't see anything. Just had a sense of her and woke up wanting to plant flowers. Are the children home?"

In their search for the perfect plant they run into Joe Snake because the seed lady called him to say the new stock has arrived and he should get some things started indoors now if they are going to be ready when the ground thaws. They talk awhile and end up going back to Ginny Mustard's house to look at Joe Snake's garden plans and Ruth decides that he has so much space they will work on it together. And though she's never had her hands in the earth she knows she needs to put them there. Joe Snake says he has to go get Harvey. He's been at the house on Bishop's Road for too long now and since Judy ran off he finds his home terribly lonely.

"We'll walk with you," says Ruth and when they arrive, decides to go in as well. Joanie's children are at home and take Joseph and Eleanor to visit in their playroom while Joe Snake tries to convince Harvey to come away with him.

"I like what you did with the kitchen," says Ruth. "If ever a place needed a once-over, it's this one."

Dorrie is coming up the front steps just as they are going down. "Oh good," she says. "This will save me some leg work. I'm opening my Barbie shop on Saturday afternoon and I want you to come, Ruth. Oh. And you too," looking at Joanie. "I heard someone with a little girl is living here now so I brought you an invitation since you're new in town and it might be nice to meet some other mothers. There's sure to be lots of them there. Get your daughter to bring her favorite Barbie. We're going to dress up and have a fashion show." Eleanor wants to go too and Ruth says, "Sure. Should be a blast."

Joanie must decline. Her daughter is not allowed to have a Barbie doll which breaks her heart sometimes because she had one when she was young and wishes John would relent. But Beth looks so hopeful that Joanie says perhaps they will. Her daughter already knows how to keep secrets from her daddy. Michael is another story. So honest it hurts. Wanting so badly to please no matter the punishment. She'll talk to him. "Yes. Yes. We can go."

Eleanor thinks it would be a really good idea if they all go together and Ruth says, "Why not? We'll come by and get you at two. How's that? And we might as well dress to the nines. I have a feeling it will be that kind of gathering." Joanie looks at them with their bright scarves and mittens sharp against the grey, wet day and can just imagine what dressed to the nines means. Sees herself a lumpy turtle in her ugly suit and old brown boots, one of them falling a good three inches below the other so she's always pulling it up and seconds later it's drooping again. But being with Eve last night has given her a spark where there was none and she surprises herself with a laugh. John won't be back until Sunday night.

When the day is over she tucks the children in and goes to the kitchen. Spreads Eve's garden plans all over the table. Wishes John hadn't thrown away the catalogues that came last month. Her parents had a garden, wild and rambling. A high fence to drown out the grumbling of the neighbours with their manicured lawns and well-paid groundskeepers. Joanie spent her young summers with her mother, digging and planting and moving things about. In the evenings they sat beneath a willow whose branches swept the ground and her mother would read to her. *The Water Babies* and *Peter Pan. Under the Lilacs* and *Little Women.* And as she grew they read to each other. All the poems of Edna St. Vincent Millay who is her mother's favorite writer in the world. And Joanie remembers. *The world is wide on either side. No wider than the heart is wide.* But the rest of it is lost. In the grass. Beneath the willow.

Joanie is missing her mother and father and her tears are falling into hands covering her eyes and spilling to soak Eve's garden plans. She hasn't heard from them since the move to this place. She has written and sent pictures of the children - no response. And if she could she'd telephone them now but John made arrangements to ensure that no out-going long-distance calls be made from the home phone. He thinks the children might accidentally call Japan.

Joanie is smart but she married stupid. It happens to some. You needn't be damaged starting off. Just too proud to admit you blew it and next thing you're jelly woman in the corner of your kitchen with not enough clothes and nowhere to go even if you had some. And if you can remember who you really are before the children come along escape might be possible but once you have them, forget it. The day dawns that the nicest thing you can say about your marriage is, "Well, at least he doesn't beat me." and by then it will take an act of God to put things right.

~

Ginny Mustard is growing thin. Her eyes are sinking and have a secret look about them. She is afraid and only now will admit it. Joe Snake is reading to her. Words that break her heart. *Let us go then, you and I, through certain half-deserted streets,* and *Shall I say, I have gone through narrow streets and watched the smoke that rises from the pipes of lonely men....?* and something about *the yellow fog that rubs its back upon the window-panes* and she starts to cry for home and her ocean and river, her own foggy, narrow, half-deserted streets. Cries to be away from this prison and her fears. Tells how Crazy Rachel watches and wants their baby for her own. How she stares at her belly and threatens to take it from her when she is asleep.

And there's no point in Joe Snake saying that can't happen, because Crazy Rachel has already stolen the guard's keys twice and can do it again whenever she wants to. She tells of waking to find Crazy Rachel taking the knife from under her pillow saying that's how she could have the baby, just wait until it's big enough and take it with the knife. And she can't tell the guard because she wasn't supposed to have a knife in the first place. And now Crazy Rachel has it and will take their baby. Joe Snake says he'll talk to the warden right away.

~

When John comes home there's hell to pay. He had telephoned on Saturday afternoon, about the same time that Joanie and Beth were putting on make-up with all the other moms and daughters and laughing at themselves for being so silly - the moms - not the daughters. Of course there was no answer and when he arrives on Sunday night he sits Joanie down. Stands over her. Towers over her. "Where were you? There's no point in lying. You'll only make it harder on yourself in the long run. Eventually you'll have to tell the truth so you might as well do it right away."

John has never raised a hand to Joanie. He doesn't have to. When he finds fault he has merely to suggest that a *woman like you* might be found unfit to raise children should the matter ever come before a judge and he would have no choice but to leave her and take Beth and Michael. If she hadn't had the awful baby blues those long first couple of months after the children were born then he wouldn't give his *woman like you* speech every time she messed up. There'd be no sword dangling over her head. But he tells her she's unstable and that's the reason he has to keep the reins so tight. If he were to relax, let her have her way all the time, then who knows what might become of her and the children. He can't take the chance. After all, don't forget what happened after Michael was born, Joanie. Don't forget that you left Beth alone in the bathtub when you went to tend him and she might have drowned if I hadn't come home when I did. You can say you were exhausted. You can say you were depressed. That's the point - not an excuse.

And Joanie can't tell him that if he had let her breastfeed the babies instead of being up half the night warming bottles and dealing with colic then perhaps she wouldn't have been such a basket case. Why bother? He won't hear her. If that was the worst thing she had ever done, leaving little Beth alone in the tub for two seconds, he might get over it. But one day she had awakened briefly to the truth of her life. Had put her babies in the car and driven away. She has no idea where she thought she was going. She can't imagine what she thought she'd do without a penny to her name. John reported the car stolen when he came home from work. Reported a kidnapping. The police found Joanie on the side of the highway, gas tank empty, eating fruit and sandwiches with the children. Chewing sweet apple to pulp and kissing little bits of it into Michael's baby mouth. And they were laughing. Kissing and laughing.

When John let her come home from the hospital the children hardly knew her. They cried when she picked them up and didn't trust her. A long time passed before they kissed and laughed again. Joanie can't risk losing them so now she tells John where they went when he was away. Waits for her punishment. "I have to take the car. When your behavior becomes erratic like this I have to ensure that you don't do anything we'll both regret. I'm doing this for your own good. You understand that, don't you, Joanie? We can't allow Beth to be warped by this sort of nonsense. You understand that, don't you Joanie?" As though she's an idiot. As though she has lost her mind. He must go to the office now to catch up. Joanie puts the children to bed and washes her panties.

~

Ruth and Patrick have set a date for their wedding. As soon as summer's over, first day of fall because Patrick won't get a vacation until then and he wants a nice long honeymoon in Maine and Vermont when the leaves turn. Ruth thinks he is crazy and tells him so. Why can't they just live together for God's sake, and why go to Maine when the leaves here are as pretty as anywhere, but he wants the whole shebang. Wants Ruth to wear a long dress and get himself done up like never before. As formal as you'd want. With a five-tiered cake and a best man.

Ruth says, "I'm not that fond of people. I can't think who I'd want to invite other than the crowd I was living with on Bishop's Road and a few of the old dolls at Zellers. Peter and Sarah. Matthew and Joanna. My side of the church is going to look pretty pathetic."

"We won't have sides. Just throw them all in together."

He brings Ruth to meet his mom. Ruth has never met anyone with Alzheimer's disease and it takes about half an hour to get used to being greeted every two minutes. "Hello. Are you Pat's friend? My you have wonderful thick curls on your head, dear." And then when Ruth finally gets the hang of it, mom decides that she must be an old friend from school a thousand years ago and wants to chat about all the badness they got up to when the nuns weren't looking. Ruth can identify with that one and they have a good time.

"I like her," she tells Patrick.

~

Dorrie's business is doing very well. She can't keep up with the demand for custom-made Barbie clothes and has hired two seamstresses to do the work while she serves tea and chats with her clientele. And the wind might be cold enough to rearrange your face and you can't remember what you look like without a winter coat, a cap pulled down over your eyes, a scarf pulled up over your nose, but if one thing in your life is strapless and sequined and elegant you'll be all right until the thaw. It's a girl thing. Not a bad thing. And if it doesn't follow the rules then you'd best question the people who wrote those rules and carry on, because there's not a woman out there who doesn't want to feel as lovely as Dorrie's dolls when the paint peels in the bathroom and the siding falls off the house and no one cares that you put cilantro in the meatloaf for a change.

~

This place is grey brown - nondescript. This place is a small bird on a winter willow. Waiting. Wanting something to sing about. If you put your ear to the city's heart you will hear life but only the mad are wont to do such things, the earth being wet and soggy and you'll never get the mud out if you lie down in it. Most people wait and listen to the trees for the beat later on - when the buds begin. But the mad need to hear now. It's lucky if you can find a little rise where the water runs down and away. Not as messy but certainly as satisfying.

Bishop's Road readies itself for spring. Mr. Palfrey, not a patient man, is digging the snow out of his backyard and dumping it on the street so it will melt a little faster. So the rhubarb won't have to work so hard. So he can find the spiderwort. Any day now the forsythia will burst into flame the way it always does and young Aiden Porter will be losing his mittens all over the place because if he can feel the sun warm on his little face then it can't be as cold as his mom says and he just leaves them wherever they land. And where the sidewalks are bare there's hopscotch and just to the side in the gravel a few alley pots. Some boys still play marbles in this place and the girls skip rope. Their songs are as old as the hills.

~

Mrs. Miflin goes to her house every day and sits on the front steps. She has taken her money from the bank and carries it around in a brown paper bag with handles. A copy of the *Catholic Chronicle* tucked over it so no one will see what she has there. She can't get anywhere with Joanie and waits for John to come home from work but her backside gets numb or she gets hungry and thirsty and it's too cold and Joanie won't let her in so she usually wanders off by three o'clock. Joanie hasn't told John about Mrs.

Miflin and she never comes by in the evenings.

Whether it is fortunate or not that John pays a surprise visit when Joe Snake comes again looking for Harvey so he can take a new picture for Ginny Mustard, is difficult to say. Might take years to find out for sure. But Mrs. Miflin is on her perch when he pulls up and is so upset with that heathen Indian in her house and she, a God-fearing woman, having to sit outside in the freezing cold, she decides to tell John all about the affair Joanie is having behind his back. "As soon as them youngsters is out of the house in the morning that one is over here and they're going at it all day long. You can hear them out in the street. You should put a stop to it right now Mister. There'll be talk for sure, if you don't."

And John races into the house to confront the lovers. Finds them in the kitchen drinking coffee and looking at drawings of some sort. It might be the sudden rise in his blood pressure that makes him appear so threatening, eyes bulging and he is shaking, even drooling. How else to explain why Harvey makes a mad dash for his throat, pushes him to the floor and holds him there, jaws wide open and teeth pressing against John's skin, just enough to let him know not to move. Growling for effect, pleased that he can, never having tried it before. Waiting for someone to say, "And who's the best dog in the world?" Rub his head and give him a treat.

Joanie stares for several seconds before going to John's rescue. Pulls Harvey away and helps her husband to his feet. He tells her she's gone too far now but what else should he have expected from a woman like her. Joanie assumes he's upset because she has company. John doesn't care for guests unless they're his.

Mrs. Miflin comes in and starts counting out her money on the kitchen counter next to the stove. "It's all here. Every last penny of it. I hardly think you'd want to be living in this place now what with your wife carrying on like that. It's a good thing I came along when I did. I knew she was no good the first time I set eyes on her. Messing around with that Indian and his pregnant wife in prison for killing my poor husband, God rest his soul. Right there in the living room she did it and I in my sick bed at the time and couldn't even get up to stop her. She got what she deserved, you know. Justice will always prevail when it comes to her kind."

Now it's John who is bewildered. "Who the hell are you?"

"I am Mrs. Jessie Miflin and I'm here to buy my house back. I made a mistake. Though not as big as the one you made by the looks of it, marrying the likes of her. I'm going to get all my lovely furniture and move in as soon as you sign it over to me. I hope that doesn't take too long. I'm just about driven cracked in old Mrs. Pretty's place. My God, but she's slovenly. There's no other word for it. I can't understand the city not shutting her down. But we'll see about that once I get settled."

~

Judy enjoys her new-found fame and fortune - to a point. "It's all fun and games," she says, "until someone loses an eye." She's making truckloads of money and even after The Great Simon Grace gets his cut there's more than she can spend. She sends Joe Snake the $1,000 she borrowed in a really fat, padded envelope and no one can tell there's cash in it. Mails it from New York so he can't trace her but since he never opens the bank statements he doesn't have a clue that he and Ginny Mustard have been ripped off and can't figure out why someone would send him so much money. Gives it to his parents so they can buy a new sofa, something nice for their house.

Judy told the officers who pulled her from the fight that

her name is Felicity so that's what she's stuck with now and just as well, though if anyone from home should see her face on a magazine cover they wouldn't recognize her anyway, she's that made over. After a few months she started to be bugged by the whole thing. Standing around in the friggin' cold waiting for a cameraman to take his friggin' pictures, and that after getting out of bed before the friggin' sun comes up. And Simon always measuring every bite of food she puts in her mouth. Telling her she has to watch her weight because no one wants to see a fatty on the catwalk. Simon getting pissed with her when she doesn't get enough sleep as if she's going to be in friggin' bed by eight just to please him. And if that wasn't bad enough, he decided to put the make on her and he says it isn't true, he was just kidding around, and if he hadn't put his hand on her backside it might have passed, but he did and she slugged him one and split his lip.

She said, "Like I'd ever let you near me for fuck sake - you're forty if you're a day. Screw you buddy, I'm going home."

"You can't do that. You signed a contract."

"Tell it to my probation officer why don't you!" Packed her bags.

~

On the other side of the earth, Maggie and her dad are tired. They have seen and done enough to last a lifetime. Just the other day Maggie said she would like to go back now. They were walking a little street in London and someone was tarring a roof and that scent and the salt fog made her homesick for this place. It happens to everyone. There's no getting around it. It may be warm and lovely, peaceful and no struggle elsewhere. No matter. Once this place gets in your bones you will find yourself longing now and then. Minding your own business and out of the blue a hunger. You need something and you think it's a sandwich or love or a new coat but it isn't. And then you know. If I can breathe that air for an hour, you say. If I can walk by the water or over the hills, surely that will cure whatever ails me now.

~

John decides quickly that they will move. It will take a few weeks to put things in order. Transfer his office. He sends Mrs. Miflin away with her bag of money. Tells her he will be in touch but she's not taking any chances. Comes by every day and parks her fanny on the front steps. No real estate agent is putting a sign on her house and she'll be waiting if one even tries to.

Ruth telephones a couple of times but John answers and tells her that Joanie is not accepting calls. Eleanor wants to see Beth. They had such fun at Dorrie's shop opening and it's been a while now, so Ruth is dispatched to the house on Bishop's Road to ring the doorbell. See if Beth can come over to play. She finds Joanie packing dishes in the kitchen.

"We're moving. I have to finish this so I can get supper started. We will probably sell the house to the same woman who sold it to us. Isn't that the funniest thing? She just happens to want it back and it couldn't have worked out better for us."

"You can cut the crap," says Ruth. "I was talking to Joe Snake and he told me what happened. Just stop for a minute will you and tell me what's really going on."

"Nothing's going on. It just didn't work out for us, business wise. John feels that Alberta might be better. Financially. This place is not exactly a boom town, you know."

"This is such bullshit," says Ruth. "Been there, done that, bought the tee-shirt. Talk to me. I'm sure I have better things to do but I can't think what they are right now."

Joanie talks. And talks. "I don't know what happened. We were so happy when we first married. Sure, John was a little controlling. Possessive. But I put it down to his loving me so much. He came from an unhappy home. His parents split up when he was young. He is so afraid of losing me that he can't stand to see me talking to other men. He just can't take any chances, you know. He loves me and the children so much. He couldn't bear to live without us. My parents haven't been in touch since we moved here. I wish I knew what's wrong. I know they don't care for John all that much but still - they would hardly write me off too. And they love their grandchildren. Oh Ruth, I don't know which end is up anymore."

And in the end Ruth says, "So who takes your mail to the post box? Let me guess. Hmmm. Could it be John? Could that be why you never hear from your folks? Come with me. You can call them from my phone. Maybe they can help you out of this mess. That husband of yours is a freak. There's no way a man like that should be anywhere near children, especially his own."

There's barely enough time to get to Ruth's and back - what with the car off limits - before the children return from school. Joanie's parents don't answer. She leaves a message with her address and Ruth's phone number and says she will call back as soon as she hears from them. Says please let Ruth know what time and it has to be between nine and three but not lunchtime when the children are home. And she starts to cry. Says she doesn't have any clothes to wear. Says she's lonely. Wants to call again to hear her mother's voice on the answering machine. But there's no time and she rushes home to meet Beth and Michael waiting for her on the front step. They were worried. Michael especially. He bites down on his bottom lip to stop its trembling. He's not allowed to cry. And she holds both of them more tightly than she has ever dared before. And she says, "It's all right. Everything is going to be all right now."

Ruth says, "There. Doesn't that feel better? You don't have to be so tough, you know. I'll get out of here before that one sneaks home to check up on you. You know where I live. You have my number. If you need me, get your ass over to my place. Take this key. Hide it though. And for God's sake don't say a word about this to his nibs. That's the worst thing you could do right now. He's only got one oar in the water and it probably wouldn't take much to set him off. Promise." And Joanie promises.

Joanie holds her tongue and if John notices that she is a touch more nervous than usual he doesn't mention it. Goes back to his office after dinner. Eve comes to the garden. Says she is pleased that Joanie phoned her mom and dad. Now she can do what she likes with the flowers.

~

When Judy's flight arrives she goes home to Ginny Mustard's house. Joe Snake hears a little rustling coming from downstairs but thinks nothing of it. He is worried sick about his wife and can't be bothered with mice or rats or anything else that may be roaming about. When she comes upstairs for coffee in the morning he says, "Hello."

"I know you're not much of a talker, Joe Snake, but I've been gone for a dog's age. You think you'd come up with more than hello."

"I have to find a way to get Ginny Mustard out of jail. She is suffering and looking poorly. I have an appointment to talk to the warden today."

"Why don't you see if they can put her under house arrest? I did that once. They put me at the YWCA and as long as someone checked my room all the time it worked pretty good. Until they found the bit of pot I had and turfed me out. Sometimes they let people serve their whole sentence at home as long as someone is keeping tabs on them. They're not allowed out at night and they can't drink and stuff. You know. Shit like that. Of course, they might not do that kind of thing for murderers. Mostly just people like me. Did you get the money I sent? Do you think if I go to school this morning they might not notice I was gone? Did anyone hear from that bitch Maggie?"

~

When Joanie's parents hear her message, her father calls Ruth and her mother books a flight through the Internet simultaneously. They aren't the kind to waste time when their children's welfare is at stake. They pack their bags and are out of the house within an hour. John wouldn't let Ruth talk to Joanie so it is a big surprise to everyone when her parents ring the doorbell at six the next morning.

John curses when he hears it. Tells Joanie not to go near the door. Whoever it is will leave in a minute or he'll call the police but the ringing doesn't stop. Cursing some more, he heads down over the stairs. Looks out a window to find out who's making this infernal racket. When he sees who has come calling he has no choice but to let them in, but not until he forces his mouth into a welcoming smile.

Joanie's father's name is David and he is a big man. Tall and strong. The kind of dad everyone wants when there's trouble afoot. Her mother is Caroline. Not so tall but you wouldn't want to be on her bad side either. When John answers the door she pushes past him. Into the house. Calling to her daughter as she searches for the stairs.

~

During their flight home Maggie and her dad remember that they have nowhere to live. Surely Judy has another roommate by now and Mr. Eldridge may not be welcome in his old house, being divorced and all. Maggie would live with him if he thought it was a good idea. But he doesn't. "You're a young woman. You should be on your own, not hanging around with an old man all the time. It's not good for you."

~

Judy finds the postcards that Maggie sent ever so faithfully from abroad. Joe Snake kept them just in case she showed up again. She has a little cry for herself while she reads them.

~

Joe Snake is making no progress in his bid to free his wife. She has never complained to the warden about Crazy Rachel's behavior. And no one thinks she looks sick enough that they need to do anything about her situation. Her shot at parole is still a long time coming and if she doesn't like it she never should have pulled the trigger and killed poor Mr. Miflin in the first place. Granted, she's not all there, but guilty nonetheless. Joe Snake is sent on to the next person and the next, in a chain of command that seems ridiculously long to be dealing with one thin woman.

~

Before Joanie's mother has even hugged her daughter she

searches out the bedroom closet. Grabs the pitiful wardrobe - hangers and all - and runs downstairs. Dumps the works on the living room sofa and stands over the sad shirts and the suit, two pairs of pants. Says quietly, "You bastard. You bastard. Look what you've done to my girl." And when John opens his mouth as though to speak she whirls around to stare at him. Raises her hands, palms inches from his face, fingers spread and claw-like. Says, "Don't. Don't make a sound."

John appeals to his father-in-law silently, expecting understanding. But David Scott smiles and turns away. "He's all yours Caroline. Do with him as you will." Puts his arm around Joanie and walks her upstairs to the children.

Caroline speaks clearly and low. Almost whispers but there's a roar at the back of her throat. "When Joanie introduced you to us, my skin crawled. Your mouth has slime written all over it, John. Your hair is too neat and you spend too much time sucking up to anyone who has more money than you do. I had hoped you would grow out of it. I had hoped that Joanie would be strong enough and good enough to help you become human. I have never interfered with my children's decisions - no matter how disastrous they appear. But when they call for assistance, God help the poor bastard who has wronged them. I want you to leave this house. Find somewhere else to stay. Pack a bag and let us know where you will be and I will forward the rest of your belongings. This is no longer your home. Tell Michael and Beth you have to take a business trip and get out. There is nothing you can say right now that can make any difference other than in helping me to decide whether the rest of the world should know how my daughter has been clothed while she raises your children. Get out. Now."

~

Patricia Hartman ignored the invitation to Ginny Mustard's wedding. Home from her visit she managed to put her sister's face away at the back of her mind, where it stays for the most part. When her father showed up out of the blue, having read of his ex-wife's death, she spent a day and a half with him before thinking to mention that he has another daughter. Her mother had done a great job of hiding her second pregnancy, running off before she was five months gone and showing. The man was shocked to learn the news, but only until he remembered other details of his former life and then it all made sense somehow.

Dr. Kamau is very tall and good looking. Sophisticated. Walks like some kind of king. As though the planet belongs to him. He has spent so much of his life poking around in its cultures that perhaps it does. He certainly knows what it has been up to all these years. People stare when he passes and he often smiles at them. A slow smile. Mostly with his eyes and they get the feeling that he likes them. Patricia thought the smile was just for her until they went out together and she saw that he treats everyone the same. It annoys her that she's nothing special. And just when she was thinking of switching her surname back to Kamau, too. Now he wants to visit that other one. Patricia becomes irritated and testy when he asks Virginia's whereabouts. If her father notices that she is very much her mother's daughter, he doesn't say.

His telephone call to the house on Bishop's Road proves fruitless. Mrs. Miflin's number is no longer in service. Patricia won't recall the names of the other women who lived there but Dr. Kamau decides to go visiting anyway.

"Surely you won't show up unannounced, Father. Virginia is not stable and your sudden arrival could cause considerable damage." She doesn't bother to mention that her sister calls herself Ginny Mustard. Let him figure that one out on his own.

Dr. Kamau is happy to go alone. He considers asking Patricia if she cares to accompany him on the trek but she has begun to look so much like her mother that the thought of spending any more time with her right now is unbearable. He will drive. Days it will take and the ferry crossing is long but he's on sabbatical with no particular place to be so no matter.

~

When Maggie and her father arrive at Ginny Mustard's house there's nobody home. Someone left the apartment door unlocked. Most likely the same someone who recently dyed her hair orange and there are spots all over the tub surround. They make themselves at home and Mr. Eldridge gets started on the newspaper to find a place to live. They thought to take a hotel for a few days but they've both had enough of that. Maggie is hoping that Judy doesn't have another roommate and is willing to let her stay. The few odds and ends she left behind are still in plain view and there's no indication that anyone else has moved in. In fact, other than the mess in the bathroom and Judy's unmade bed, it seems no one has been here in months. There's dust all over the place and milk soured solid in the fridge. The unmistakable sound of Judy's footsteps interrupts Maggie's inspection and she braces herself for the worst, which is no less than what she gets when Judy comes tearing into the apartment.

"What the hell are you doing here? You got some nerve showing up now after taking off and leaving me by myself with no one to talk to! Hello Mr. Eldridge. Did you have a nice trip? Don't you dare talk to me Maggs! I am really pissed! That friggin' teacher went and called Patrick and he's probably on his way over here right now to cart me off to the cop shop on account of I went missing! I practically begged her not to but - no - she had to go and tell on me! So now I've got to get packing again! I don't know where the fuck I'm going either and it's all your fault! If you didn't run off like that I'd still be in school most likely and doing just fine. I don't know how you could be such a bitch, Maggs. I never did anything to you."

"What are you talking about? Why haven't you been in school? You didn't need me to get you there, you know. There's nothing keeping you from going on your own."

"Shut up! I told you not to talk to me! I wasn't in school because I took off. To Vancouver, not that it's any of your friggin' business. But I got a job there and made lots of money too. I was modeling, don't you know. It was pretty good as long as I didn't open my mouth. I don't know what's wrong with those upalongs. You'd swear they never heard anyone talk before the way they were all the time asking me to say stuff. Said I had a quaint accent. I'd like to show them friggin' quaint. Made me feel like some sort of retard. And then that creep put the make on me and I had to hit him. They hardly let you eat anything. Especially meat. I never had bacon and eggs the whole time there. And I had to sleep about twenty hours a day so I wouldn't have circles under my eyes. Like, who the hell cares? I tell you, that crowd wouldn't know fun if it up and bit them. They're friggin' crazy so I came home. Now it looks like I have to take off again. I don't want to, Maggs. I want to stay here and have things the way they were before." And she's crying just a little and her nose is running.

Maggie finds a tissue in her backpack and hands it over. "Maybe if we talk to Patrick. I'm sure we can figure out a way for you to stay out of trouble permanantly this time. I mean, you were working. That shows some initiative. You're obviously good at something."

"Geez, thanks Maggs. You're making me feel a whole lot better."

"I didn't mean it to sound that way, Judy. It's just tha you've never done anything for money before that wasn't agains one law or another, have you."

Mr. Eldridge has been listening quietly to the conversa tion. Smiling. "I can speak to Patrick if you like. Or your proba tion officer. Or both. It must have been difficult to have Margare leave just when you had become good friends. That would b rough on anyone. Why don't I see what I can do. I'm sure tha with a little time and patience we can work this out."

"Well okay," says Judy. "Do you want to go and have swing in the schoolyard Maggs? I think I miss that more than any thing. Though you're sounding kind of grand compared to wha you used to. I suppose you're too good for that sort of thing now are you?"

"Not likely," says Maggie and they're off. Mr. Eldridge set tles back with his paper to wait for whatever will be.

~

Sarah has become inquisitive. She wants to know wh Peter's father is. Wants the story of Ruth's life from beginning t now. Ruth is none too pleased.

"I knew bloody well you wouldn't be able to leave it alone You can forget about it right now. I really don't feel like airing m laundry in front of you, if you don't mind." Ruth might as wel give up. It's not that Sarah nags. She doesn't have the mouth fo it. Not enough lines and she can't make it go all tiny and pinche the way a true nag does but damn it, she is persistent. Last wee she showed up at work just as Ruth was taking a break. Wrappe her arm through Ruth's and said, "Why don't I take you to lunc and you can tell me all about Peter's father." And a couple o nights later she popped by with tickets to a jazz concert. "Let' have a drink first and you can tell me all about Peter's father."

Another time she invited Ruth to drive with her out to Pottle's Cove. "We can watch for whales while you tell me all about Peter's father."

"You're like a crackie with a bone," says Ruth. "Do you ever give up?"

"Not often. It's a gift."

"I suppose that's one way of looking at it."

~

Joe Snake's mom and dad never did do anything with the money he sent. His sister Lucy talked them into buying a second-hand barge of a car that one of the cousins had fixed and was selling cheap. It took the better part of the winter and half the spring to get her license. The cousin repaired the new dents and scratches free of charge when she was done. Lucy is not the best driver on the island but she's as good as most. The folks try to talk her out of going to visit her brother. It's a long trek and she can barely see over the steering wheel but she's determined.

"It'll be nice now that summer's coming. Joseph must be lonely with Ginny Mustard in jail. Annie Paul can look after the garden. I need to get away from here for awhile. Just for a couple of months."

Her mother says, "Over my dead body. A couple of months! No! And that's final." She'll need help making fish soon and putting up berries later.

"Get with the program, Mom," says Lucy. "Nobody eats salt fish anymore. It pickles your heart. And anyway, you've got enough food preserved around here to feed you for a hundred years. And I'll be back in plenty of time to help you pick the damned berries. There's barely leaves on them yet, for God's sake."

"Well that's a fine way to talk to your mother."

But she gives in, though if Lucy thinks she's going all tha way alone - forget it. Mom is not about to let the flighty girl ou of her sight for too long and so they all pack up and head east Dad in the backseat with his earplugs and a pillow. The women ir the front arguing over radio stations.

~

"There's an old woman in the backyard, Joanie. I don' think she has anything on her feet. She must be freezing! Shoulc I see if she's all right?"

"It's okay, Mom," says Joanie. "That's Eve and she seem to be impervious to cold. She doesn't usually come around durin the day. She used to live here. In this house. She tended the gar den and can't leave it alone for some reason. I'll go and talk tc her."

Eve is concerned about the birds. "There's really no much for them to eat yet. I used to put out suet and seeds bu someone has taken down my feeders. Where are they?"

"John threw them away. He was going to get more but jus for the hummingbirds. He's gone, Eve. My parents came anc forced him to leave this morning. I don't know what I am goin to do now. I don't know if he'll ever come back. All I wanted wa to have him be nicer to me. Less impatient with the children. Jus to bend a little and not be so controlling all of the time. I'm sur we can work this out if he makes a few changes. Now the childre will grow up without a father and that doesn't work for anyone."

"I think," says Eve, "that if he was ever going to make a few changes, he'd have done so by now. Your children were sac little people with him. I don't think his going can make them an more unhappy. Better they have one parent who can laugh witl them than two who don't. You just have to find something to smile about and everything will be fine. Ducks are good for that. When there's nothing else can do it, you should go down to the lake and watch the ducks. It's only a few streets over. Will you have enough money to get by? It's harder if you don't but it can still be done, you know. As long as you find something to laugh about. And if you're going to feel sorry for yourself you'd best do it when the youngsters aren't looking. After they go to bed, maybe. Children are silly. They always think things are their fault. I expect Patrick knows how to build nice bird feeders. He's handy. I should ask Ruth if she will mention it. The ones in the stores are too fussy. Birds don't like fussy things."

And she's gone. Walking or fading - it's hard to tell.

"Well. That was strange," says Joanie to her parents when she goes back into the house. "Eve said there's a lake around here somewhere with ducks. Will you stay with the children while I take a walk?"

When she opens the door Harvey races in, followed closely by Joe Snake who does not want to cause any more trouble for Joanie and has been running a few steps behind the dog since he got away.

"Hello, Joe Snake. Go in and meet my parents. I'm looking for ducks. My husband is gone and I can have all the company I want now. Why don't you show my father where he can buy some good wine - John still has the key to the liquor cabinet - and please stay for supper."

Joanie is crying and Joe Snake is not too sure what she said but he goes into the house anyway. Introduces himself to David and Caroline. "Joanie wants me to help you find wine that will go with duck. I think. I could be wrong."

~

Crazy Rachel has had about enough of prison. Torturing Ginny Mustard only takes up so much of her time and she's in the devil's playground. She instigated an all-out brawl with Becky Norris but got the worst of it, not being as good with her fists as she is with her tongue and now she's in solitary confinement again. "For two cents, I'd slit my wrists," she says to the room that seems a little smaller than last time she was locked down. She has bruises on her face and arms and one of her feet was stomped on several times in the ruckus so she's hurting. But only physically. She has never felt pain of any other kind. She hasn't cried since she left the womb. No one ever noticed that. If she was dry-eyed when she didn't get her way, the screaming and yelling made up for it.

Prison officials decide that regular psychotherapy is in order to make sure this batch of criminals never comes back to haunt them when their time is up. The women will have two hours each a week and group sessions on Saturdays. The warden thinks this is a crock of shit and has no qualms about saying so but she makes up a schedule and pretends to be nice to young Alice Paine when she comes in. Alice is fresh out of school and, if you don't count her friends and relations, Crazy Rachel is her very first client. She is shocked by the bruises and says so.

"This happens a lot around here," says Crazy Rachel. "You can be minding your own business and next thing you know they're all over you. The guards." She whispers now, "If you put out they leave you alone. I just can't do that. I was raised different than some of them, I guess, so I get the worst of it. You might think I'm just a common criminal but mine was a crime of passion. The man I love cheated on me and I lost my mind and tried to kill him. I'm all right now except for the beatings. The one I really feel sorry for is Ginny Mustard. She's pregnant, you know, and not looking so good lately. I don't think they hit her but they can be pretty mean in other ways. Telling her that they will take her baby. Things like that. She seems terrified all of the time, the poor woman. There's no point in asking her about it. No point asking anyone about anything. They are all scared to death of the guards. They'll never tell the truth. They'll probably say I got the bruises from fighting or something. That wouldn't surprise me one bit."

Alice Paine is upset by Crazy Rachel's disclosure but promises that she won't mention it to anyone. "Because it will be worse for all of us if you do. Oh, if only the other women felt safe enough. They might say something too. But a few of them have parole hearings coming up you know, and they can't take any chances. It's okay with me if I never get out of here. My Howard won't see me again and I don't care if I live or die. That's the truth. I don't know how much more mistreatment I can bear, though. Sitting in solitary and nursing my wounds. They won't give me anything for the pain. Promise not to say a word about this to anyone."

~

"Eve wants bird feeders and you have to build them."

"I don't have a lot of time for that, right now," says Patrick. "Things are busy at the station. What do you mean, Eve wants bird feeders. Eve is dead, Ruth."

"No matter. She wants bird feeders. Seems that idiot who moved into Mrs. Miflin's house threw hers out and the birds are hungry. Don't ask me how I know that. I just do, okay? If you can't make them maybe I can."

"Have you ever built anything?"

"No, but how hard can it be? Whack a few pieces of wood together and voila. Bird feeder. I don't think they're all that picky.

As long as there's a few seeds or whatever. Up high where the cats can't get at them. Instead of going to the movie tonight why don't we go to your workshop and you can show me the ropes."

In the morning she brings her creation to Joanie. Hears the news of John's eviction and meets David and Caroline. They are pleased to know the woman who saved their daughter.

Caroline wraps her arms around Ruth. "You can't possibly imagine how grateful we are for your intervention, Ruth. We had no idea where Joanie and the children were. We've searched high and low but John is very good at covering his tracks. We were worried sick." She begins to cry and Ruth pulls away only to be hugged by David.

"The police were no help at all. Thank you for getting involved, Ruth. We were detemined never to give up but we have been so discouraged and have feared the worst for such a long time. Thank you. I wish there was something we could do to repay you."

"It was nothing," says Ruth, peeling him away. Almost embarrassed. "I might have done it for anyone. You can stop thanking me. Joanie, Eve wants that bird feeder put up in the birch tree at the back of the garden. You'll need a ladder. Better you than me especially if you use that old one she had. I'll build a couple more to go on the shed and in the prickly hedge. I forget what she called it. I don't mind saying, that woman is a lot more demanding now that she's dead. She never seemed to want much of anything before. I was going to paint a picture on the side of it but all I can draw is horses and that doesn't make any sense. What do you think, though? My first piece of woodwork. I'm rather proud of it. Not bad, if I do say so."

"Eve is dead?" says Joanie. "The old woman who comes around all the time?"

"You've seen her? I just get a sense of her now and then. She made me buy a plant once and now I'm building bird feeders.

And she's worried about Ginny Mustard. I'm going to see if I can locate Joe Snake when I leave to find out what's going on. How does she look? I thought she'd start from the beginning again. You know, baby, teenager, adult. Maybe that's not the way it works. Anyway, what odds. Just put up the bird feeder so she'll get off my case."

"You're joking, Ruth. There's no way that woman is a ghost."

"I didn't come here to argue. I'm delivering a bird feeder. That's it. Believe what you want but, as old what's-his-face said - *there are more things in heaven and earth, Horatio, than are dreamt of in your philosophy* blah blah blah."

Caroline is fascinated with Ruth and her ramblings. Wants to meet Eve next time she comes around. Tells her husband they should plan to stay awhile.

~

Dr. Kamau has been travelling for six days. He might have been here ages ago but there are dozens of small towns along the way and he can't resist a visit to each of them. There are even more places off the beaten track and so far he has clocked 2400 km on a 1500 km trip and not even halfway done. He has been sitting around with fisherfolk and truckdrivers. Farmers and steelworkers. Today he had lunch with handful of nuns who grow lettuce for a living. Fifteen different kinds with no pesticides and they charge a small fortune for them at the market on Saturday morning. A few times he has forgotten where he's going until someone asks and then he drives all night to make up for lost time. He's not so much absent-minded as easily led astray. Not unlike that daughter he never knew he had.

There are tiny fish that come ashore each year. Called

caplin. They are much like smelts but mostly in size. You can eat them fried fresh or dry them for later or use them for bait to catch bigger fish. In some places people dig them into their vegetable gardens as fertilizer and the smell is awful for a few days but worth it in the end. The caplin come to spawn. Millions of them. On the tide. Find out when it will be high and go to the ocean. If you look out a little way you'll see them, a dark cloud in the water. And then they are rolling on the beaches. Gleaming silver. A flood of silver in the sun setting. You can fill a bucket in a minute. They are especially delicious cooked in butter with the tiniest new potatoes - boiled - and some steamed turnip tops or dandelion greens.

Following the caplin are the codfish in a good year and whales. Cod is tasty too and the whales are better than a circus any day. Take cold beer and sandwiches and a friend and find a grassy spot on a hill overlooking the ocean. You won't need binoculars, they are that close. If you are lucky enough to know people with a boat, go out with them. The whales might play with you. Might let you touch their tough wet skin.

Dr. Kamau happened upon a crowded beach just before sundown one evening and had to investigate. Someone handed him a colander and he helped fill a wheelbarrow with the wriggling silver. Minnie Osborne had never seen an African man before except on television and invited him home for tea and he ended up staying in the twins' bedroom for the night and they were sent outside to sleep in the camper trailer which suited them fine. And the next day Minnie was drying the caplin and he had to watch the process. Then they all went out to the beach to pick mussels for the fundraiser at the church hall that night. He ended up staying for three days and had a marvelous time.

~

Ginny Mustard is very unhappy. She is thin as a rail except where the baby grows. She looks like a brown egg on stilts. If only someone would listen to Joe Snake as he pleads on her behalf. If only someone could help her out of this sad and dreary mess. If only. She has been listening to Ella pray all day every day for months and might get down on her own two knees if it seemed to be helping at all. But Ella is as pathetic as ever. Moaning and crying out to her Lord and Savior. Begging forgiveness. If she would shut up for a minute she might hear the answer. Or not. Even God must tire of repeating Himself.

When Ginny Mustard had her first encounter with Alice Paine she didn't have anything to say. Alice was sweet and almost pleading but Ginny Mustard has given up talking. Only the baby hears her anymore and there's no need to speak aloud for her. Alice tells the warden that Ginny Mustard is suffering from severe depression and that she fears the worst. The warden doesn't really give a damn. She's been running this show for long enough and is planning early retirement. She and her husband have finally finished the cottage that's been under construction for twenty-odd years and she spends most of her time building a Web page to show it off to the rest of the world. She was never interested in that pack of criminals to start with. This was the first job to come along when she and Bill decided they needed a summer place. Every cent she makes goes into it. Their home is a shack by comparison. She will put in her notice as soon as the trout pond has been stocked. Ginny Mustard is of no more concern than the rest of this sorry lot.

The food around here is inedible again. Ginny Mustard takes no care and more often than not most meals go into the garbage barely touched. Some of the inmates are talking riot but they're too hungry to pull it off. They complain to the guards who complain to the warden but she's at the computer most of the time with her door locked. "Some of those cows can stand to lose a few pounds," is all she says.

The guards have been spoiled. Ginny Mustard is the best cook to come along ever. They are none too happy with the warden's response. Mae Foley says, "You know, now that I come to think on it, Ginny Mustard is not looking all that good these days. Do you suppose there's something wrong with her? She looks awful. And she never opens her mouth any more. It doesn't surprise me her cooking's gone all to hell. We're going to have to find someone else to take over the kitchen but do you think we should get the nurse to check her out? I don't know what they're doing putting a pregnant woman in this place. We've got enough on our hands as it is without having to watch out for her. What if she goes into labour one of these nights and the nurse is not around? I don't want that kind of responsibility. I find it real stressful, myself. I don't know about the rest of you but I think something ought to be done about this. We don't get paid enough to be liable for whatever happens to her, do we now. I wouldn't mind her being here after that youngster is born but this isn't sensible."

~

The problem with travelling this time of year is moose. They are everywhere. The yearlings have been turfed out of house and home to make way for the spring crop and they haven't a clue where to go. So they wander aimlessly, often on the highways and straight toward your car. Dusk is the worst time because you can't see all that well and perhaps they can't either. How else to explain the number of collisions between car and beast every year. Mrs. Benoit is adamant about getting off the road long before sunset and there is no point arguing though Lucy gives it a good shot anyway.

In the lobby of a motel, which turns out to serve a mean

hot turkey sandwich, they run into a very tall African man also looking for shelter. Someone in the last town he visited told him all about moose but it wasn't until he saw one clambering out of the bushes and up over the shoulder of the road toward him that he really believed the stories. He waits patiently while the Benoits check in, observing that they are native and hoping to get a chance to pick their brains later. Hears them ask if the dining room is open and decides he is hungry as well. Waits until they are settled before taking a table next to theirs. Mrs. Benoit thinks he must be lonely and a long way from home since the only other black person she has ever met is her daughter-in-law. They are as scarce as hen's teeth around here. Besides, the room is empty but he's practically sitting in their laps. He must be lonely. And so she strikes up a conversation, bewildering the poor man. He's come to expect fast talkers on the island but she can outdo the best of them. It will be some time before he gets a word in to find out what these people are about. No matter. The food is good and she will have to wind down sooner or later. He shares his wine and listens to her ramble while Lucy fills in the blanks. Mr. Benoit sits quietly for the duration and when he heads outside with his pipe, even though the waitress says not to bother, there's no one else around and she loves the smell of tobacco, Dr. Kamau is on his heels.

Getting Francis Benoit to talk is almost as difficult as convincing his wife to stop but Dr. Kamau is persistent and hears the history of his people as Mr. Benoit knows it. The myths and stories, the trials and triumphs. When the others are long gone to bed they are still at it but inside, with brandy and coffee and cigars, what the hell. Mr. Benoit has many friends. The men he has lived with and worked with all his life. Good neighbours. But they sometimes take themselves for granted. Easy enough to do in a small town. Not often does someone come along to make you really look at who you are deep at the bone, so that you remember with pride a little something special that sets you apart from others. It's a cheerful man who snuggles down next to his wife that night.

~

Mrs. Miflin is sitting on the front porch of the house on Bishop's Road when Ruth comes back to visit. David and Caroline were adamant that she join them for dinner this evening. Joanie and her parents have explained to Mrs. Miflin several times in the last few days that the house is not for sale right now and that they will contact her as soon as it is. But the shrewd bird doesn't trust them. Will sit on her perch every day until the house is hers again. They had considered calling the police and having her arrested for trespassing but really, she's not doing any harm, just filling up space and making it difficult to get by. They have taken to using the back door more often than not.

"Well old trout," says Ruth. " You don't give up easy, do you? Why don't you just find yourself a nice little house somewhere else? Or two. God knows you can probably afford it. And do you really think you should be carrying all that money around with you?"

Mrs. Miflin has been looking at pictures in the magazine she uses to cover her stash and now shoves it back in the bag. "I don't know that it's any of your business, Ruth. This is my house and I'm having it. And don't you think for a minute you'll ever get your nose inside of it once I do, Missy. You can die on the street for all I care and that's the truth of it."

"Whatever," says Ruth as she struggles past the little round woman. Calls out, "I'm here," as she opens the door.

Caroline corners her the minute she enters. "I really want to hear more about Eve. She hasn't come around again and I was hoping you have some way to contact her."

"Well hardly. She's dead. I don't know where one looks for the dead. Besides, Joanie is the one who's seen her. I'm just a messenger. This seems to be the only place she wants to be when she wants to be anywhere."

"I don't understand why she hasn't returned. Do you think we frightened her away? I would feel terrible if I thought that were the case."

"Eve is - was - an odd person, Caroline. She was happiest in her garden or helping people out. She hasn't changed much since she died except for having me traipsing all over hell's half acre. Maybe she figures Joanie's okay now. And the birds are fed. She seems to have moved on to the plight of Ginny Mustard. Joe Snake is having a tough time trying to get the poor thing out of prison. She really shouldn't be there, I guess. I was about to suggest that she's not a threat to society but I may be wrong. If she runs into another Mr. Miflin type she might just up and do him in too. The woman doesn't think. Especially when it comes to babies. If there were more like her in the world there'd be a lot less misery for some but the bodies would be piling up faster than we could dig holes to put them in."

"Joe Snake didn't tell us anything when he was here. He seems a lonely man but he didn't mention his wife."

"Well, he wouldn't. A bit closed is Joe Snake. All I know is she's not well. She's thin, he says, and won't talk to anyone. He met with the new therapist at the prison and she thinks Ginny Mustard may harm herself. I can't imagine her doing that. Even as depressed as he says she is she would never do anything that might hurt the baby."

And Ruth proceeds to tell Caroline all about the bones in the attic and the circumstances that led to Ginny Mustard's incarceration.

"That is the saddest story I have ever heard," says Caroline.

"Sad? Well I guess it might seem sad the way I'm telling it but really there was lots of sweet with the bitter. God knows it was the best wedding the likes of us had ever been near. And Dorrie's tea party was a fine affair. I discovered a good man among the ruins. Some of us did more living in those months before Missus sold the house than we had in years. I fought it for awhile. I'm glad I gave up that foolishness. No. I think sad is a woman with one foot in the grave. Living every minute we have is the way to go even if it breaks your heart half the time. Because it breaks your heart half the time. At least you end up laughing louder when you can. God! That sounds like something Eve would say. I brought some wine. Found it at Mr. Miflin's funeral. I'll dig out the glasses if you go get a corkscrew."

Caroline has a strong connection with the Patron Saint of Lost Causes. Together, she and Jude feed the hungry, clothe the naked, house the homeless and spring the wrongfully imprisoned. The fact that Ginny Mustard hasn't been locked up for political affiliations or toppling nasty governments or even writing about such things, is irrelevant. In prison she is and from prison she must be released. When David comes into the living room and helps himself to a glass of wine he sees the look in her eye and sighs. Loudly. A here we go again kind of sound and he sucks back his drink in one large swallow.

"What's up, sweetheart. Not enough to worry about right now? Who are we planning to rescue this time?"

"Ginny Mustard. Joe Snake's wife." And she gives him the sordid details. Resisting the urge to embellish. Not that there's any need.

Ruth smiles. "Perhaps we should get Joe Snake to come over so he can be in on this. He's already been working his ass off and there's no point in re-inventing the wheel now, is there?"

"Excellent idea," says Caroline. "You call him, David, and Ruth and I will see what Joanie is up to. The last I heard she was going to take a bath. Bring your glass, Ruth."

Joanie has been sitting in a tub of very cold water for about an hour. She has forgotten all about dinner. She has no idea where the children are. The palms of her hands are wrinkled. She stares at them. Wonders if she'll look like that all over when she is an old woman.

"Joanie," calls Caroline through the bathroom door. "Ruth is here and we've already gone through a bottle of wine. Do you want me to start dinner?"

"Sure. I'll be out in a minute."

While Joanie dries her pruny skin, Ruth and Caroline track down the children and begin meal preparations. David has contacted Joe Snake and he is on his way over, surprised and pleased that someone is prepared to lighten his burden.

~

From their seat on the wall in front of the orphanage, Judy and Maggie observe Mrs. Miflin's vigil. They see Ruth arrive and go inside. A little later they notice Joe Snake lope up the road. Step around the old landlady and ring the doorbell.

"Well now," says Judy. "I do believe there's something going on at the house. Want to check it out?"

"Sounds like a plan to me," says Maggie. And they're off. Almost falling over Mrs. Miflin, who leaps to her feet when she sees them running toward her. Nervous perhaps.

Judy doesn't bother to knock. Just barges in with Maggie holding back a touch. Collides with Caroline who heard the commotion from the kitchen and came to see what's up.

"Hello there. You must be Judy. I'd know you anywhere from Ruth's description. When did you get back in town? I understood you had disappeared. Do come in. And you're Maggie, of course. We are just about to have dinner. Will you join us? There's plenty. And we're also going to come up with a way to get Ginny Mustard out of prison. I'm Caroline, Joanie's mother."

"Well I don't have a clue who Joanie is but I sure wouldn't mind something to eat, thanks. I told Joe Snake he should try to get Ginny Mustard to finish up under house arrest. I did that a couple of times. It didn't work because I can't seem to stay out of trouble no matter what they do with me but Ginny Mustard is different. I bet he never even talked to anyone about it. No one pays me much mind until I do something stupid. Are you staying too, Maggs? Smells awful good whatever they got on the go."

"Yes. If that's all right, Mrs., uh, Caroline."

"Of course it is. The more the merrier. It will be nice for Joanie to have some company. She's had a difficult time lately and could use a few friends."

And it's old home week. Even Joe Snake looks a little less serious than he has lately. Smiling. Accepting a glass of wine. Comfortable in his skin again the way he used to be. David puts a leaf in the table to make room for the invaders and Joanie sets a few more places. Judy asks Beth and Michael if they ever swing in the schoolyard. Says the next time she goes over she'll come and get them. So now they both have to sit next to her and Michael is smitten for sure by this very tall girl with the brilliant orange hair. He doesn't tell her that anyone who goes on those swings will most certainly be killed when the ropes give way.

~

Dr. Kamau is lollygagging again. After his evening with the Benoits he turned around and headed back to where they came from. With the key to their house and a note from Mrs. Benoit for Annie Paul, explaining that the African man can stay as long as he wants and be nice to him and make sure to take him around so he can meet the neighbours. Get out the good sheets for the bed in the spare room because she thinks she might have left the old ones on with the yellow stripes. And a quilt since he might not be used to how cold the nights can get in this country. She must have been talking herself when he mentioned he's been away from home forever. She must have been. P.S. Don't forget to weed the flower bed.

~

Ginny Mustard is starving, starving. And there is nothing can quench her thirst. She lies on her cot with her hands on her belly and may die of the wanting. She eats the wretched food she prepares. She pours salt in the water she drinks. Smells it for ocean but there is none. She will not speak. She cannot recall the music. Her heart is as cold as her eyes. If we were to look inside there would be nothing to see but a tiny girl baby. And she holds fast. Tries to make her mother sing. Tries to feel some warmth from the hands pressed hard against her. But there is nothing and so she is quiet and her own small heart slows. She will not kick or turn and the nurse says this is not good, something is wrong. Tells the warden that Ginny Mustard must be moved to a hospital where her pregnancy can be monitored properly. And the warden says she doesn't give a damn just get her out of here because nothing's going to screw up her plans to vacate this hellhole with her pension intact. Signs a few papers and sends Ginny Mustard on her way.

~

Joe Snake's parents and Lucy arrive to find the house empty but for Mr. Eldridge fallen asleep in the downstairs apartment. The doors are unlocked and so they make themselves at home. Missus puts the kettle on and takes a look in the fridge to see what her boy is living on these days. Cheese and a few eggs. Some sad lettuce and fuzzy things growing in yogurt containers. A dead carrot. And in the pantry, potatoes sprouting a trail across the floor. She tut-tuts her way through the rest of the house. Takes the cats off the beds and puts them outside where cats are supposed to be. Starts a load of laundry. Opens windows to air the place. Makes a grocery list and heads to the market on the corner.

Mr. Eldridge wakes from his nap to the unmistakable scent of cod and scrunchions. Turnip greens. And he goes upstairs to say hello. Informs the Benoits that Joe Snake was summoned to the house on Bishop's Road and Lucy says, "Well you might as well have his share or Mom will put it in the soup tomorrow and make us eat it all over again." And he does. Manages to get a few words in about his trip to see the world and hears about the African man they met on their way.

~

"I was going to visit Eve's grave tomorrow," says Judy. "if I'm not arrested when Patrick tracks me down. Don't tell him you saw me, Ruth. Does anyone else want to come?"

Ruth tells her that she probably won't find Eve at home since she's forever gallivanting around these days. Though the only place to really see her is in the garden and she hasn't been here since last week.

"You're trying to freak me out, Ruth. Don't be telling lies."

"It's the God's truth, Judy. Joanie has seen her several times. Only ever in the garden and not for a few weeks now but she has been around."

"I'm not listening." And Judy puts her fingers in her ears and sings *Jingle Bells* as loud as she can. The children giggle.

"I've been thinking," says Judy when it appears Ruth has stopped talking. "And I think the best way for us to get Ginny Mustard out of jail is to all go there and make a lot of noise. I find that's the only way to get what you want. Make a lot of noise. Joe Snake can talk as good as anyone when he puts his mind to it but he's a bit soft. No one is going to take him serious. No offence Joe Snake, but you know what you're like."

"None taken," says Joe Snake.

"Ah," says David. "The old squeaky wheel ploy. It might help. Remember when you tried it with that transition house a few years back, Caroline? They wouldn't allow a seventeen-year-old boy in when his mother went to stay there. Caroline made such a racket that eventually they had no choice." He is proud of his wife. You can see it all over his face the way he looks at her.

"Well, I don't think the prison is the place to go. I think we have to camp on some judge's doorstep," says Ruth. " I had a fling with one of them once. I don't know if they are all strange but he sure was. I digress. Forget that last statement. If we knew someone with clout. A politician or some such. Does anyone in this room know someone with clout?"

"You know Patrick," says Judy. "Course he's the one who arrested her in the first place. Never mind."

Maggie's voice is low and she has to repeat herself when they finally realize she has spoken. "My dad might know someone. He used to be a lawyer before he had his heart problems. He might be able to help."

"Well," says Judy, "it's about friggin' time you said something. What were you waiting for, Maggs? A letter from the Queen? How come you never mentioned anything about your dad being a lawyer?"

"It didn't seem important before."

"I think we should call him over and see what he has to say. Should we go get him Ruth? He's at Ginny Mustard's house. No. Wait. Maggs, you go by yourself. I bet Patrick is there just waiting to cart me off. And if he is, don't tell him where I am."

"Judy," says Ruth. "Do you think you can hide from him forever?"

"Yes. If I have to sleep in a friggin' ditch. There's no way I'm going to some friggin' detention place with a bunch of losers. He'll find something better to do one of these days and stop looking. I ran away from home once and it was six months before anyone bothered to find me. And I was living under their noses the whole time. I don't know if you've noticed Ruth, but adults aren't all that friggin' smart when you get right down to it. They only see what they want to see and the likes of me gets pretty boring after a while."

~

Ginny Mustard wakes to sunlight but she doesn't move. Closes her eyes again quickly. Perhaps she is dreaming. Perhaps she is dead and this place heaven. In which case might her mother be here somewhere? She tries to think of anyone else she knows who died. Little Jimmy Batstone with the runny nose at the orphanage did when he fell off a snowbank in front of the bus that time and Mrs. Janes who ran the candy store next to the movie theatre before they tore it down. She died. And Eve. Ginny Mustard would like to see Eve again. They might all be here somewhere. Should she look for them? What if Mr. Miflin is here? What if God let him in with all the other dead people? Forgave him the sin of killing Mrs. Miflin's baby. What if the baby is here too? It is so quiet. She had always thought there'd be singing or at least some music. But nothing. If it is heaven they will have to do something about the smell. Like a toilet that was really dirty and someone scrubbed it with bleach as hard as she could but it never will come clean. Ever.

When the nurse comes in she can tell that Ginny Mustard is awake because people don't sleep with their eyes all scrunched up like that. She is wearing soft-soled shoes and when she speaks Ginny Mustard jumps as far as the handcuff that holds her to the bed frame will allow. But she keeps her eyes closed.

"I don't like that we have to tie you down, dear, but those are the orders. If you need to go to the bathroom you just press that button with your free hand and we'll unlock you. What did you do to get yourself in this kind of mess? Murder someone? I know there's a few around that I wouldn't mind doing in myself if I had half a chance. Funny way for a nurse to be talking I guess, being as I'm sworn to save people left right and centre. But we're none of us perfect that's for sure. They told us you don't talk but that's all right. I can do enough for ten. That's what my husband says and he should know, listening to me all these years, poor fellow. And he in a wheelchair too. Can't even get away when he wants. I tell him jokes to hold his interest. Throw one in now and then when he's not expecting. Keeps him on his toes, so to speak, if he could get out of that chair." And she's laughing. The kind of laugh that makes you smile when you hear it. Makes you wish you could follow her around just in case something else strikes her funny.

"Well, now. It seems you can smile, anyway. Let me check that baby of yours. They say she's not doing so good lately. Her little heart slows down and she won't move." And Ginny Mustard opens her eyes.

"Are you an angel?"

"So you can talk. The lies they get on with around here. Yes, darling. I'm an angel of mercy and don't ever let anyone tell you different."

"And this is heaven?"

"No, sweetheart. This is a hospital. They brought you over last night because you were doing poorly. But never you mind. We'll have you happy as a clam in no time. You just do as Edna says and everything will be all right. I'm Edna. And I'm pleased to meet you, Ginny Mustard. Where on earth did you get a name like that?"

"It's short for Virginia."

"Not Ginny, silly goose, Mustard."

"It's my hair. The nuns said it's the colour of mustard. Not hot dog mustard. The fancy one. Dijon. And all the kids started calling me that. And I didn't have any last name already so it's all right."

"No last name! Well isn't that the strangest thing? You know if you want one you can just make it up. If you use it often enough and get someone to put it on a piece of ID you can have it. I read that somewhere. And it won't even cost you. Though you can't always believe what you read so maybe you should ask a lawyer. Do you know any lawyers?"

"Only the woman who was in court with me."

"Well, I wouldn't bother with her. She can't be all that good what with you tied to a bed frame like you are. Why don't you ask our resident man of God when he comes round to hear your sins? He might know something besides the Our Father, though I wouldn't put my life savings on it if I were you. No matter, darling. We'll figure something out. You just think of a nice name that doesn't have anything to do with food." And she busies herself with machines and gadgets for a few minutes. Says, "Well this baby seems to be doing all right. But Edna will be in to check again in a little while. I'm on shift until eight this evening so you'll be seeing plenty of me whether you want to or not. I'll bring you something to eat in a few minutes and I don't want to see any leftovers. You're as thin as a promise." And she's gone in a gale of laughter. Ginny Mustard smiles.

When Father Doherty comes around she has broken her fast with porridge and milk, oranges and two bowls of lime jelly that Edna found in the kitchen, left over from the last supper. When Edna opened the window shades the sun was shouting off the waves between the hills and far beyond. And when she opened the little window below the big one the breeze came running in as though missing Ginny Mustard for a long time now and very happy to see her. Played with her hair awhile before settling under the bed blanket to cool her toes.

The good priest is determined to save this woman's soul and sets about praying with a sad face and his eyes soft. He reminds Ginny Mustard of Jesus in the pictures at Mrs. Miflin's house but he has no beard. Speaks so low that she has to strain to hear him. In a little while she gives up the effort and just listens to him drone on and on slow as cold molasses. Drifts off and still he talks until Edna comes in and shoos him away.

"You've gone and bored the poor thing to sleep. You should be coming around at night when they're all yelling for pills, Father. Save the hospital a bundle, you would. You're as good as anesthesia. Now go and see Mr. Maloney. He's in a state. They can't find anything wrong with him and he doesn't want to go home. They got two nurses in there trying to stuff him into his clothes. Like dressing a squid, they said. Go talk some sense into him. Your work here is done, by the looks of it. Go on, now."

~

When Maggie goes to fetch her father, Joe Snake's family comes along to the house on Bishop's Road with him. Supper is over and Lucy is itching for excitement. Joe Snake is surprised to see them. No one had called to say they were coming. Lucy insists that her mother said she would and Mrs. Benoit says, "No, you were supposed to." So they have to argue for a few minutes which holds up the introductions but eventually everybody knows who's who and they get back to business.

Mr. Eldridge is aquainted with a few people in power but is not so sure anything can be done at this stage. Judy wants to re-visit her original idea to gang up and make a lot of noise.

"We could start with that and see what happens. It's not like we've got anything to lose. She's already in jail, right? But I'm not coming. I'll just be the brains of the operation. Behind the scenes."

"I don't know if it will help but you may be right," says Ruth. "It can't hurt."

~

"Is it okay if I call my husband? Maybe no one told him I'm here and he might visit me at the prison."

"You have a husband! Well I am happy to hear that. I was thinking you'd be one of those girls having to give up your baby to God knows what. You tell me the phone number and I'll make sure he comes to see you. Nobody said anything about you not having visitors and if they do we'll just sneak him in for you. What's his name, darling?"

"Joe Snake."

"You're a queer crowd for names, aren't you? What were they thinking to christen a baby, Joe Snake?"

"His true name is Joseph Benoit."

"French, is he?"

"I think he's mostly Indian."

"So you'd be Mrs. Benoit. You don't need to make up a name at all. How is it you don't have a wedding ring?"

"I had one but someone took it from me at the prison."

"What a sin! Well I'll call your husband as soon as I'm done my rounds and we'll have him here in a flash." And Edna is away, phone number, or at least the last four digits, tucked in her head. It won't be hard to figure out the first three, only so many on the go. Not to worry, Ginny Mustard, if you can't remember all of them with Edna on your side.

When the gathering at Mrs. Miflin's house breaks up Mr. and Mrs. Benoit, Lucy, Mr. Eldridge in spare rooms, Judy and Maggie in the apartment downstairs, retire for the night. There isn't a chance that they will find a way to spring Ginny Mustard from prison but what a team! And Joe Snake the loner, tall and thin, straightens his shoulders and shrugs off the load he'd thought was there for good. Waits until his mother is sound asleep before letting the little cats inside to snuggle down on his bed.

When Edna calls to say his wife has been relocated everyone else is up and around, his mom making pancakes and Judy on her second helping.

"Can we all go to see her?" asks Judy, wiping her mouth with the end of the tablecloth. Mrs. Benoit gives her a smack.

"Ow. What did you do that for? That friggin' hurts."

"You've got the manners of a slug, girl. Don't you ever let me see you doing that again. Use your napkin and mind your mouth."

"Better do as she says if you know what's good for you," says Lucy. "I think Joseph should go by himself first. See what's up. Then maybe we can all visit later. What do you think Joseph? I'm sure you'd like a few quiet minutes with your wife, wouldn't you now?" And she smiles.

"Yes. I'll call after I've seen her. I hope there's nothing wrong with the baby. Her heart would never mend. I'll call." And he's away, his mom following with a plate of food. "Do you want me to keep this warm for later?"

Joe Snake finds Edna in the nursery kissing babies. "I love

these little ones. I could never have any of my own what with the old man being broke from the waist down, you know. So I come in here whenever I get a free minute. Stay half the night sometimes when one of them can't sleep. That rocking chair in the corner's got my arse print worn right through the cushion." She laughs as though that's the funniest thing she's ever heard tell of. "Come with me, dear. I'll take you to Virginia's room. Such a darling little wife you have. Bit thin, though. But you're not much more than a bag of bones yourself now, are you. Pity she's a criminal but I daresay she couldn't help doing whatever she did. That should be one fine looking youngster. Tall, judging by the two of you. Nice colour I would imagine. I always thought there was enough red hair and freckles around here to sink a ship. What did she do to end up in jail, anyway?"

"She killed a man."

"Well, I'm sure she had her reasons. Here's her room. She was supposed to eat everything on her tray so I'll just check and make sure she did and leave you alone. Virginia, look who I brought to see you. Wait now. I'll just undo those handcuffs so you two can have a quick hug but I have to chain you down again as soon as you're done."

And she does. And they do. A long hug like no one has ever hugged before and Sweet Polly feels the warmth and kicks her heels with baby joy. Hard. So they both can feel it. They laugh. Edna laughs. She snaps the cuffs shut and is gone. Still laughing.

They sit and stare at each other for awhile. Nothing to say. Holding hands.

"The baby was not so good so they brought me here. I thought I was dead when I woke up but I'm not. It's nice here. The sun was on the water and there was a little wind. I can smell the ocean and the fish. Oh Joe Snake, how can I go back to that place? I can't live there. I feel all mashed up inside myself and my heart is a hard thing."

"Perhaps we can keep you in the hospital until the baby is born. Our friends are trying to find a way to have you released but I don't see there's any way around it, Ginny Mustard. I think you'll have to be there until your parole hearing." And he tells her about Joanie and her parents, the others, trying to come up with a solution to this dreadful problem.

It seems to help. It seems she's less alone. It seems Joe Snake has people in their corner and so he is less alone as well. She has imagined him in their big bed. Cooking solitary meals. Dusting empty rooms. And has been sad for him.

"When the baby comes I'll bring it to visit. It will know you well when your time is done."

"Her. Bring her to visit. Her name is Polly. Becky read a book to me called *Five Little Peppers and How They Grew* and there was a girl named Polly. And she had a food name. Edna thinks I shouldn't have a food name. So I want to be Ginny Benoit now. Is that all right?"

"That's perfect." And he gives her a kiss for punctuation. "I can bring people to visit, you know. Mom and Dad and Lucy are here. I have no idea why or how long they plan to stay, but if you'd like to see them I can ask Edna if it's kosher. And Judy. Maggie. Everyone wants to see you. Would you like that?"

"Yes. Call them. If Edna says it's - what did you say - kosher?"

~

Dr. Kamau has signed up for the native cultural immersion course. Who better to teach him than Annie Paul who knows almost everything and has no qualms about making up the little she doesn't, borrows from the Sioux and Cree if she has to, reasoning that they are all brothers and sisters so what the hell. Annie

Paul found herself a few years ago in the archives on a trip to the city. Has since taken to making her own boots and coats - mostly of rabbit skins since that's about all there is around here but for the odd fox. She wears lovely pointed hats for special occasions, weddings and christenings, decorated with porcupine quills. Her moccasins and boots are covered with beads. She has to order the quills from away. And the beads. She lives in a teepee that Old Cecil helped her to build and cooks over a fire. Smokes salmon, trout and cod for the winter and sells some to make a few dollars for flour and sugar. Butter. Eggs, since she doesn't like to see animals penned and hens scratch too much in the vegetable garden when they're free.

The neighbours thinks she's crazy and perhaps she is but they all say nobody can cure a fish like Annie Paul and they don't mind paying what she asks. The only things she can't get enough of are steak and a baked potato with Caesar salad on the side and she never got the hang of stir-frying over her fire so she trades her soul's work for a few trips to town and the best restaurants therein.

Annie Paul can see. Might be the pot she smokes or the fact that she's the seventh daughter of a seventh daughter. Either way she knows what Dr. Kamau is about, though she waits a day or two to tell him where he should be since she dearly enjoys his questions and company.

"Someone needs you now and I think you'd better get yourself away. To the city. I'm not sure who she is but she's pregnant and important to you."

"That must be my daughter, Virginia. I have been told she's there but I didn't know she is pregnant."

"She's not only pregnant, she's in a sorry state for some reason. If I can find someone to look after my garden - and Sadie Benoit's - I wouldn't mind a trip myself. All right if I tag along? I can't pay for gas but seeing as you're going anyway that's no big deal. I'll bring a lunch. Let me go talk to Old Cecil. I'm sure he owes me something by now and he's got a house full of grandchildren doing frig all these days. A little gardening won't do them any harm. Keep them out of trouble."

Dr. Kamau is pleased to have Annie Paul's company. She is a delightful woman and funny and has the most beautiful hands he has ever seen. He watches her face as she stares into her fire. Annie Paul broods. Sits so still she could be a dead woman. Doesn't blink. And then she looks right into a person - slowly - so as to get all there is - and swallows hard before she speaks.

~

"So," says Ruth to Sarah, "you missed a fine reunion at Mrs. Miflin's house the other night. Maggie and her father are back from their wanderings and Joe Snake's folks arrived out of the blue and we all ended up drinking too much and trying to figure out how to spring Ginny Mustard from her lonely prison cell. A good time all around. The only thing lacking was a mournful violin. I can't see how anything can be done but, on the up side, Joe Snake told me this morning that they've seen fit to transfer her to a hospital so at least she'll be getting proper care for awhile. It would be great if they can manage to keep her there."

"Good. I wouldn't mind going over to see her if that's allowed. I wonder why you still refer to that place as Mrs. Miflin's house. She hasn't lived in it for ages now."

"Might be the fact that she camps out there every day all day sun-up to sundown. You should see her Sarah. Little tub, she is, squatting on the front porch, sweating in her old winter coat with a bag of money tucked under her arm and a few sandwiches in her pocket." And Ruth laughs.

"Poor thing."

"Poor thing, my ass. The woman is trouble and I wouldn't put it past her to do something dangerous one of these days if she doesn't soon get her own way. She's a few bricks short of a load and that's the truth. Joanie and her folks have no idea what she's made of. They step around her and tolerate her foolishness as though she's just a bit of local colour and nothing more to it than that. Quaint is probably the word they use when they see her there. They'll have her in for a cup of tea one of these days and that will be the end of life as they know it."

"What do you mean? Do you really think she's that much of a problem?"

"Damn straight, she is. You have no idea how she can worm her way into every situation and work it to her advantage. She has a knack for finding your weak spots and whipping them into festering wounds. The only mistake she ever made was bringing Judy into the house. That girl has a built-in bullshit sensor."

"Speaking of bullshit. When are you going to tell me about Peter's father? I don't think I can nag much more. It really is wearing on a person, you know."

"There's an understatement! I don't even answer my phone half the time just in case it's you. And the other day? When you came over? I was in. Saw you through the window and hid. Why in God's name is it so important to you anyway?"

"So many reasons. If we can find him then the children would have another grandparent."

"Come on, Sarah, you can do better than that."

"I think Peter should know who his father is."

"He knows Matthew's his father. I don't see any reason to believe he's not content with that situation."

"What if someone needs a kidney one of these days and the only match is Peter's biological father? What about that for a reason? And what if there are some hereditary diseases or disor ders that I should be on the look out for? Like diabetes or such?"

"Now you're getting a little carried away, Sarah. Come on, girl, get your brain in gear. You've got to get out of the house more. This kind of obsession isn't healthy. There are tons of people in the world who haven't a clue where they came from and they get over it. Eventually. Actually I never thought of it before. Maybe they don't."

"Don't you think that your future husband should know you have a son?"

"Perhaps. But then he'd want to know everything else I've ever done and once we open that can of worms we'll never get any sleep. Besides, what does that have to do with telling you who Peter's father is?"

"Oh hell. Nothing. I'm just curious. For some reason I'm stuck on it. I think about it all the time. I've taken to looking at the kids differently. And Peter. I keep watching for things about them that don't remind me of anyone I know. And there are things. All sorts of mannerisms that I can't pin down."

"Good Lord, Sarah! It's not like they come out of a cereal box with a nice neat list of ingredients. You're really losing it, darling. Maybe you should get some help for this."

"Now you're mocking me. Be fair, Ruth. Why can't you just tell me?"

"Don't you have better things to do? Where are the kids? I only came over here to take Eleanor to Dorrie's for a new Barbie dress. I promised I would last time I saw her and I don't get another day off until next Saturday. Let's just leave this be, Sarah. It can't do anyone any good and it could very well fuck things up."

"Eleanor is at a birthday party and Joseph went with Peter to get the groceries. They won't be home for ages."

"Oh for God's sake! Get me something to drink and I'll put you out of your misery but don't ask me anything else ever again as long as you live, okay? And this doesn't mean you can tell anyone else, Missy, don't think that it does. I don't want to be screwing up Peter's life with unnecessary crap. He's a happy man. Content. Let's leave it that way."

"All right!" says Sarah tearing back from the kitchen with a couple of beers. "Here. Do you want a glass?"

"No. Why do I have the feeling I'll regret this?" And she takes a long drink, finishing half the bottle before looking at Sarah again. "Bring me another one. Bring a few. If I know you at all this will take some time."

~

Bill was tall and good-looking and if it weren't for the moustache and the fact that he screwed one of Ruth's co-worker and was a little shell-shocked who knows, they might have made something of the affair. It happened in Central where there were still a few American servicemen stationed back then and little else to choose from. Ruth was not one to be overlooked and Bill made a beeline for her section of the bar the first time he laid eyes on her. Stared at her the whole night while she busied herself sling-ing booze and snacks, snapping at customers, cleaning up the mess when they spilled beer and throwing them out when they pissed her off. He ignored the strippers in their cheap sequin which irritated Ruth no end because those girls were her friend in some odd sense of the word and worked friggin' hard for the lousy few dollars they made on the floor, but he was taller than most and a better tipper too and she thought to herself, I would-n't throw him out of bed for eating crackers.

During a break, while she was having a beer with Candy Apple, the stripper with the biggest tits in creation and the back-ache to go with them, Bill strolled up to the bar and asked what time her shift was over and would she like to go out for a coffee later on, in a Texas drawl to melt your heart. But this is Ruth's heart we're talking about here and she said, "Sure Candy Apple is done for the night. Why don't you two take off now. Have a ball. I'll talk to you tomorrow, Apple girl." And the Apple girl, who knew exactly what Ruth was up to because guys like this one never gave her the time of day, hooked her arm through Bill's and led him to the door, past his fellow soldiers who clapped and whistled until his gorgeous face turned red and Candy Apple almost felt sorry for him.

Anyone less a gentleman would have dumped the pretty stripper in a flash but Bill actually took her out for coffee and talked to her for an hour and then another and asked questions as though he was interested in what she had to say. And she ended up telling him her greatest secret which was saving money so she could have her boobs lopped off to a normal size and be taken seriously enough to get into med school because it was hard enough getting the first degree being deformed and just once she'd like someone to look into her face.

Then she confessed that Ruth had done a very bitchy thing pretending that he had invited the Apple girl instead of herself when she knew better. Bill laughed and they talked for another hour even though he knew the difference now and the Apple girl couldn't help it, she had to plot with the fellow and figure out a way to get Ruth interested.

It wasn't so difficult. After they left the bar Ruth had become even nastier than usual and felt the fool for having sent Bill away. Every man in the place just got uglier and uglier as she worked and he became an Adonis so when he showed up the next night she was only too happy to sail off with him into the dark.

For a few months all went as well as could be expected. They spent most of their time screwing their brains out and the rest of it thinking of screwing their brains out. She wouldn't sleep in his bed and the odd time she stayed the night she slept on the couch. He had a nasty reaction to movement that gave her the creeps. Probably too much Vietnam. Probably never got over it Any sound or stirring at all and he was awake. Swinging. The firs night she got up to pee and disturbed him. Half asleep, he began to yell and punch at the air, landing a good one right on her chin Enough of that crap, thought Ruth, and moved out to the living room.

He was sweet and a charmer and he treated her like a goddess which is probably why, when Ava got into his pants, Ava who worked the early shift and plied him with liquor one afternoon while he was waiting for Ruth, she told him right where to get off I don't deserve this kind of treatment. Who do you think I am I'm better than this, because she actually believed she belonged on that pedestal. He begged and made promises, he loved her afte all, but Ruth wanted nothing to do with anyone who could hur someone as special as he had convinced her she was.

When she found out she was pregnant a week or so late she didn't bother to tell him about it. He was heading back to the States. He wanted her to come with him. He loved her so much and they could have a good life. She looked at his beautiful face and his long strong body and all she could see was Ava under it or over it, and she had never been jealous before and mistook the feeling for hatred and told him to fuck off she never wanted to see him again.

And that might have been that but she couldn't afford an abortion back in the day when a person had to come up with plane fare to New York as well as money for the dirty deed so sh decided to go ahead and have the kid. And somewhere around month five she started talking to it and somewhere around month seven she fell in love with it and when her time was up she knew it was the most important thing in her life and gave him away. Ran as far as she could go from the place and the baby and the memory of his father. And now Sarah you pain in the ass I have to relive the whole works thank you very much.

"Oh Ruth. I am sorry. But I am so happy that you told me. And now we have to find him."

"Find him? Find him? Are you out of your mind? I should have known. What the hell was I thinking? That is the last thing on earth I want to do."

"Well, no. The last thing on earth you want to do is tell me your deep dark secret and you've gone and done that so what's stopping you from finding Bill? Hmmm? Come on Ruth. You know you want to. I saw the look on your face when you were talking about him. I can tell you still have feelings. Strong ones, I might add. It is so obvious I can't believe you haven't gone looking for him by now."

"Well, actually, I did think about him awhile back. Even started a letter but I never finished it and probably wouldn't have mailed it if I had since I don't even know where he is. Shut up Sarah! I have a good man in Patrick. We're going to be married. Why the hell am I even talking to you? Tell Eleanor I came by. No don't. Oh shit! What the hell was I thinking?"

Ruth storms away, forgetting her umbrella and she's drenched to the bone in two minutes which doesn't help at all. When Patrick comes to take her out to dinner she's still soggy and tells him to go by himself - she's in no mood for company.

~

Down the hall from the maternity ward where Ginny Mustard rests is a little room with nothing more than a bed and a chair that no one ever sits in. On the bed is a broken boy, asleep for almost a year now. Most of the people who knew him have forgotten he ever existed. And perhaps he never did. His mother carries on. Goes to work and looks after her home and what remains of her family. When her son was found, battered beyond recognition behind the school on Bishop's Road, when she was told he might never really live again, her husband decided to get out and took off for Australia. She hasn't heard from him since. And then her oldest daughter went to university in Toronto leaving just her and the two little ones. It wasn't easy getting a babysitter and often one of them needed help with homework or a drive to soccer practice same time as visiting hours, so after a few months she got on with her life and moved to a small apartment with just enough room for three, and pretended she never had a son at all. She finds it easier this way than sitting in that chair and watching his face for a sign that he is still in there somewhere.

She gave his clothes and games away, his hockey stick, his school yearbook, and threw out all but one picture which she keeps in an envelope under a stack of old magazines in a trunk. And though times have changed when it comes to this sort of pain, she hasn't, and the boy's little sisters are forbidden to mention his name and only talk of him in whispers when their mother is asleep. And they dress his old teddy bear, rescued from the garbage, in doll clothes, and tuck it away at the back of their closet.

The boy's body has healed nicely. It is young and healthy, after all. When there are no other demands on the physiotherapy department someone manages to move his legs a little. His arms. So that the muscles don't atrophy. On the off chance that he might choose to move them of his own accord some day. And there is always fluid of sorts going in to and coming out of his body. Someone bathes him a couple of times a week. But that's about it. For all intents and purposes the boy might never have lived.

If Judy hadn't decided to go see Ginny Mustard at the same time Patrick had chosen to visit, that boy might still be alone in the little room. When Judy hears the familiar voice she takes off and in no time is at the boy's door. When she runs out of hall and the only escape seems to be back past Ginny Mustard's room she steps inside. Stares at the curled thin body on the narrow bed.

"Frank? Frankie? Is that you? Holy shit, Frankie! I was looking for you ages ago. I was feeling pretty bad about what happened. I went to ask your mother where you were but she moved or something. Does Jimmy know you're here? I bet he doesn't or he'd have you killed for sure by now. He said that if you ever came out of it he'd be up shit creek. I was half tempted to tell on him but I figured you went away and everything was fine. Besides, I don't know who'd believe me anyway, being as I'm not what you'd call the most trustworthy person in town. Are you okay Frankie? You got awful thin, boy. What's all this shit they got you hooked up to. Are you okay? Wake up, Frankie, for fuck sake."

Judy steps closer to look into his face and sees that nobody's home in there. She pulls the little chair close and sits. Stares. A nurse comes in to change one of the bags that feed the boy and asks if she's Frank's friend.

"No. I don't think so. No. But I knew him once. Is he okay?"

"Not by a long shot. He was in a coma when I started working here and he'll probably be in the same state when I retire. Do you know you're the first person I've ever seen in this room besides staff? It's unbelievable how people can just dump each other like that. I often say to the other nurses that if anyone gave a damn about him he might have a chance. Do you think you'll come back? You can, you know. In fact, it doesn't even have to be at regular visiting hours. If you want to just come and talk to him. Or read. Hell, sing him a song. Anything would be better than what's he's got going on now."

"But he wouldn't be able to hear me, would he?"

"You know, you never can tell with situations like this one. I've heard tell of folks coming out of comas and saying they heard every word that people around them said. That's why you're supposed to be a bit upbeat and positive when you talk to them. Though in Frank's case I don't know that it matters. He's been out of it so long I'm surprised they haven't pulled the plug on him by now."

"Shit, lady. You better hope he can't hear you the way you're talking. Poor fucker. Just wait until I get my hands on that bastard, Jimmy."

"Who's Jimmy?"

"No one you'd know. Never mind. If I was to read him a book, what kind should it be?"

"Doesn't matter. Read him the newspaper if you want."

"Well that ought to cheer him right up. I'll ask Ruth. She knows about books. Are you sure I can come back whenever I want?"

"I'll let the desk know that you'll be in. Come down so they can have a look at you and they'll know you when you come around."

"Well, okay. But first I have to go see Ginny Mustard over in the pregnant section. Can you check her room to make sure no one else is there? I really want to see her alone. She's the reason I came here in the first place. Will you do that for me?"

~

"Joanie, sweetheart, don't you think it's time to do a little clothes shopping?" Caroline has been wondering if her daughter will come up with the idea on her own but it's not looking likely. She's still wearing the same old rags that John dressed her in. Still washing her underpants every night before bed. "Let's go to Ayres. I walked by there yesterday and they have some lovely things in the windows. Your father can stay with the children and we can have a girls' day out. You haven't been away from the house since John left, you know, except for that duck pond. I think it's time. What say you, darling?"

"Well for one thing, I have no money. Everything is in John's name. There's only ever enough in my account to pay for groceries. John deposits it on Friday so I can stock the pantry."

"Christ! Well, in all the goings on around here we haven't thought of that at all. An important detail that's been overlooked. Perhaps we should be calling a divorce lawyer now. We can go shopping tomorrow. I don't suppose you have anyone in mind?"

"Divorce? Do you really think it has to come to that? Yesterday Michael asked when his daddy will be coming home. I told him soon. If we could see a counselor maybe we can work this out. Maybe John will be a little more the man I married."

"He is the man you married. He has never been anyone other. You had blinders on. I don't know why. Maybe he's the greatest lover in the world. Maybe you're a masochist. The man is an ass, Joanie. Always was. Always will be. He'll need more than counseling to change that. A lobotomy perhaps. It's time to wake up, Joanie. Did you ask Michael why he wants to know when his daddy is coming home? Did it occur to you that he is terrified by the thought of John's return? I do know one thing, sweatheart. You are not the person you were when you married him. I'd stake my life on that one. You were a vibrant, special person. Quiet and soft - spoken but your body used to sing when you walked. Now you creep around like an apology. I know you don't want to hear this but I have to say it. And there was a time when you would have said the same to any woman in your position. Let go of whatever fantasy you carry in your precious head about this marriage working out. It will never happen. I've known it from day one."

"Well with that kind of negativity going on there's no wonder it couldn't work. You're a powerful woman, Mom. Maybe you're the reason we didn't make it. Did you ever think of that? Did you ever think that those horrid, nasty, negative vibes might have been too much?"

"You're clutching at straws, Joanie. You know damn well that's bullshit."

Joanie cries hard. Wipes her eyes with the sleeve of her ugly shirt. She knows there's no truth in what she says. Love would have conquered any negativity from outside. But there was no love on John's part. There was nothing but John the taker and Joanie the prize. The pretty woman, educated, refined, well-heeled as it were, with old money to take the sting out of John's nouveau riche plans. Well. If he could see me now. Wiping my nose in the front of my crappy old shirt.

"Okay," she says. "Let's go shopping. But it will be on your tab. I'm a little strapped right now."

~

Finding poor Frankie may be the answer to at least one of Judy's problems. She has been hiding out in the strangest places ever since she came back and is tired of the rambling. Calling the cop shop from various phone booths and asking for Patrick. Hanging up when he answers and going to Ginny Mustard's house for a bite to eat. Taking cover again if he isn't in. It's been a long time since Judy has had to run and being somewhat settled for awhile got into her bones. It's that much harder now to worry about keeping out of sight since she got used to walking free in the world. It's not easy being broke again either but she lost her bank card and is too afraid of running into a cop to go get a new one. Other than the cash in her pocket she's pretty much penniless.

If she knew that Patrick isn't actively looking, that in fact he's so busy tracking the latest drug ring in town he doesn't give her much thought, assuming the others are looking out for her, that he has better things to do at the moment, that her probation officer never even noticed she left town in the first place, Judy might relax. But she hasn't a clue and is feeling somewhat desperate.

So she packs herself a little bag of necessities, jeans, shirts, make-up, jewelry box and borrows a few books - for a friend - from Joe Snake. Nosy old Ruth had to ask who are they for, how can I suggest reading material if I don't know who wants it, and Joe Snake just said help yourself so she chose *No Exit* by someone named Sartre because it seems appropriate on so many levels. And *East of Eden* because she remembers that *The Red Pony* was the only thing she liked about grade eight and the same fellow wrote this one. *Care of the Soul* which sounds like a good thing to read to someone half dead. *A Book of Bees* because she's missing Eve.

She comes calling early and tells the nurse at reception that she will stay as long as poor Frankie is in his coma and the nurse, who has heard that one before and knows it's lies, all lies, is up to her ears in paperwork and says, "Sure. Whatever," and doesn't even look up at the girl with the hunted look on her face.

If Nurse Edna had known there is a Frankie way down the other end of the hall you can bet she'd have been there by now. But as it is she is so taken up with the nervous new moms who aren't quite sure what they've gotten themselves into and those others, not as many thanks be to God, out of their minds with grief, whose little ones didn't make it or who might have been better off if they hadn't with their bodies all wrong and their small brains not wired properly, that she rarely makes it off her own ward. Edna is nothing, though, if not observant so it's only a matter of days before she begins to wonder about that tall girl she sees walking by the nursery every few hours, day and night, coming back again with a meal or a can of pop and heading down the long hall. And when she decides to follow her and sees the poor boy and meets the girl come to sit with him until he wakes, she digs out a roll-away cot so Judy doesn't have to sleep on the floor and they both work their arms off getting the windows unstuck so there'll be some fresh air to breathe.

There's no way Judy would be allowed to do what she's doing if anyone who cared found out. Edna doesn't mind that. If Judy wants to hang around with a boy no one else seems to give a damn about, fine, and there's no reason she shouldn't be comfortable while she's at it. This room is as close as a nightmare. Nothing wrong with cracking a window and cheering things up a bit. Edna got her daffodils from the Cancer Society fundraiser yesterday and she'll bring them in as soon as she gets a chance, along with a little table to set them on. She gives Judy a quick hug before she leaves with a promise to be back soon.

~

"Seems to me," says Annie Paul, "you'd have a little more of a rush on to see your daughter than this. What is your problem, anyway? I've told you she's in trouble. That she's pregnant. And here you are friggin' around in this hole of a place. Believe you me it'll still be here in a month. No panic to check it out today. I'm starting to think you're afraid to find her. Either that or you really don't give a sweet damn. What's going on?"

Dr. Kamau has taken yet another jaunt off the beaten track. To yet another half dead end fishing village. Bunch of ne'er-do-wells hanging around a dart board sucking back beer. One general store and a chicken take-out. A hundred or so residents of dubious mentality languishing in, as one beloved son of the nation declared, *a gene pool the size of a teacup*.

"What the hell are we doing here? If you aren't interested I'll get going myself. We're that close to the city I can almost hear the poor thing. Lend me fifty dollars and I'll find a taxi or a bus or whatever they use around here to get from A to B. Though I'm not sure any of this crowd has ventured that far in a while."

But the doctor can't hear her and so she trots back to his car and flinging caution and his wallet to the wind - after helping herself to enough cash to fill up at the next gas station - she's gone in a spray of dust and crushed stone. One of the locals says,

"Buddy, your missus there just took off with your car. You two have a fight or what?" and Dr. Kamau turns slowly to see the rear end of his black Mercedes for the last time.

The first few days with the fine anthropologist was a good time. After that Annie Paul became dreadfully bogged down in his all-consuming lectures. Because if he isn't listening he has to teach which would be just fine if she was half interested in what he had to say but when he began repeating himself she drifted. And once Annie Paul drifts there's no returning. If he didn't look so good she wouldn't have lasted this long.

"Oh well. He'll be fine where he is. I'll check on the way home and if he's still there I'll give him back his car. I must be wanting to get laid awful bad to put up with that foolishness. Onward through the fog."

Since the journey began Annie Paul has been visited in her head on more than one occasion by an odd old woman in a red sweater who wants her to get a move on. Something to do with the doctor's daughter and there's a hospital involved so that's where she's heading as fast as she dares what with no driver's license and a stolen car.

~

Nurse Edna is in a bit of a quandary. It has something to do with Virginia Benoit's baby. Lately she's taken to dreaming.

Mostly when she's asleep but now and then when she's on her feet and moving about. Since she has no recollection of ever having dreamed before it is a bother. The dreams are of a baby and sometimes an old woman and sometimes the baby is the old woman and sometimes the old woman is the baby and last night she woke to find the old woman sitting on her side of the bed looking at her. Didn't say a word. And she nudged her husband and said, "There's an old woman in the bedroom." And he, not the most pleasant person on earth when you wake him suddenly, said, "What do you want me to do about it, you're the one with the working legs?" and went right back to sleep. Edna stared at the woman for a few seconds but she didn't seem to want anything so she went back to sleep as well. And then there was that baby again for the rest of the night and the baby was shrinking and then the old woman was there again and she shrinking too until there was nothing left of either but a little black space in Edna's sleep.

This morning she is worried. So much so that she doesn't even ask Dr. Boland how his date went with the new teacher on the sick kids' ward. Doesn't speak, in fact, until she goes to Ginny Mustard's room to see how she's doing. The mother-to-be is beaming but back of her smile is a small case of nerves. She wants to stay here in this room. Even cuffed to a bed she is happier than she ever could be in prison. Her free hand is resting on her belly and she's been humming sunny tunes to Sweet Polly for an hour. When she sees Nurse Edna's face she stops and stares.

"I'm about to do something I have never done in my life that I can recall," says Edna. "I am going to tell a lie. That sounds like I might be perfect I know, but don't think for a minute that I am. I just never told an untruth and I was thinking I might stay that way to my grave. I did a lot of things that are bad. Not as bad as you did, killing a man, but who's to say really. I guess our maker gets to cast the deciding vote on that one. I mind once when I was little how I locked my brother in an old truck and forgot about him until he never showed up for dinner and everybody went looking. By the time I remembered, he was just about dead for want of air and I got in more old trouble. And once me and my friend Jessie were in a mood because I wasn't allowed to go to the time at the church hall. To this day I can't think why I had to stay home but me and Jessie went into my mother's room and cut all the pretty tassels off her curtains and bedspread. They matched you know, and she was so proud to have such nice things for once but we hacked them off anyway because she wouldn't let me go out.

And now I've got to tell a lie for you, Mrs. Virginia Benoit, so that baby can have a fighting chance. I know damn well if I say everything is fine they'll ship you on over to that place again and I also know if they do, you'll get so sad your little baby won't make it. But they are not going to believe that for a minute so I'm going to have to lie and tell them you're still doing poorly and you have to stay here until your time. If any of the others come to check on you it would be best if you could stop looking so content and well fed. Can you do that? Can you pretend for a while that you're still feeling bad? There's always someone screaming for a bed around here. They don't want to be footing the bill for a healthy person when there's so many lined up for space. And God knows you're healthy. You were just having a hard time of it in that jail and who can blame you. I got to tell you, Virginia, I've been dreaming about that baby for nights now. Days too, truth be told. At least I think it's that baby. There's an old woman too but I don't have a clue who she might be."

Nurse Edna needn't worry further about breaking commandments. Annie Paul has just now pulled into the hospital parking lot - staff only - and is on her way to the rescue. Eve is tired, if the spirit can be tired, of arranging the pieces and should stop fretting as well. Annie Paul checks out every ward in the place without interruption. A year or so ago someone shot a movie about the last of the Beothuks and people became accustomed to seeing extras wandering around town in full dress between takes. Perhaps they are at it again and no one pays her any mind except to comment among themselves that it looks like they've finally got the costume design figured out, thank God. When she remembers that the woman she seeks is pregnant she heads for the maternity ward but not before everyone who could see got a good look at her.

At the front desk she asks the whereabouts of a young woman who might be black or brown or at the very least coffee-coloured but probably not as white as themselves. Someone points her in the direction of Ginny Mustard's room and it's a good thing the door has a window because now Annie Paul is inclined to rush and if Nurse Edna hadn't seen her coming she'd have suffered one terrible whack to the head when Annie Paul came barelling through.

"Another visitor," says Nurse Edna. "I think it best that you not stay too long, dear. The young mother here has had quite a week of callers and needs some rest." Trying the edges of her lie to see if it will fit. See if she can follow through.

~

Joanie has seen John. He watched the house until her parents went out, and came knocking. Poor Joanie. She has not had enough time and freedom to strengthen her resolve and it only takes a few words from her husband to convince her that she's made a dreadful mistake. That no one could ever love her as much as he does. That her children will grow up delinquent without their dad around. That no one else will ever want her the way he wants her. That she cannot possibly make it on her own. No matter that she is feeling rather pretty today in a soft purple blouse and new jeans. That her underpants are silk and risqué and her hair shiny clean and she found just the right lipstick. Watch her crumble and join the sisterhood of floppy women with jelly where the backbone was. If her parents were to return from their walk right now they would find her the same Joanie she has been since she said I do.

She never should have opened the door, looked into his face, listened to his smooth talk. But she did. And here she is in her bedroom with her husband and if she's not careful she'll be making another baby and whacking more nails in her coffin. Too late. Too late. And now she's packing her new clothes and her children's clothes and some toys and going to the school to bring them home early today because she has a surprise for them and now they are heading for the airport in a taxi to go to their new home away from this place and its sad memories.

"Everything will be different, now," says John. "Yes," says Joanie and she stares straight ahead through the windshield but she really can't see anything.

When her parents arrive at Mrs. Miflin's house they are met by a security guard who tells them they are trespassing and have to get their things and leave because the house has been sold and they are no longer welcome. Clever John had the foresight to take Mrs. Miflin's offer to buy and gave her back the keys which she can use to her heart's content as soon as the rest of his belongings have been crated and sent to where he is going. Ask until they're blue in the face, Joanie's mom and dad will never get that address from the movers.

Mrs. Miflin is trying to locate her own furniture and round up a few tenants. She has lit all the candles in front of the Holy Blessed Virgin at the church as a thank-you for the miracle though she only put money in the collection box when Father Delaney came out of the confessional and looked at her funny.

~

Judy was a full six pages into *No Exit* before she realized the characters were all dead in a really nasty hell and not going to cheer anyone up, least of all a boy in a coma, so she wasn't long shoving the book into her backpack and starting another. She won't return it to Joe Snake yet though, because she really does want to find out what happens. How the fools got themselves into such a mess in the first place. Maybe she can figure out what not to do so she won't end up there herself.

She has pulled her cot close to Frankie's bed, the better to read to him quietly, and sometimes at night she holds his hand, cold as it is, almost stiff, and the warmth from her strong body lights a small spark in his. Now and then she cries a little for him. Cries for herself. Cries for total strangers who seem to hurt. For the sad old goats in their wheelchairs sitting alone in the hospital cafeteria when she steps out of the room for a sandwich. The girl with no hair, nothing but skin and bones and freckles standing out hard on her thin face walking ever so slowly with her worn out mother. She can't help it really. Anyone who finds herself in such stillness for any length of time would probably do the same. Once when she was crying the sadness was so unbearable that she crawled into Frankie's bed and snuggled like a spoon into his back and got tears all over his neck. Warm salty tears all over his neck and she didn't want to move away so she licked them off and her salt mixed with his tasted odd on her tongue. Not bad. Just odd.

Sometimes she talks to him about things that come to her mind. About Eve and Ruth and the others and what a good time they had because she can't remember it being any other way now. She talks about her mom and dad as though they were the people she needed them to be. Talks about watching her dad shave before going to work as if he did that every day and not just now and then when someone was fool enough to hire him for a week. Talks about the times her mom made cookies and how delicious they were and she can almost taste them even though it only happened once and they were store bought and all her mom did was put some ready made icing on them. She's making up stories but it's okay. Sometimes you have to do that to get yourself out of bed in the morning. To be able to see the flowers bloom and the leaves fall. Smile. Say hello. And the only one who hears is Frankie if he's listening so it's not really telling lies now, is it?

~

Ruth's life has taken a turn for the worse since she gave in to Sarah and told one of her secrets. You can be sure that will never happen again. Sarah has been calling and coming by at all hours, even bugging Ruth at work when she's busy but there's no way Ruth will speak another word to the woman until she bloody well feels like it and it probably won't be tomorrow. She can't remember if she told Sarah Bill's surname. Is worried she did because it shouldn't be too difficult for that bloodhound to track him down. There are only so many American soldiers who might have been hanging out in this part of the world back in '72 and she can't remember if she told Sarah where he was from. Did she? Damn it all to hell!

Patrick is as sweet as ever he was with no idea the turmoil consuming Ruth right now. Their sex life is all but non-existent. "It's menopause," says Ruth. "I haven't had a period for two months and my estrogen production is shot so I don't feel like doing it. I don't know if I ever will again. Do you still want to marry me?"

Of course he does. There's more to life than sex but he buys a couple of books on the subject of the change. Talks to his sisters to see if their fun days are indeed over. Most likely they aren't but it would help if he could get her to eat a little tofu now and then so he takes her to Chinese restaurants often in hope that she will but she says it tastes like shit and forget it. When he suggests progesterone cream or at least evening primrose oil, she suggests he take a flying leap.

Ruth is telling lies. Fact is she's as horny as she's ever been, maybe more so, but the last time they were going at it she couldn't stop thinking about Bill and is afraid it will happen again and she just can't do that to someone as nice as Patrick. Well actually she could, but she's not about to.

Sarah is hell bent and determined to lay claim to Peter's father. She has been checking those Web sites aimed at helping people find their old classmates and neighbours and loves but isn't getting very far though she did find her best friend from college. Not a big deal since she has been in touch with her for years anyway. Still it was fun to see her name in cyberspace. Ruth was wise not to tell Sarah Bill's last name or where he came from and there have been thousands of Bills, Wills, and Williams in uniform at any given time. Even if someone in Washington felt like helping it still might take forever to pinpoint the one Ruth had been messing around with.

~

"I think I know you," says Annie Paul to Ginny Mustard. "I'm pretty sure I just spent the last few days with your father. What's the problem anyway? Are you sick? I came as quick as I could. Your old man can be damned annoying. Of course you wouldn't know that, would you, since you've never met. I left him in some hole in the ground about an hour out of town. God knows where he is at this point."

"Who are you?" This from Nurse Edna. "Are you a friend of Virginia's?"

"And that I am. I have to get her out of here now. I can't say why but that's what my gut is telling me to do and I find if I go along with it I manage to do right. What have you got her cuffed to the bed for?"

"She's a prisoner. Just here on loan while she gets better and then she has to go back."

"Well I'm feeling that she's not going to get better unless she comes with me. Do you have a key for those things?"

"Yes, but I can't unlock her. I'll never hear the end of it if I do that. I'll be fired for sure."

"Well, how about I just whack you over the head with something and take it? They can hardly fault you for that, can they? I'm serious, lady. I have to take her away with me now."

"Why don't we ask Virginia what she thinks of all this before we get carried away. As far as I'm concerned she shouldn't be going back to the jail but there's not enough wrong with her to keep her in this place. What do you think Virginia? Do you want to go with this Indian woman?"

"Yes. She knows my father," says Ginny Mustard. "I want to go with her."

"Well, all right. I was planning to tell a pack of lies anyway. Let me think how we can get around this situation. I spend a lot of time with babies that no one wants. Here's one on the way already loved to bits and won't make it if her mother ends up back in jail. Where are you going to take her anyway? No. Don't tell me. I have a pretty good feeling about you. You don't look the dangerous type even if you did say you'd whack me over the head. Let's just sit quiet a minute while I work this out."

And a minute is all it takes for Nurse Edna to make her plan. "Okay. Here's what I'm going to do. I will let the doctors know that I think she is in good enough shape to be heading back to jail now. One of them will come in to check and see that I'm right. Once I have everything written up all neat and tidy I'll pretend to call the jail and tell them to come and get her. I'm on the desk for a few hours this afternoon and no one will know what's going on. I'll probably get my walking papers over this but I don't think I care. That baby is not going to make it if Virginia has to go back. But you have to promise to look after her. When the baby comes let me know. If I'm still here we can make a plan to get Virginia put back to do her time. If I'm gone then no one will ever know where she is anyway so it'll be all right either way. I'll time it so the doctor doesn't release her until I'm on the desk and you can sneak out this evening. God, I hope this works."

Nurse Edna tells Annie Paul to make herself scarce. "Get out of here until around six o'clock. Do you have anything else to wear besides movie clothes? You might have a better chance not being noticed if you didn't have feathers hanging from your ear, you know."

As she accompanies Doctor Hopkirk for Virginia's examination, Nurse Edna is all stiff and starched and professional and the doctor asks if she is feeling all right herself. It's not like Edna to be quiet and calm like this. When she realizes she's over-doing it, Nurse Edna relaxes and even puts up a small argument against the move to prison. For future reference. Should she ever need an alibi. Back at the desk she fakes a call telling the warden that her prisoner is ready to be picked up. She goes to Ginny Mustard's room and takes the handcuffs off. With a quick hug and kisses on both cheeks she hands the prisoner over to Annie Paul.

"Put all her jail things in this bag and take it with you." Another hug and she's gone.

"Right. I don't have a clue how we'll get away with this," says Annie Paul. "We're not the most inconspicuous pair to walk these halls, I'd put money on that. Where are your clothes?"

"In the little closet there."

Annie Paul stuffs pants and shirt - ugly as sin with numbers on the pocket - and handcuffs into the bag. "Now listen to me. We have to be cool. We're going to walk - can you walk? - not run - no rushing - out the door and down the hall and with any luck I'll remember which way to turn after that. If you can manage to look as though this is all fine and legal and we have every right in the world to be doing it, we should be okay. I have found in my sweet short life that if you appear to know what you are doing, people assume you actually do and pretty much leave you be. Are you ready? Let's go, girl and for God's sake don't look guilty or we're screwed."

Ginny Mustard couldn't look guilty if you paid her. Slowly, nonchalantly, even stopping to look through the nursery windows at the brand new babies for a minute, she and her new friend make their way out of the hospital and toward the stolen car just as security is slapping a ticket on the windshield. Annie Paul pulls Ginny Mustard behind a shelter where a dozen nurses are having a smoke break and they wait a few minutes while the fellow makes his way through the staff parking lot.

"This thing is like driving on a cloud," says Annie Paul as she helps Ginny Mustard fasten the seat belt over her belly. "I'm half hoping we don't find your father so I can keep it, though they say parts cost an arm and a leg. You don't talk much do you? So why is it that you never met your dad before? Geez, I hope I got the right woman. There could be half a dozen Virginias in that place. Probably none looking like you, though. Wouldn't that be a laugh! I don't usually get things wrong but it did happen once - my gut messed up and I went over to the grocery store because I knew the owner was going to have a heart attack with no one else in the place. Turned out it wasn't him at all, but old Doris Tom, and it wasn't even a heart attack but her falling off the ladder in her basement. She only broke her arm. Some say I can't see at all but I'm pretty sure I can. Not that I want to but certain things you're just stuck with, like it or lump it. I expect it's a good thing I came to get you when I did. Have you ever lived in a teepee?"

Of course she hasn't. How many of us have, really, in this time and place? Annie Paul talks most of the way and the lilt of her voice reminds Ginny Mustard of lullabies on the CDs she bought when she lived at Mrs. Miflin's house. She listens as best she can, looking out the window at the wonderful world she has never seen before, never knew existed, miles and miles of trees and rivers, lakes. When darkness comes she naps. Annie Paul can't remember where the turnoff is to the last place she saw Dr. Kamau so she keeps driving.

At confession early next morning, Nurse Edna tells the priest she told a lie - they never need details so it was okay. She does the Stations of the Cross and a couple of Rosaries and conveniently forgets her indiscretion until Joe Snake comes looking for his wife. She tells the tale. The truth. And while she doesn't know where Virginia is, at least she's not in that dreadful jail which is some comfort to Joe Snake and he goes back to his garden to think.

~

Annie Paul's home is like nothing Ginny Mustard has ever seen and she loves it. The teepee sits on a large lot of land with the house that her brother gave her when he left to work in the Territories. Annie Paul never goes inside except to use the bathroom or do laundry and once to sleep when they had the worst weather on record and she had to dig her way out of her own home through twelve-foot drifts. "I'm cool," she says. "But I'm damned if I'll die of it." She buried a very long extension cord from the house to the teepee so she can listen to the CDs her brother left - everything Tom Waits ever recorded and Chopin's greatest hits. The only bill she pays regularly is the electric, for the music and warmth when she needs it.

She keeps toasty during the winter with two old duvets that she covered with rabbit skins. She wanted polar bear or wolf to wrap up in but can't bring herself to kill anything she wouldn't want to eat even if she could find it. The wolves died out years ago - the only one left is stuffed in a museum in the city - and no one's ever heard tell of polar bears in these parts. In the summer she sleeps outside unless it rains. She brings an old wooden lawn chair from the basement of her brother's house for her pregnant guest and sets it outside the teepee. "You don't want to be sitting on the damp ground in your condition." She sets up a camp cot. "That's probably more comfortable than hauling yourself up off the floor in the morning."

Annie Paul tells anyone who wants to know that Virginia is a friend who's come to stay until her baby is born. She borrows maternity clothes from Peggy who recently had her fourth youngster and sent her husband off to be fixed or he's never coming near her again and that's the truth, damn it.

Ginny Mustard learns how to start a good fire - you need blasty boughs - and weed the gardens - Annie Paul's and her mother-in-law's, though she has no idea there's any relationship between herself and the woman whose vegetables she tends since the latter's name has never come up. If she were to go into Sadie's living room she would see pictures of Joe Snake on the mantle and put it all together but she has no reason to do that. She misses her husband. Wonders if she can tell him where she is, but never aloud, so Annie Paul has no idea what's on her mind.

Annie Paul teaches her to fish trout in the lake - the wonderful lake - a minute down the path from home. How to gut and clean and cook them to perfection and Ginny Mustard can't get enough of the taste. And the stars - amazing stars - ablaze in the black sky so that she sleeps outside as well. She has never seen such a sight, away from the city lights where they are dim at best. When the sun goes down and the mosquitos come out, so do the little brown bats and if you sit as still as a tree they will come close enough to grab - if you want to do such a terrible thing - as they snatch their dinner from where it swarms your head. Such peace Ginny Mustard has never known and she grows soft from the joy of it overnight, her body rounding where before it had been sharp points and straight lines.

~

Joanie's parents are going home. They can't find out where their daughter is and when they reported her disappearance to the authorities, were told there's nothing can be done. As far as the police are concerned the woman left town with her husband willingly and until they have evidence to the contrary it's none of their business. They won't question the moving company regarding Joanie's whereabouts. They won't ask cops in the rest of the country to keep an eye out for her. They won't find out where John relocated his company. Until Joanie shows up dead one of these days - which she surely will since nothing good can come of the situation and eventually keeping her under lock and key won't be enough for John and he'll lose it altogether - no one cares, except for her mom and dad and they are on their own with their grief.

Patrick is no help either, for all the pleading Ruth has done on Joanie's behalf, and she is having second thoughts about marrying him. She knows that Joanie is in trouble but has no proof. So what that he kept her in rags? So what that he kept a tight rein on her movements? So what that Ruth knows - truly knows - that one of these days Joanie will breathe her last in agony and terror? No proof. No proof. Until a woman's knowing becomes something to bank on and applaud, proof will have to be measured tangibly in ransom notes and blood on the walls, Joanies of the world be damned.

If Ruth were a younger woman she could give in to Patrick's reasoning but she's old enough now to trust herself and put stock in her magic and she gives back her pretty engagement ring which he figures is just a symptom of menopause and tells her so. Big mistake. He'll be lucky if she ever speaks to him again.

~

Ginny Mustard tells Annie Paul that she can smell salt water. "Of course you can. We're just a spit away from it. Get in the car and I'll take you there." Now Ginny Mustard has lived with the ocean all her life but the part of it she knows is rather dirty and rock-bound and she has never once touched it. The ocean Annie Paul brings her to is wide and wavy with sand running along it for miles. "It's damned cold until August but sometimes I go in now anyway. Take your shoes off and check it out."

And Ginny Mustard does that. Stands for the first time in real water. Until her feet turn blue. She tastes it. "Like tears but not so warm." She sits on the sand and lets it run through her fingers a hundred times before she's ready to leave and doesn't say another word until the next morning.

"When is that baby due, anyway? You're starting to look like you could pop any minute."

"I was pregnant in November. After the wedding."

"So. Let's figure another month or so. We should find you a doctor, I guess. Old Cecil's wife used to deliver babies. Probably still would if we asked her nicely. I daresay it's not the sort of thing you forget how to do. Most women around here go off to the hospital these days but I don't think that's the best place to be yanking a kid into the world. Full of sick people and all. Would you rather have it here or in the hospital? Up to you." Ginny Mustard wants to have her baby in the teepee. "Smart move," says Annie Paul.

~

Joe Snake has confided in Ruth. Has told her what he knows about his wife's whereabouts, which is nothing really. Ruth says, "I can't believe that you haven't figured out how to track down one of your own. There can't be too many places for a native woman to hide around here. Aren't there reserves or something? I know there was a crowd out around Central and some on the French Shore. Have you even checked to see if she's there? God, you men are such friggin' bricks sometimes! Did you find out what she looks like? Whoever took her? Did you ask your parents if they know anyone fits the description? No. I bet you didn't. Just holed up with your misery. Go talk to that nurse again will you, for God's sake. Exhaust the possiblities before you start sitting around feeling sorry for yourself."

Anyone looking for sympathy these days would do better than to ask it of Ruth. She's pissed with the world again and has little time for its whimpering and moaning. "So. I was going to frig around in your garden today but I'm not in the mood any more. Where do I sign up for university courses? Walk over with me, will you? I have a vicious need to learn something interesting. I'll go with you to the hospital and you come with me to the university. It's a gorgeous day. You won't need that sweater. "

~

"I think he moved," says Judy. "I'm sure I saw one of his

yelids twitch a few minutes ago. Come with me." Judy tugs Nurse dna's sleeve and guides her to the little room at the end of the all. But Frankie, if he did move at all, isn't going to do it on command and they both stare at him for a few minutes before Nurse dna is called away.

At the front desk she is met by Joe Snake and Ruth who ant to know more about the mystery woman who stole Ginny lustard away. "I can't tell you much. Other than she was dressed ind of odd, she seemed like an all right person. I figured she ould be trusted, you know, and so did Virginia. She went with her ast enough."

"Well, how old was she? How tall? Did she have long hair r short? And what do you mean dressed kind of odd. What did he have on for God's sake?" Ruth is not very patient at the noment. Humankind is really beginning to annoy her.

"She dressed like those Indians you see in the movies. Natives I think you're supposed to call them now. She's tall, hough not so tall as Virginia, and she looks strong, like she might hop wood for a pastime. She had her hair done in a couple of ong braids and she had slipper things on her feet. Moccasins I uess they were. Her dress was real pretty. Looked like leather vith some little beads sewed on up around the neck. I remember hinking she must be hot wearing it this time of year. She had a nice necklace too and an earring with a long red feather hanging off it. That's all I know so it's no good to be asking me anything lse. I'm after going over it and over it in my head ever since it appened. I think your wife is okay. I'm sure she's in good hands."

"Well there you have it," says Ruth as she and Joe Snake valk along the river to the university in search of Ruth's enrichment. "She's probably right, you know. She doesn't seem the type o go along with something like this if it didn't feel right. And if he prison thinks Ginny Mustard is in the hospital, and the hospital thinks she's in jail, sounds to me like she's a free woman. Shit!

Do you know what will screw this up? Her parole hearing. When is it?"

"Not until December. Long after the baby is born."

"Good enough," says Ruth. "All we have to do is find her and stick her in somewhere before that. No. That's not true. We have to get her back now, before the baby comes. Someone is going to be looking for her the minute her time is up. You're just going to have to convince her to fucking hang on for a couple more months. For God's sake take that look off your face. Moping around is not going to get us anywhere. Us! Who the hell is 'us'? This is your problem, buddy. Not mine. I just told Patrick to go to hell and now I'm getting on with my life. I don't need this kind of crap."

It's a good thing Joe Snake has nothing to say because Ruth's battle with herself continues all the way to the university and for the full length of time she waits in line at the Registrar's office to pay eight dollars for a course calendar. "Eight friggin bucks! I can see where this is heading."

Back at Ginny Mustard's house they tell Sadie Benoit their story. She's upset that she wasn't told earlier but only for a few minutes. Her first questions were what did she look like, how old was she, what was she wearing and Ruth says, "See? See? Women know how to get to the heart of the matter. What is it with you men?" And she's off on another rant. Sadie asks if she's going through the change, dear, and offers to send her all the medicine she needs from her pantry when she gets home. "I grow most of it myself."

When Sadie hears Annie Paul's description she knows exactly where her daughter-in-law is. "There's no one else crazy enough to pull something like that."

"Well? Call her and find out," says Ruth. To which Sadie replies that Annie Paul doesn't have a telephone but she will try to get in touch with a neighbour who can tell them if a stranger i taying in the teepee.

~

The only fellows who venture into Dorrie's shop are gay. 'he only fellows who want to talk to Dorrie about Barbie are gay. nd since she lives upstairs and is usually buried to her ears in ork anyway, the only fellows Dorrie knows are gay. When Phil ame in to buy her wares she naturally assumed that he is gay as ell. But it turns out he was running an errand for his sister who as sick as a dog with the flu and trying to put together a nice irthday for her twin daughters who each wanted Barbie cars and 'hil was dispatched to find them. It didn't take long for Dorrie to ealize that she had an honest to God heterosexual on her hands nd she was quick enough asking him if he wanted to go to a novie to which he replied not tonight because of the birthday nd all, but if she could wait until tomorrow he'd love to.

Before their fifth date they were talking about marriage. fter she got him into bed he wanted to set the date, the sooner ne better, he being just as hungry as Dorrie is for love and regu- r skin contact.

Invitations come in the mail to Maggie and Judy's apart- nent and when Judy's remains unopened for a week, Maggie real- zes the girl hasn't been home all that time and is hunting her own. She has no idea where to look and even thinks of asking 'atrick's help but doesn't, since he seems to be of the impression nat Judy is keeping well away from trouble these days and Maggie oesn't want to put a stick in her spokes if she can avoid it. She sks Joe Snake if he knows anything. And Ruth who tells her to et it to music and leave her alone when Maggie cries that she is ightened for her friend. "She hasn't been home for a week and ou're only now out looking for her? What the hell kind of friend does that?"

"I thought she was just going out early in the mornings or something. Her bed wasn't made so I really thought she was sleeping there. She stays out late sometimes, you know. It was only when she didn't open Dorrie's mail that I thought she might be missing."

"Right," says Ruth. "Like that girl ever got up early when she didn't have to."

If Maggie hadn't taken up with the crowd she met at church that time when her dad wanted her to come along she'd have been concerned before now, surely, but all of a sudden she has a social life where there was none and is busy having a good time. Everyone who should, thinks that Ginny Mustard has been returned to prison so there's no point in asking at the hospital if Judy has come to visit and one would have to be gifted with a wilder imagination than Maggie's to figure out what's really going on around here.

Judy will not leave Frankie's side. Now that she's convinced he moved she refuses to go anywhere at all. She hasn't seen the light of day for ages and is terribly pale for want of sun and fresh air. Nurse Edna brings her meals and snacks when other patients refuse to eat what can best be described as airline food without the fun of going anywhere, but Judy is not interested and the magic has left her eyes. Everything she has goes to Frankie. She gives willingly and he sucks the life out of her. Wraps her arms around him and prays harder than she ought. If there's any justice the boy will wake while there's still something left of her. Nurse Edna is worried to death but there's not much she can do.

~

Joe Snake and his mom are heading home. Sadie called

ne of the neighbours who told her that an odd-looking woman as taken up with Annie Paul and yes, she is pregnant. No one nows her name because Annie Paul will only say she's a friend om away but she sure sounds like the one Sadie describes. Lucy nd Mr. Benoit have opted to remain in the city. Lucy, because she ants to and Mr. Benoit to keep an eye on her at Sadie's insis- nce.

~

"...the rain is full of ghosts tonight, that tap and sigh Upon the glass nd listen for reply, And in my heart there stirs a quiet pain..."

If Ruth were to be honest with herself - and she is of an ge to do that now, because at this point on the journey one must ake to drugs or develop a close relationship with the demon rum r similar in order to avoid face to face confrontation with what- ver ails one - she would admit that Patrick's indifference to oanie's plight has little to do with her telling him to frig off.

The rain is full of ghosts tonight, Ruth's ghosts in particular nd the one who stands out is Bill, less fuzzy than all the others ince they were mere substitutes for the real thing anyway. And he can damn Sarah all to hell if she wants to, which she does reg- larly, but if it weren't for her meddling Ruth might have kept the ecret from herself that she loves Bill and has forever.

The dampness is in her bones - she's of an age to feel that s well - and it saddens her. The sky was boiling with clouds efore six o'clock and there was no purple on the hills when the un went down and if there's a moon tonight how would anyone now? Ruth prepared a little dinner for herself and ate it right out f the saucepan with a wooden spoon, staring through the win- ow at the black rain which is a sure sign that a woman's heart is eavy.

This afternoon she thought of looking for Bill and h been trying to talk herself out of it for hours.

"Even if I could track him down, a big if since all I ha to go on is a name and a town, he probably looks old by now, f and ugly."

"He said it was the smallest town in Texas, how ha could it be to find him? And you're no spring chicken yourse you know."

"At least I'm not fat and ugly."

"What makes you so sure that he is?"

"Shut up!"

"No, you shut up!"

But Ruth doesn't shut up and gets no sleep at all with th argument going on in her head and she's crabbier than she's ev been when she leaves for work in the morning.

~

Patrick is a most patient man. Always has been. He ha finally realized that Ruth's reasons for dumping him are not tru and has resigned himself to the waiting game. He's thinking asking Sarah if she knows what's really going on but is in no rus Ruth will come around again. He refuses to believe that their rel tionship is done and over with no matter what she says. Patric has had several close encounters with women but never wi someone like Ruth. All of the others had looked out for hir Plied him with home cooking and made sure he had gloves on the winter, talked him into buying decent clothes now and the and told him which tie to wear with what shirt. They feigned inte est in the things he likes and bought him cards for no reason an finally left when they realized he wasn't going to marry them. Rut has never done anything for him that he can recall and doesr are one way or the other how he dresses or if his shoes are polhed. She says he's big enough and ugly enough to look after himelf and he loves that about her.

If he knew what she is thinking right now he might be aclined to worry but maybe not. Perhaps he knows that the way hings were don't exist but in a people's minds and there's nothing an be done to make them real again. It's always a shock to go ome to the house you grew in if you've been away for long. Iouses shrink when you don't live in them. So do parents when ou aren't looking. The taffeta dress you wore that time rustles hen you wear it in dreams far more than it ever did for real, and he boy who loved you and held you smells better, tastes better in nemory than he will at the reunion.

Somewhere else on this planet but at this very moment, ill is musing the same thoughts. Wife Four is packing her bags nd heading out - for good this time she says - and he is thinking ondly of the first woman who tossed him aside and wondering hat she's up to. He never got over her really, though anyone ooking wouldn't have guessed it in a million years the way he cares on. In his mind's eye he can see her if he thinks hard enough. eing dumped at an early age has the same effect as being nacked around by a parent when you are only six or seven. You mp with it for the rest of your life unless you get professional elp and even then it will take close to forever to heal yourself. ometimes you must return to the scene of the crime and do the elling you couldn't at the time. If the same person dumped you r smacked you after you've lived fifty years you'd just say piss off nd get out of my sight you big jerk, and go about your business. here are advantages to age that youth cannot imagine. Bill knows hat he and Ruth will never be what they were to each other and hat's fine, but he's been drinking while Four gathers her underear and books and is at that point when a person is inclined to e to himself to feel better, three scotch rocks no water on an empty stomach, six if he's had a bite to eat lately.

Bill has no idea where Ruth may be, but he does recall tha
she has or had a brother and he does recall where that brothe
lives or lived and he does recall that somewhere in the attic i
everything he ever owned, including address books from earlie
times. He's comfortable in his armchair though, and waits until h
hears the front door slam - harder than last time - maybe she really means it - before hauling himself up over the stairs to shake th
dust off his ghosts.

There are photographs, cruel photographs that neve
change, to keep memory alive as we curse reality. Better we al
have portraits, as did the enviable Dorian Grey, to keep us slim
and smooth, glowing on the outside, with calories and wrinkle
visited on canvas, safe under wraps among useless toasters an
three-legged chairs and carvings of spotty cows that Grandm
made that time she lived in the country and thank God we don'
have to bring them out every time she visits now that she's dea
and buried.

Only two pictures of Ruth. She was never one to pose an
Bill liked to set the scene so by the time he was ready to snap sh
had wandered off. These were taken by a buddy. On a beac
where they had gone to boil lobsters and he'd had his first taste o
June snow. Ruth in his big old flight jacket with his dogtag
around her neck. He had given them to her when his stint wa
over. When he didn't need them any more to prove he was wh
he was if he'd been blown to bits and those bits carried home i
a box. He wonders if she has them still.

~

Joe Snake does not care to return to the place of his birt
It never became a source of comfort with the distance he p

etween it and himself. It was always too small for him and he has o fond memories of fishing with his dad or chatting with the eighbours, of celebrations or old friends. He recalls too clearly ne tightness of it with everyone breathing down his neck and mothering him with thinking they knew him inside out. He can't nagine how his wife can possibly cope without her treasured soli-ude. A small town is a hard place for an introvert.

No need to trouble yourself, Joe Snake. Ginny Mustard is ne. Annie Paul has taught her to swim and she is this very minute loating baby side up on the lake with the full moon, following a rail of light that turns the water on her naked belly to a stream of iamonds. She will stay there until Annie Paul comes down to the hore and calls her home. Ginny Mustard has no problem with he smallness of the town. She rarely goes beyond the garden and vhen she does happen upon a stranger she smiles a silent hello nd carries on. No one else comes to the lake at night and that's er time to swim since she likes to take off all her clothes and Annie Paul suggested she not do that in broad daylight if she can ossibly help it.

When Joe Snake arrives she is overjoyed to see him. When he makes all the connections she marvels again at how little the vorld really is. Annie Paul is irritated that she couldn't see it com-ng but recovers in time to whip up a celebratory meal of mussel howder and trout with all of the spinach and chard thinnings rom the garden and wild little dandelion leaf salad which they eat nder the stars, except for Sadie Benoit who takes her share to her wn kitchen table, thank you anyway.

Ginny Mustard does not want to return to the city. She vants to stay here in the clean air and live forever. Joe Snake says ne hates to disappoint her but unless she is returned to prison efore anyone finds she's missing, it will take that much longer for ner to be free. There's always the chance of parole in December. And if not, she'll be out anyway in another eighteen months. And yes, she can live here then if she wants to and yes, he will build her a teepee just like Annie Paul's and he will bring her trout from the lake and shellfish from the ocean and he will dig a garden and help her plant flowers and vegetables and he will hunt rabbits and sea birds and swim with her in the moonlight, gather moss and old man's beard to stuff her mattress and feathers for her hair if that's what she wants but not yet, precious, not yet. "First we have to get you back under lock and key."

They set out in the morning after Ginny Mustard says goodbye to the water, Annie Paul leading in Dr. Kamau's car so they can return it on the way. But when they find the place she lef him no one has ever heard tell of the man. "We'd sure remember a black fellow around here wouldn't we now? Why don't you check in Alder Bight just over the road? Maybe that's where he go off." Annie Paul doesn't believe those layabouts for a minute bu won't tell the others so they waste plenty of time searching every town between there and the city.

Once at Ginny Mustard's house, after she has greeted the cats and Harvey who is beside himself with joy to see her, they must devise a plan to put her in place. Annie Paul enlists the help of Nurse Edna who calls the prison and tells them to come and get Ginny Mustard who is waiting for them in the lobby and no she can't stay any longer since she's fine and they've given her bed to someone else so get over here now before she escapes or some thing. She digs out the release documents and spills a little cold coffee to smudge the date. Joe Snake runs out to buy paper and coloured pencils since Ginny Mustard feels like drawing again and the captive leaves smiling, with memories of seeds sprouting and speckled fish frying and blue water lapping at her toes - enough for hundreds of pictures - enough to tolerate even Crazy Rachel enough.

When she has been bundled into the prison van Joe Snak and Annie Paul walk home slowly. "He's gone, you know. He ather is gone," says Annie Paul. "Those idiots were lying. They now exactly where he is, dead or alive. Don't ask me how I know hat. I really get tired of people asking me how I know things. I ould smell evil in that town the first time I was there and it was tronger yesterday."

"What does evil smell like?"

"Imagine something the flies wouldn't touch. Worse than hat."

"Perhaps we should go back and check it out. At least eport him missing. I can call Patrick. He's a cop I know."

"That's probably a good idea as long as he doesn't ask too nany questions. My life has more complications than I care for ately and I'd just as soon get back to some peace and quiet. Are ou really planning to come home? I can't imagine you living here. I remember when you were a kid. You never seemed to fit n with the others. Always by yourself. I used to watch you down y the water just staring off into space like you were the only person on earth. Like you had the best secrets."

Joe Snake laughs. "I have no secrets. But I don't think I vas meant to live small. I'm not sure what that means, really. Here can go about my life with no interference. No one telling me vhat to do, when to do it. Pure childishness on my part, I suspect. No one ever tried to talk me out of following my dreams. I don't nave any. No aspirations. I seem to need to be alone more than ome. Here I can go for days without seeing anyone who wants to alk to me about the weather. And if I choose to stay behind closed doors there's no one asking if I'm okay. No one worrying about me. I have no secrets Annie Paul. It's all very simple."

"So how are you going to cope with small once Virginia's out in the free world? You know she'll want to head back right away."

"I can spend time there. For her I'll do that. But I'll need o get away often. She'll understand. Well, maybe not understand, but she doesn't have to understand things to accept them. She's a rare one that way."

Mr. Benoit and Lucy are awake when they reach the house and sad to have missed Ginny Mustard but they were sound asleep at her arrival and still at it when she left.

"I heard that silly dog barking and thought something was up. Why didn't you tell us she was here?" cries Lucy. "Now I'm all depressed. Can we go somewhere for breakfast to cheer me up?"

"I'm game," says Annie Paul and they head out, leaving the men to drink coffee and not say much in the backyard.

~

Judy is ice cold. Her lips are as blue as her eyes used to be and her legs are prickly where she hasn't shaved them for so long but she barely feels the irritation any more. She barely feels anything any more. When Frankie finally wakes up he has to shove her to get her out of his way on the little bed, which takes most of his energy and when she comes to he's sleeping again but in a different position than before so she knows for certain that he moved and that she didn't dream he was pushing her around. She pinches his upper arm ever so gently and then his cheek a little harder and he raises his hand to swat her.

"Hello Frankie," says Judy.

"I could eat a horse," whispers Frankie in a voice not used to exercise.

"I'm pretty sure they have that here," says Judy but the cafeteria is closed and the best she can come up with is jelly and a few dry rolls from the tray trolley that hasn't been emptied yet of dinner's leftovers. She brings the feast to Frankie's room. Of course he can't eat, having been without food for so long, and she devours the works. It sits heavy in her stomach.

"I guess I should tell someone that you're awake." Judy eads to the nurses' station with her news and in two minutes ıey're all over Frankie, picking and prodding and announcing a ıiracle and Judy is lost in the shuffle wondering what she is to do ow that her cover's been blown. She leaves a note for the doctor elling him to keep an eye on Frankie and not let anyone named mmy Snelgrove come visiting since he's the one who beat the rap out of him in the first place and to call the cops and have him rrested. She doesn't sign her name.

When she goes home she tells Joe Snake everything that's oing on. She's not disapppointed to hear that Patrick rarely asks fter her but her ego smarts a little.

"Well. I think I'd like to get out of town anyway. I'm real- hungry, you know. Is there anything to eat?"

Mr. Benoit scrambles eggs and sets them in front of her vith some toast but after a bite she has to run to the bathroom nd throw up. Her poor tummy can't take it and she settles for a andful of soda crackers.

"You look like hell," says Annie Paul when she returns vith Lucy and is introduced to Judy, hears her tale of woe. "Have ou ever lived in a teepee?"

"I thought you'd had enough complications in your life," ays Joe Snake.

"So did I but when the spirit flings things at your feet I hink it only best to pick them up. Come on Judy. I know the per- ect place to mend. Get your things and meet me in that gorgeous lack Mercedes out in the driveway. Joseph, I don't think you hould bother your cop friend with word of the good doctor's lisappearance. He's gone, for sure, and I think looking for him vill only cause more trouble for the living. Leave it be. Can you give me money for gas?"

~

Nobody thought to tell Ginny Mustard not to mention her adventure in the beautiful country. She's been drawing up a storm. Pictures of a loon and a lake, the moon on the water, a teepee and a native woman staring into a fire. From the little she says her fellow inmates figure she's out of her mind and even young Alice Paine is inclined to go along with the diagnosis. She is pleased that Ginny Mustard is talking to her now and thrilled that she seems so healthy - physically - but believes her patient is heading off the deep end for sure this time and tells the warden so.

"She is completely delusional. She thinks she's been to the country and living in a teepee. She could snap any day, though she certainly seems to be happy with her fantasy."

"What do you mean snap? So you figure she's dangerous?"

"Well, not exactly dangerous. It's hard to say really."

"Oh for God's sake! Is she dangerous or not? That seems a simple enough question. Never mind. Go on back to your other lunatics and leave this one to me." And has Ginny Mustard placed in solitary to keep the peace around here.

In her tiny cell, Ginny Mustard can't hear anything but the guards when they bring her meals. She can't see anything but four walls and a ceiling. The light is false and pale, there is no window. She doesn't have pencils or paper. When Joe Snake comes to visit he's told he can't see her. Neither can he talk to the warden to find out why, though he sits outside her office for a long time until several guards escort him away. The same happens the following week and the one after that. He talks to Alice Paine. She looks too worried to be of any help but she does tell him she's keeping an eye on his wife and that she's okay.

When her water breaks in the middle of the night Ginny Mustard is surprised but doesn't call out. She takes off her clothes nd lies down on the hard cot. When the pain becomes unbear-ble she walks back and forth. Sometimes she crawls. She mas-ages her belly and feels each rock hard contraction consume her. etween them she laughs. She hears Annie Paul telling her to be good little Buddhist and eat the pain, the only advice on child-irth she could come up with, not, she said, that she knew any-ning on the topic, and she certainly doesn't think there is any ense in being a Buddhist but they sure know how to deal with uffering. Ginny Mustard laughs again and eats the next contrac-on and the next one after that, on into the night. When the time omes to push she does with all her might - squatting on the cold loor - and with strong arms brings her baby to her belly, lies own and the afterbirth comes and she stares in wonder as the iny creature crawls to her breast and suckles.

That's how the guards find her at breakfast time. Nursing bloody little baby with afterbirth all over herself and Sweet Polly till attached. And now Ginny Mustard is back in the hospital and Nurse Edna is holding "the most beautiful creature I have ever een in my life" clean and shining and ready to live again. If any-one were to walk by Eve's grave right now the peace emanating rom its depths would drive him to his knees.

"She's early according to the doctor, but they don't know verything. Some babies are just in a hurry. And she's a real good veight. And long. I was right. She's going to be a tall one."

Nurse Edna hands the baby back to Ginny Mustard who mmediately removes the little one's clothes and examines her ead to toe. She's not looking for anything in particular, just doing vhat every new mother does if no one stops her. She stares into lark eyes, blue black eyes. "She has blue eyes," she remarks to no one and Nurse Edna tells her they'll change later on. Most likely e very brown. "Her hair is black. The other kids won't call her Mustard."

"No," says Nurse Edna. "But I'm sure they'll come up

with something else. Kids always do, you know."

"She's pretty."

"And that she is, dear. Prettiest thing I ever laid eyes on," says Nurse Edna, wondering what's to become of the sweet bab when her mother is hauled off to jail again.

Joe Snake has been here already. He held his daughter a though he knew what he was doing. Stared into her small face fo the longest time before a nurse took her away for more of check-up. He sat with his wife. Held her hand. Smiled. Only whe Ginny Mustard said he should tell his mom and dad, did he leav to make a few phone calls. "And Annie Paul. Tell Annie Paul wha a nice baby we have."

~

When prison officials got wind of the goings-on the were furious. The warden is being raked over the coals for stick ing a pregnant woman in solitary with no one watching her. Wha the hell was she thinking? Where were the guards when th woman went into labour? No! They were not where they wer supposed to be or they would have heard her! How can you no hear a woman yelling when she's in labour? Impossible! What d you mean they heard her laughing? Woman don't laugh when the are having babies! She might be crazy as the crows but guaranteed she'd be yelling - not laughing - in that situation! Doesn't matte what you say!

They question Alice Paine and learn that as far as she' concerned Ginny Mustard was not well enough to be there in th first place, found out why she had been sent to the hospital orig inally. And what the hell was she doing in solitary confinement Delusional? She pretended she'd been living in a bloody teepee So fucking what? She killed a guy. Sane women don't run arounc killing people! Why would a stupid fantasy set her apart from the others in the first place? There's no one in here with both oars in the water! What are you going to do - stick them all in solitary?

Now they are in a huddle. We could have a lawsuit on our hands like you wouldn't believe! They wonder if maybe they should have a parole hearing now instead of waiting until December. Strings are pulled, stretched to breaking, and it is decided that as soon as their prisoner is on her feet and back behind bars they will proceed. If they set her free there's less chance that this will explode in their faces.

~

Joe Snake goes to Ruth's apartment to leave a note about the news. He tried to call but she's not answering her telephone. When he arrives she's sitting outside on her little porch making decisions, university calendar in hand and notepaper everywhere.

"I'm going to study forensic science," she tells him. "I'm going to eat my vegetables and some whole-wheat chicken and free range fruit so I can live for a few years after I'm done choking down the education. Maybe I'm a late bloomer but it's about time I got off my ass and on with it. What do you think, Joe Snake? Do you think I can get it together at this late date? I don't know how I'll pay for it. I'll have to keep working and get a student loan. From what I hear if you have a job they don't give you enough to pay the friggin' tuition so forget about rent and food and I'm not giving up the cigarettes, that's for damn sure. I'll have to lie about a few things, I daresay. Help me fill out these forms, will you? And you'll have to teach me how to use your computer. Can I borrow time on it now and then? What brings you by, anyway?"

Joe Snake smiles. Tells her she can certainly use his computer. "The baby is here. She was born last night."

"Wonderful! A bit early. Is she okay? How much does she weigh? How long is she?"

"She's fine. They're both fine. I don't know how much she weighs. How long."

"God! You men are all alike. When can I see her?"

"Ginny Mustard is sleeping now but if you want to come later on we can go together."

"Did you get flowers?"

"No."

"Joe Snake! You have to bring flowers! We'll get some on the way. Lots of them. I remember how much she liked the ones I got from Patrick when we were living at Mrs. Miflin's house. Daisies were her favourites. I'll bet old Eve is happy as a lark now. She really had a concern going for that baby."

"Eve is dead, Ruth."

"Yeah, yeah. Whatever. Give me a hand with these forms, will you? I think you need a PhD to figure them out."

~

Annie Paul says, "The baby is here. Sadie Benoit just told me. She wants to see her so I said I'd drive in tomorrow."

"I want to go too. I need to check on Frankie. Make sure Jimmy doesn't get him again. I want to tell Patrick what happened. I was thinking about it you know, and I figure it's the right thing to do. Tell Patrick and say what I know about Jimmy beating the crap out of Frankie. He shouldn't be allowed to just walk around like nothing happened, should he? I mean, Frankie was lying there for ages missing a whole lot of his life and his mom went and moved without him and no one knows he's even alive any more except me and those people at the friggin' hospital. I'm scared

Annie Paul. Jimmy's got a lot of mean friends. What if they hunt me down when I tell on him?"

"I can't imagine that anyone would ever find you in this hole in the wall. You can stay here until the coast is clear. Why don't you tell this Patrick of yours what you know and see what happens. I have a feeling it's going to work out okay for you. I'll come with you to see him if you want me to."

"Okay. Thank you."

Judy's time with Annie Paul has been good for her. "You put me in mind of Eve, only for she was real old, but she was kind of peaceful, you know. Like nothing bothered her much and you're sort of that way. I don't think I ever saw her get flustered except that one time when she wanted us to tell about Ginny Mustard killing Mr. Miflin but then she was fine again. She liked growing things. And birds. She was forever feeding them scraps of bread and stuff. She used to keep the bacon and sausage fat in the fridge in a milk carton. She'd put seeds in it and just throw the fat on top and when it was full she'd put it out for those birds. She said His eye is on the sparrow but sometimes He wants us to give it a morsel now and then especially in the winter when the worms and bugs are hiding. I really miss her a lot."

Annie Paul enjoys Judy's company. The girl has a knack for weeding and the garden is spotless. And she's smart as a whip. Show her something once and she's got it. She knows which weeds to throw away and which ones they'll have with supper. She cleans trout faster than anyone but she won't eat them. She chops wood better than three people put together and is tireless. When Annie Paul ran out of things for her to do she wandered off and met up with some of the other young people and they seem to have accepted her, taking her with them to the local hang-out to play pool in the evenings but more often than not she'd just as soon be around the older folks, give them a hand with whatever they're up to. Most days there's a crowd of little kids close at her heels because she comes up with the best ideas for having fun and the noise from the lake is deafening at times with a dozen or so youngsters and Judy the ringleader splashing like there's no tomorrow. She asks Annie Paul if the lake is good for skating in the winter because she's thinking it might be fun to get a hockey team together.

"If Patrick doesn't arrest me for running off is it okay if I stay longer? I have some money in the bank but I lost my card so I can't get it out until they give me a new one. I could pay for whatever I eat, you know. I feel real comfortable here. If you don't want me to live in your teepee maybe I could find another place. Maybe Mrs. Benoit could rent me a room and I could still help you with things."

"Why don't you stay in my brother's house? It's empty."

"I think I need to live with people. I always get in trouble when I don't. Sometimes even when I do but not so much."

Annie Paul looks at the girl who wants so badly to do the right thing. Since her arrival the spark has come back and she's usually smiling. Other than smoking pot with her new friends now and then and the subsequent giggles and munchies when she gets home. The racket when she's swimming with the little kids. Shaving her head that time because orange hair looks out of place around here, don't you think Annie Paul, and I'm going to see what colour it is - I've been friggin' around with it since I was eleven and I can't remember - Judy is a joy. Annie Paul is not sure she wants the responsibility of looking out for the girl but she doesn't want to piss off the spirits either.

She smiles. "Why don't we wait and see what happens after you talk to your Patrick. Time enough to make decisions when we know what we're dealing with. Okay?"

"Okay. I'm going to see if Mrs. Benoit has any more of that stuff she makes for fly bites. I'm itching like crazy. Bye."

~

Ruth and Joe Snake are on their way to the hospital, arms full of flowers for Ginny Mustard, dozens of daisies in every colour but blue. "They're too weird," said Ruth. " They must dye them. They sure as hell don't look natural to me."

She asks why Joe Snake didn't make it to Dorrie's wedding. "It was worth the cash. What a show. He's a friggin' biker in his spare time, you know. And his buddies were all there and I don't care how you dress them up they still look like hoods. Dorrie's friends came as Barbie dolls, whether they meant to or not, and her parents are the straightest pair you'd ever want to meet. Butter wouldn't melt in their mouths so you can just imagine what the church looked like, a bunch of Pentecostals on one side and Hell's Angels on the other. I sat with the bikers. Couldn't take the chance of all that goodness rubbing off on me. You could almost taste it."

"What does 'goodness' taste like?"

"Sticky. You'd never get it off the roof of your mouth." And she laughs. "The honeymoon is a trip to some big Harley convention. Phil gave the bride a motorcycle helmet for a wedding present. She all but disappeared when she put it on. There's about fifty of them going together. Dear Dorrie is officially a biker babe. In my wildest dreams I wouldn't have seen her in that role."

Ruth stops walking. "You never can tell, can you, Joe Snake."

"No, Ruth. You never can."

They carry on in silence. Ruth has no more to say today and when she holds Sweet Polly, looks into her eyes and smiles. The baby wraps her little brown hand around one of Ruth's fingers and Ruth cries - in her heart - where stirs that quiet pain again.

~

Three days after she had the baby Ginny Mustard was whisked away to jail. She nursed Sweet Polly one last time and handed her over to Joe Snake's care. Mrs. Benoit has brought along all of the paraphernalia necessary for the clothing and feeding of a baby. She dug out the cradle her own children had slept in for the first few of months of their lives, close by her bed so she could rock them with her foot when they stirred in the night and didn't need to wake yet. She cleaned it and packed in gently in Annie Paul's stolen car along with one special blanket she had made for her son while she was carrying him.

She teaches Joe Snake how to wash the little one, how to test the temperature of the milk, how to burp her, and a few lullabies in the old language to sing her to sleep. "When she grows out of the cradle she should sleep with you until she's ready for her own bed. I think that makes for happier people. And don't haul her around in a stroller until she's too big for this carrier. Put it on your front first and on your back when she starts wanting to look around. You have to get a rocking chair." Joe Snake makes notes but there's no need because his mother plans to stay in the city awhile if he wants her to. "Young Judy might go back with Annie Paul and she can look after things for me. She's a real good worker that one, when you can drag her away from the water."

~

Judy goes to see Patrick as soon as she arrives. Tells him what she knows about Frankie's situation. Frankie has had total recall and is ready to do battle. Patrick agrees that Judy should stay out of sight until the trial which won't happen until there's an arrest made and Jimmy is nowhere to be found. Frankie will be tucked away in a safe place and yes, it's okay for Judy to go back with Annie Paul. The investigation will be a quiet one. If Jimmy is in town they don't want him to find out what's going on until they nab him but she shouldn't let anyone know where she's going. No. Not even Maggie. No one. Jimmy is well known as a hard ass and has a faithful following. Patrick is pleased to have something tangible on the dirty little bastard. He has long suspected that Jimmy and his crew are responsible for every gay-bashing in town but can't prove a thing. If he can get him behind bars for a few years maybe the queer young fellows can breathe easier when they finally come up with the courage to step out of the closet.

Judy wants Frankie to come with her and Annie Paul but Patrick says no. But what if Jimmy finds him? He won't. Patrick will be in touch with Judy as soon as he needs her to testify. He talks to Annie Paul. Now she'll have to watch over that girl whether she wants to or not. He provides a police escort to see the two safely home. He's not too confident that some loose-lipped member of the medical profession hasn't spilled the beans and he knows how quickly news travels around here. All it will take is for doctor so and so to tell the family all about the lastest coma marvel and for one of his youngsters to mention it to the best friend of someone's sister who remembers the rumours she heard last year and that will be the end of his case. For all its airs this city is a village at the core.

Judy is shipped off before she sees the baby or Frankie or Maggie or anyone else who matters and that is very sad, but on the up side, she's free to be where she wants to be right now. She slides back into the new world as though born to it.

~

Matthew calls Ruth with the news that someone named Bill is trying to find her. "I told him I couldn't give him your phone number so he asked me to give you his. Also his addresses, street and e-mail. Do you want them?"

Ruth is almost speechless. Almost. "This is wild! I've been thinking about him lately. Haven't seen him in eons. I'm not so sure I want to talk to him but give me the information. I'll keep it. Just in case."

"Oh God!" says Ruth after she hangs up. After she tells Matthew that she won't be marrying Patrick. After she tells him she's going to school in the fall if she can come up with the money. After she pours herself a beer and settles down for a bath. After she drops her ashtray into the tub. "Oh God! Oh God! Oh God! And don't be getting all excited thinking that's a prayer, Mister high and mighty. What makes you think you can waltz around screwing with people's lives, anyway? You can be such a bastard sometimes, you know that? But still and all it might be interesting to see him again. No! No it wouldn't. I have things to do now. I have things to do. Miles to go. Promises to keep. Whatever."

Ruth paces for a couple of miles in the apartment. Slowly. When the stars come out she takes her troubles to the streets. Walks another few miles. Along the river and down to the waterfront. She finds herself in front of the police station but has no idea how she got there.

Patrick is finally leaving after a very long shift and happens upon her standing at the bottom of the big stone stairs - looking up at his office window.

"Have you come back?" he asks.

"I don't think so. I don't know what I'm doing, really. Do you want to have a coffee? I'm a bit messed up at the moment and could use a friend."

"I'm not all that interested in being a friend," says Patrick. "But I will have coffee with you."

Settled in a dirty booth with torn seat covers, the only thing open in the vicinity this time of night, Ruth bares her soul. She hadn't intended to. Stops now and then to shake her head as though the next thought needs work to put itself into words. She finds herself telling all. About her son. About her life. Her dirty little secrets. "I don't know how I feel about him. Bill. I don't know if I should bother to find out or leave it alone. I just don't know."

"You know Ruth, I'd really like to help you, but I happen to be in love with you and I'm the last person on earth you should be looking to right now. I'm not your best buddy. If you need advice on whether or not to call an old lover go to someone else. What do you think I'm made of? It's great that you're talking. Good to hear what's been haunting you. But for God's sake, Ruth, give me a break."

"Well fuck you."

"No. Fuck you, Ruth. You're with me or you aren't. I'm not some sensitive new age guy. I'm not big enough to sit here and help you figure out if you should contact this Bill character and pretend it doesn't hurt like hell. It does. I'm out of here. Let me know what you decide to do." And he's gone.

People are staring. "What are you numbnuts looking at?" yells Ruth storming across the dining room and through the door. She mutters to herself all the way home and into the wee hours. When the sun comes up she heads to Ginny Mustard's house. Joe Snake wakes to find that she has dug up half the grass in the back yard and constructed a couple of sloppy flower beds.

"Is it too late to plant things? Never mind. I'm going to the seed store to see what they've got."

"What is the matter, Ruth? Do you want to talk?"

"No. I tried that a few hours ago and believe you me, it's

not worth shit. I'll be fine. I just need to muck about in the garden for a while. Thanks, but leave me alone, okay?"

Joe Snake goes inside to make coffee. Ruth heads out to buy plants and comes back in a taxi with boxes of spindly end-of-the-season marigolds and zinnias and asters. "They were on sale. Some of them were free. I think they're half dead but you never know. I spent all my cash so can you pay buddy in the cab?"

She calls Zellers and tells her boss she won't be in. She accepts a cup of coffee and starts digging. Joe Snake asks his parents not to speak to her until she's finished. Not to go out back. Ignore her. By the end of the day the pathetic flowers have been freed of the cruel boxes that bound their roots. Breathing gratefully. Sucking up the generous water.

"There. I think that just about does it. Invite me to dinner, will you? I don't want to talk but I don't want to be alone right now, either. You talk. I need to stop dwelling on me for a few minutes. Tell me what's going on with the wife and kid. Tell me anything that has nothing to do with Ruth. Better still, just let your mother and Lucy go wild. I've got a fridge full of salad makings at my place. I'll get them. You come up with meat."

~

Those in charge of such things, are debating Ginny Mustard's fate. Once they see her the action heats up considerably. "I didn't know she's black. This is worse than I thought. If the black community gets wind of this we'll really be up the creek."

"What black community? You're watching too much TV. You wouldn't need both hands to count the number like her in this place. That hardly makes for a community. Still, the problem remains. I'm surprised the shit hasn't already hit the fan. If anything had gone wrong with that baby I'd hate to think where we'd be right now. Meantime, I'm certain we can appease the victim in this case by setting her free as soon as possible. Has anyone spoken to the father? He could be the one to cause trouble. Unless he's as simple as she is. Talk to Judge Steeves. Tell him what's going on and that we need to get her out of here. Get her to sign something saying we aren't responsible for anything that happens to that kid in the future. If it doesn't get straight As in school or can't figure out how to play basketball or pass its bloody driver's test we don't want the justice system having to compensate for our negligence."

Such nasty people to be talking this way. Ginny Mustard would never think to sue anyone. Neither would Joe Snake. Still and all it's just as well they don't know that because now Sweet Polly won't have to spend her baby time without her momma. The hearing is swift and painless. There is some confusion when Ginny Mustard tells the board that she is going to go live in a teepee with her baby but they come to order again when one whispers to another and she to another that Ginny Mustard is clearly out of her mind and they will simply forward pertinent information to the parole officer and forget all about it.

Since Ginny Mustard didn't know she was to be released so soon and had no idea why those women wanted to meet with her, it comes as a shock to Joe Snake that she is free. When she calls to ask him to come and get her he can't quite believe what he is hearing and the old warden is packing up to leave and the new one waiting for space to put her own junk. There's no one around but a guard who just came on duty for the evening and doesn't know what Joe Snake is talking about. She checks with a few of the inmates and is told that, yes, Ginny Mustard is free, after which she goes to the office and finds proof on paper. "You might as well come pick her up."

Ginny Mustard takes Joe Snake's travel time to say goodbye to the others. Some of them shed a few tears. Some don't give a damn. Crazy Rachel is angry beyond angry. When the place settles down for the night she sits on the floor and bangs her head against the wall and wails like something dying until the guards put her in solitary which is worse because you can still smell birth in that little room. She tears her shirt to shreds and has eaten a sleeve and the collar by morning so they ship her out to the insane asylum where she spends her time making pictures of really ugly babies with dry beans and pasta.

At home - Ginny Mustard's home - such a wonderful night! Dinner was over when she called with the news. Much wine had been consumed and Sadie Benoit was beside herself with wanting to pick Ruth's brain. Once Joe Snake had left to drive to the prison - a little too fast - he got a speeding ticket - she dove in and Ruth was just drunk enough to let her.

After she spills her guts, Sadie Benoit says, "You know what your problem is Ruth? You don't laugh enough. You make all kinds of wise-cracks but you really don't have any humour in your soul. I really think you should lighten up. Life is not that serious, you know. And not that long either. If you can relax a bit before you're completely over the hill you might find the trip down the other side more enjoyable. And that's all I have to say."

"Sure it is," says Ruth. "Did hell freeze over when I wasn't looking?"

"See what I mean? Your tongue is too sharp. You'll cut yourself bad on that one of these days if you're not careful, Missy."

"Yeah yeah - whatever. Tell the happy family I'll see them around. I'm sure I have something better to do than listen to this tripe." She leaves in a huff and people walking by step aside when they see her coming. Some of them cross the street. One old fellow takes the Rosary beads out of his pocket and kisses the crucifix. A little cold wind whips over Eve's grave, all the way downtown and in through Ruth's kitchen window.

~

When Ginny Mustard arrives the first thing she does is snuggle her baby. And since no one thought to give her anything to dry up her milk and it's only been a couple of days, Sweet Polly nuzzles in wanting a meal and Mrs. Benoit gathers up all the bottles she bought and puts them in back of the cupboard.

The second thing Ginny Mustard does is start packing to move to her new home in the country. Joe Snake talks for an hour or more before she sees reason.

"Let's stay here until next spring. I can get most of the courses I need at the university done by then."

"But I want to sleep outside."

"We can put a tent on the little bit of grass that Ruth didn't dig up."

"But there is no water."

"We'll build a pond."

"There are no bats."

"We'll stick houses for them in the trees and maybe some will show up."

"I want to catch fish."

"We'll find a lake."

"Okay. But only until spring. We have to go see Annie Paul."

"Yes. As often as you like."

~

Ruth's apartment is so cold that she has to put on a sweater and mittens and even then she is chilled. She sleeps under every blanket she owns. When Sarah comes banging at the door bright and early she is still freezing and won't get up for the longest time.

"I know you're in there, Ruth. I really need to talk to you. I'll kick this thing down if I have to."

"What do you want, Sarah? I'm not in any mood for your shit right now."

Sarah starts to cry. "I've done the worst thing, Ruth. I told Peter about Matthew not being his father. That you're his mother. We couldn't find you. Matthew and Joanna are at the house. You have to come and get this straightened out. Please, Ruth."

"What is there to straighten out? I'm sure you've told them everything I said. That's all there is there ain't no more, darlin'. Though I do have Bill's phone number. How about you just take it and traipse on home and give it to Peter and if he wants to call his daddy he can. By the way, make sure you tell him that Bill doesn't have a clue about any of this. Not a clue. You go on now. We can talk about this until the second coming but it won't change anything and you sure as hell don't need my input." She finds the paper with Bill's address and hands it to Sarah. "Here, girl. Knock yourself out."

Ruth packs clothes, can opener, frying pan, bowl, plate, knife, fork, spoon, coffee cup, kettle in an old duffel bag and lugs it over to Ginny Mustard's house. Yells out to Joe Snake that she wants to see him. "I need a favour. Lend me some money and give me a ride away from this friggin' place. I have some more thinking to do. No. That's not the truth. I've done enough of that. I want to be by myself. Completely by myself. Here's the key to my place. Take my plant and look after it will you? And my books. I'm going to buy as many groceries, beer and smokes as you can afford and then you're driving me off into the sunset. Just don't tell anyone where you left me. Deal?"

"Deal. I'll let the others know that I'm going. When can I

say I'll be back?

"Give it half the day."

"Right. Why are you wearing winter clothes? The sun is splitting the rocks."

"Not where I'm standing, it isn't."

~

On Bishop's Road Mrs. Miflin's tenants wake to the day. One heads around back to walk in the garden. Another slides like a ghost out the front door and down to the river. Someone lies on her bed and tries to remember where she was yesterday and on the third floor landing a very sad woman sits in an old chair near the window. If she squints real hard she can see all the way through the trees and into the park from here.

The End

Acknowledgements

Some of the words quoted in Bishop's Road are found in *The Love Song of J. Alfred Prufrock* by T.S. Eliot, *What Lips My Lips Have Kissed* and *Renascence*, by Edna St. Vincent Millay, *The Unstrung Harp; or, Mr. Earbrass Writes a Novel*, by Edward Gorey and *Hamlet* by William Shakespeare. Others are from *Hush Little Baby*, author unknown.

Author's Note

Bishop's Road does not exist. Nor do the characters in this novel. But St. John's does and it is by far the most magical place on earth.